Marlyn & Nor[illegible]
Don't worry

SILVER LINING

Love
Wendy x
April 2013

Wendy Soliman

ROMANCE

BookStrand
www.BookStrand.com

A SIREN-BOOKSTRAND TITLE
IMPRINT: Romance

SILVER LINING

ISBN-10: 1-61926-645-8
ISBN-13: 978-1-61926-645-2

First Printing: March 2012

Cover design by Jinger Heaston

Printed in the U.S.A.

PUBLISHER
www.BookStrand.com

SILVER LINING

WENDY SOLIMAN

Chapter One

"Lauren Miller was released from prison this morning."

At last! Jeff Williams leant back in his expensive leather chair, careful to hide his elated reaction behind a casual elevation of one eyebrow. "It's thoughtful of you to let me know, Inspector."

"All part of the service, sir."

"Well, it's appreciated." Jeff tilted his head, unsure why the inspector had bothered to stop by to break the news in person. "Actually, I thought it was another two weeks before she was due out."

"Yes, but a combination of overcrowding and the unnatural interest the press continue to take in her case persuaded the authorities to let her out early. She was released from East Sutton Park first thing today, into her mother's care."

"Everyone wants to know what happened to the money she stole, I suppose," Jeff said pensively.

"She's a good-looking girl from a privileged background who wanted for nothing, so that makes her newsworthy. No one's managed to figure out what made her throw a promising career away when she must have known she'd be caught eventually." Jeff nodded, hoping there was nothing sinister behind Read's shrewd observations. "Had any further thoughts on that one, sir?"

"None whatsoever, Inspector, and believe me, I've wasted a lot of hours mulling it over." Jeff stood up, turned his back on the inspector, and stared out of the triple-glazed, tinted windows that protected his privileged eerie from any direct contact with the hoi polloi crowding the polluted city streets several storeys below. "As you well know, her actions had major ramifications for this firm."

"And her accusations about an affair with you, her initial insistence that she was acting on your orders when she diverted that money, can't have made your life any easier."

"Well, yes, but she soon stopped making those silly claims when she realized no one believed a word of it." He expelled a prolonged sigh. "Even so, it was a bitter pill for me to swallow after everything I tried to do for her."

"I'm sure it must have been."

Jeff adopted a suitably avuncular expression. "I thought the girl had talent, you see. She certainly had all the right qualifications to survive in this jungle, plus enthusiasm, a positive attitude, and a willingness to put in all the hours God sent."

"So she couldn't have had much of a social life, not if she worked so hard."

"I wouldn't know about that. As I told you at the time, our relationship was strictly professional."

"Ah yes, so you did."

"I tried to encourage her by offering her a guiding hand." Jeff noticed that the inspector was showing a little too much interest in his declamation and made do with a self-depreciating shrug. "Much good it did me."

"Well, that's all behind you now, sir. I just wanted to let you know that she's out. As a condition of her probation, she isn't allowed to contact you or your family. If she tries to, just let me know." Read slid his card across the smooth marble surface. "She'll soon be back inside to serve out the rest of her sentence, if she does anything daft like that."

"Thank you, Inspector, that's very reassuring." Jeff placed a hand on Read's shoulder as he led the way across the wide expanse of thick carpet toward his office door. "But Lauren was never silly, you know, far from it, so I don't anticipate that she'll try and get in touch." Jeff injected a casual note into his tone. "She'll be living with her parents now, I suppose."

"I'm not at liberty to reveal her whereabouts, sir. This protection thing works both ways, even though she's now an ex-con." Read paused, his hand on the doorknob, his eyes raking Jeff's face in a disconcertingly speculative manner. "Anyway, why are you so interested in where she's living?"

"Oh, no reason." Jeff rapidly backpedalled. "It's just that, in spite of everything she's done, I still feel a modicum of sympathy for the girl. I obviously overestimated her talents and put too much pressure on her. It's the only explanation I've been able to come up with for what she did, so I feel partly to blame." He lifted his shoulders. "I wouldn't like to think of her out there all on her own."

"You don't need to worry about that. The probation service will make sure she's looked after."

"Ah, I see. Well, that's all right then."

"Good day to you, sir."

"Good day, Inspector, and thanks for dropping by."

Jeff closed the door behind his visitor, crossed back to his desk, and returned his attention to the view, deep in thought. At last she was out, and he'd be able to get his hands on the money he so badly needed. *His* money. He'd get his hands on Lauren, too, whilst he was at it and give her a mercy shag for old time's sake. She was the best he'd ever had—she'd ruined him for all the rest—so she owed him at least that much. He picked up his private phone and dialled a number from memory. It was answered on the second ring.

"They let her out this morning," he said without introducing himself.

"I see."

"Find her and let me know where she's living."

"I'm on it."

Jeff hung up and continued his rather pleasant speculations about his forthcoming reunion with Lauren.

* * * *

Nate Black bought two pints of lager and carried them across to a quiet corner table in the otherwise-crowded city pub. He slid one across to Peter Read, a man who still owed him a few favours ever since Nate had gone out of his way a while back to help him catch some particularly vicious killers through carefully planted information in his newspaper column. Something told Nate that Read's unexpected request for this meeting might signify payback time.

"Thanks, Nate. Cheers."

"Cheers." Nate crossed one denim-clad leg over his opposite knee and leant back in his chair. "So," he said in a voice that still bore distinct traces of his native Colorado, "they've let Lauren Miller out early, have they?"

"Yep, this morning. Thought you'd like to know, given your intense interest in her case."

"Hum, it's just a shame she wouldn't let me visit her inside. Perhaps I could have helped her."

"No one visited her the whole time she was banged up."

Nate's head shot up. "What, not even her family?"

"Nope, she wouldn't see them."

"What did she do in there all that time then? Do you know?"

"Course I do."

Nate chuckled. "Take that much interest in the entire prison population, do you, or do you reserve your attention for the good-looking ones?"

"Do you want to know how she spent her time or not?" Read asked calmly, not rising to the bait.

"Sure I wanna know, Peter, and you know I do. Why else would you be telling me all this?"

"Typical bloody journalist," complained Read, "always answering questions with questions."

He took a sip of his lager, seeming to enjoy dragging this thing out. Nate, an experienced journalist used to worming information out of reluctant sources, sat back, savoured his beer, and said nothing. Eventually his patience was rewarded.

"She worked in the library and studied for an A-level in psychology. She passed it with an A-star, by the way. Other than that, she survived by acting as an unofficial jail-house lawyer for some of the girls on remand."

"Clever!" Nate nodded his admiration. "No one would give her the sort of grief you associate with those places if she made herself useful to the right people."

"I guess that's how she looked upon it."

"But she didn't appeal her own sentence?"

"How could she when she pled guilty? She got off lightly with a six-year sentence, and she knew it, especially as she only served three years for defrauding her stockbroker employers of over three million quid."

"*If* she did."

"Why plead guilty if she didn't?"

"To avoid a murder charge, perhaps?" Nate grinned at his friend. "What do you think?"

"She wasn't charged with murder."

"That's because she didn't commit one."

It was Read's turn to smile. "You don't know that, Nate. Just because she's a looker, she's got you thinking with your prick instead of that pea-sized brain of yours. Pretty girls from good backgrounds are just as capable of committing crimes as anyone else." He waggled his brows in a world-weary sort of way. "Believe me, I know about what I speak."

"I may not be able to prove that she didn't kill anyone, but you sure as hell can't prove that she did. If you could, you'd have charged her."

"Just because we didn't have enough evidence to pin Drake's murder on her, it doesn't mean I don't think she did it."

"Come on, Peter. I know you." Nate shook a thick lock of hair out of his eyes and flashed a smile at the contact who'd become a friend over the years. "If you really thought she was a killer, you would have moved heaven and earth to prove it."

Read nodded with transparent reluctance. "Perhaps, but she still stole a shed-load of money."

"They do that on Wall Street every day, and in your City of London, too. It's called speculating, or profit-taking, in polite circles."

"Yeah, but they get prosecuted if they get caught *speculating* with money they don't have."

Nate took a long swallow of beer, disregarding the two women at a nearby table who were staring at him with their tongues almost hanging out. "Yeah well, what she did was wrong, but from what I've found out about her, I'm convinced she was coerced into it somehow. She isn't the type to do something like that off her own bat."

"Good luck proving it."

Nate shook his head, ignoring the interruption. "No, she wasn't in it alone, but some clever bastard was pulling her strings, and when it all went wrong, he left her to take the fall. My money's on that sleaze-bag boss of hers, Jeff Williams. I'm convinced he's in it up to his grubby little neck. The tosser's far too smooth for my liking."

"Good luck trying to prove that, as well."

"Ah, so now I get it!" A slow smile spread across Nate's features. "I wondered why you were telling me all this. You've tried to prove it and failed, so you think yours truly, with the strength of the press at his disposal, might have a better shot at it."

Read gave a noncommittal shrug. "Williams is whiter than white."

Nate blew air through his lips and refrained from comment. "No known debts, top-notch credit rating, happy family life, spotless record with the firm, golf handicap in single figures, does the funny handshake bit." He shrugged. "What more do you want?"

"Sounds too good to be true, if you ask me. Everyone has something to hide." Nate drained his pint. "So where's she living, our Ms. Miller, now that she's out?"

"Couldn't possibly tell you that. It's between her and her probation officer."

"Not with her parents then?" Read shook his head. "Thought not. I gather they haven't actually been pillars of support. Too busy maintaining their social position and worrying about what they'll say at the country club about their daughter's rather dramatic fall from grace to look out for the girl's interests."

"You could say that."

"Poor kid."

"She's hardly a kid, Nate. She's twenty-eight, and she knew precisely what risks she was taking when she stole that dosh."

"So why are you telling me all this, Peter? You know I want to talk to her, but if you won't tell me where to find her, what chance do I…hey, hang on a minute." Nate smirked, offering a flash of perfect American dentistry for the women at the adjoining table to drool over. "Between her and her probation officer, you say?" Read nodded, not quite managing to suppress a smile of his own. "And most people return to the area they know best when they get out. She wouldn't want to be back in the city after what happened to her there, and anyway, she'd never get another job in finance a month of Sundays. So"—Nate paused, rubbing a chin adorned with five-o'clock shadow as he thought it through—"she'll have gone back to her roots, which are in the New Forest." He looked enquiringly at Read, who maintained a neutral expression but didn't actually deny it. "Which means her nearest probation service will be in Southampton, right?"

Read downed the last of his pint and stood up. "I never said a word, remember."

"Course you didn't."

Read waved over his shoulder as he pushed his way through the crowded bar and disappeared from view. Nate waited a moment and then followed him out the door, winking at the two gawping women as he passed their table. What contacts did he have in the Southampton Probation Service who'd be prepared to give him the inside track on Lauren Miller's whereabouts?

* * * *

Lauren huddled in the passenger seat of a nondescript Ford Fiesta and stared out the window until the drab prison buildings receded from view. She thought about the eclectic mix of people she'd come into contact with during her time inside. Women with pathetically sad reasons for finishing up incarcerated, almost always thanks to the machinations of the men in their lives. She watched the barren hedgerows hurtling past her window without really seeing them, idly wondering whose car it was that she was riding in. It didn't belong to her parents, that was for sure. They wouldn't normally be seen dead in such a common vehicle and had obviously commandeered it for reasons of anonymity. Marian Miller would never live it down if she was seen hanging about outside a prison or, worse yet, was photographed by the paparazzi as she drove Lauren away. That would account for the sun glasses, presumably, even though it was a drab day and rain was forecast.

So this was freedom. Lauren had spent countless hours wondering how she'd feel when the day finally came. Now she knew. She felt nothing at all, other than the overwhelming desire for revenge, of course. That had never gone away and was the only emotion she'd permitted herself to feel throughout this entire terrifying ordeal. Sometimes she thought it was the only thing that had got her through it. The bitter taste of betrayal was as fresh on her tongue now as it had been on the day when her world fell apart over three years before. She could still recall the moment when it dawned on her that everything she'd done had been based on a pack of lies and that she'd fallen for the oldest line in the book. She'd been used, exploited, and then left to carry the can alone.

Lauren grimaced. She'd been an idiot, but if nothing else, prison had taught her the value of patience. She wouldn't rush into anything now but would let Williams sweat a bit first. He'd know she was out and would wonder what she intended to do about him. She'd served her time, couldn't be tried for the same offence again, and as her life was in ruins anyway, she had nothing to lose by going after him. Williams was a controlling bastard, and he'd want to see her. He probably imagined that she was still the same naive, trusting individual she'd once been and that he could bend her to his will with a pat on the head and a few carefully chosen endearments.

Dream on, you evil bastard!

"It's so lovely to have you back with us, darling." Her mother glanced at her and plastered on an artificial smile. "But you look so pale."

"Being locked up all day tends to do that to you, Mother."

"Yes, but still, you need to get some sun."

"Are we going on holiday, then?" Lauren knew they weren't—apart from anything else, she was on probation and wasn't allowed to leave the country without permission—but she wanted to see how her mother would respond.

"Well no, darling, not right now because—"

"Then where am I going to get any sunshine in the middle of March in bloody England?"

Her mother shuddered. "That place has made you coarse, Lauren."

Lauren almost smiled as she watched her mother's perfectly made-up face twist into an expression of distaste, but guilt immediately banished all thoughts of smiling from her head. She knew how badly she'd let her parents down. She also knew that they didn't believe her version of events, even though they pretended that they did. That was one of the reasons why she hadn't let them come to visit her. Not that they'd tried too hard and were probably relieved when she'd said she didn't want to see them.

"Where's Father?"

"Oh, he wanted to come, darling, really he did. He's anxious to see you, but he had a meeting he simply couldn't get out of."

Lauren rolled her eyes. Some things never changed. "Never mind, I'll see him at home then later, shall I?"

"Well…er, no."

Lauren watched her mother struggling with her acute embarrassment, temporarily forgetting that she was the cause of it. She'd never felt less connected to her than she did now but would give what few possessions she could still call her own if her mother would say, just once, that she truly believed she wasn't solely responsible for what she'd done. They had never been close, but wasn't blood supposed to be thicker than water? She had visited unnecessary troubles upon them as a family and ought to be glad they were still standing by her, but still…

Lauren concentrated on the passing scenery as they sped down the motorway. Maybe it would be better if the connection was broken altogether. Prison, and the events that led to Lauren's incarceration, had changed her—how could they not have done?—and she would now never be the person she'd worked so hard to become in an effort to make an impression upon her ambitious parents.

"Then where am I going?" she asked, her face still turned away from her mother.

"Well, the thing is—" Her mother removed one hand from the steering wheel and wiped imaginary sweat from her brow. "The thing is, darling, since talk of your release found its way into the press, we've been besieged with reporters, and much as we'd like to have you there, you'd never be left in peace if you came home."

"Me or you, Mother?"

"Don't be like that, Lauren," she snapped. "I'm doing my best here."

Lauren regretted her outburst. "It's all right," she said, sighing. "I know you've paid the rent on a cottage in the forest for me. They told me that before I was released, and I'm grateful to you, really I am. I'd like to go straight there now if that's okay with you."

Her mother breathed an audible sigh of relief. "And so you shall, darling, if it's what you really want. I expect you're anxious to get back to normal."

Normal? Her mother really did live in cloud cuckoo land. Lauren knew very well that her life would never be remotely normal ever again.

"Yes," she said quietly, "that's what I want."

Chapter Two

Lauren was already awake when her alarm went off at five in the morning. She shut it off and lay immobile for a minute or two, listening to the crystalline silence. The soothing sound of dawn in the forest vied with the urge to pull the covers over her head and sleep for the next five years. In prison, constant noise and lack of privacy were the two things she'd found hardest to deal with. Now that she had both in abundance, she struggled to make the adjustment.

Aware of time passing, Lauren pushed the covers aside. The temperature in the bedroom couldn't have been much above freezing. She shivered as she shoved her feet into slippers and pulled a thick dressing gown on over the baggy T-shirt she slept in. To call this place a cottage would trouble the conscience of even the most silver-tongued estate agent. A shack would better describe her current accommodation, but Lauren didn't care about her reduced circumstances that she had chosen by not returning to luxury living at her parents' home. At least she had her freedom. Rents in this part of the world were ruinously expensive, and her mother, to her credit, had done what she could to make the place seem homely. Just as well because Lauren didn't have the energy to care and so wouldn't have bothered.

The minuscule lounge was spotlessly clean, with fresh curtains at the window and a huge supply of logs for the open fire—her only form of heating. The old-fashioned kitchen was kitted out with a mishmash of crockery and pots and pans that she recognized as her mother's cast-offs. The ancient fridge hummed and rattled in the otherwise-silent room, stocked with the sort of foods that Lauren could no longer stomach after three years of prison fare. The downstairs bathroom, a much-later addition to the shack, was furnished with piles of fluffy towels that looked incongruous draped over the rusty tub. The expensive bath foam, also supplied by her mother, was one of the few touches Lauren genuinely appreciated since no matter how often she bathed, she couldn't seem to get the desperate smell of prison off her body.

Upstairs, the one bedroom was supplied with an electric fan heater that spewed dust every time she turned it on, making her sneeze. The bed was piled with blankets, crisp cotton sheets, and the old patchwork quilt from Lauren's room at home. The wardrobe was full of clothes her mother had brought over ahead of her release, presumably so Lauren wouldn't embarrass them by returning home and collecting them herself. The shelves were crammed with books, much-loved soft toys from her childhood, and photographs of the family group in happier times.

Lauren made a dash down the rickety stairs, moving fast in an effort to retain the heat from her bed, and crashed through the bathroom door. The ancient and temperamental water heater wasn't up to producing hot water at this ridiculously early hour—or at any hour at all, come to that, unless it was in an especially accommodating mood—so Lauren forced herself to endure thirty seconds under a cold spray, which was enough to wake her up completely. She dried herself off and jumped into a pair of jeans and a thick sweatshirt but didn't bother with breakfast. She wasn't hungry, and anyway there would be ample time to eat at the greasy spoon on the bypass where she worked the graveyard shift. She thrust her arms into her old sheepskin jacket, wound a scarf several times round her neck, pulled on a pair of gloves, and left the shack, double-locking the door behind her. It wasn't much of a place, but it was hers—at least for the next year—and she didn't want anyone invading her privacy ever again.

In the two weeks since she'd left prison, Lauren had already fallen into a routine that was almost comforting in its banality. She'd told her mother in a letter that she'd prefer to live somewhere isolated, and her mother had certainly delivered. It couldn't get much more isolated than this quiet unmade track. As far as she was aware, no casual passers-by had ventured this far into the forest since she'd taken up residence, and she had no immediate neighbours to give her grief. Her breath came out in misty clouds in front of her face as she wheeled out the ancient bicycle that she'd bought from a secondhand shop in town when she got tired of covering the two-mile distance to the bus stop on foot each morning. It had an old-fashioned basket on the handlebars and a bell that jingled every time she rode over rough ground. On the plus side, it was in good working order and unlikely to attract the attention of even the most desperate thief. With a sigh at the pointlessness of her existence, she mounted up, switched on the headlamp, and pedalled off into the predawn stillness.

Lauren got up early six days a week and went to work for minimum wage at the transport café where everyone except the owner thought her name was Louise. She chose the graveyard shift because no one was awake enough to talk to her, or to care much about who she was, where she'd suddenly come from, and why she chose to work in such a dead-end job. The lorry drivers who frequented the place leered at her, sometimes suggesting ways in which she might like to supplement her meagre income. She ignored them, and they eventually got tired of the game and left her alone.

At the end of each shift she caught the bus back to Brockenhurst, usually stopping at the general store for a few supplies. She didn't care what she ate as long as it was cheap and kept her alive. And Lauren had a very good reason for wanting to stay alive. It was the same one that had got her through the terrifying ordeal of prison and the stigma of being branded a criminal.

It was the one they called revenge.

Gradually she started to recognize a few faces about town but avoided all the friendly, inquisitive questions about her sudden appearance in the district and kept herself to herself as much as possible. On the one occasion so far that she'd been to Southampton to report to her probation officer, she took the opportunity to descend upon the library and stock up on reading material. She had no television, stereo, or radio at the shack and no telephone either, which was just the way she wanted it. The television in the corner of the café was permanently tuned to Sky News, which kept her informed about current affairs, whether she liked it or not. She didn't particularly. Lauren supposed that she'd developed a hard shell since going inside. Distressing scenes of displaced refugees in war-torn countries living in tents and surviving on handfuls of rice—scenes that would once have reduced her to tears and had her reaching for her chequebook—now left her cold.

At home she had large log fires each evening, curled up in front of them with a book, and lost herself in a fictional world that bore no resemblance to her own bleak existence. Eventually her eyes dropped, and she fell into a dreamless sleep, only to wake before dawn and do it all over again.

Her mother gave her a pay-as-you-go mobile, making her promise to keep it charged and topped up. She threw it into a drawer the moment she left, and there it languished still. Lauren didn't want to speak to anyone and was fairly sure no one was gagging to get in touch with her. Except, perhaps, one person, and she fully intended to keep him waiting for a lot longer yet.

She'd phoned home a couple of times from the café. Her mother made vague noises about her and her father coming down to visit, but Lauren knew it was unlikely to happen and really didn't mind about the rift.

Lauren opened the back door to the café and heaved an overflowing bin of scraps toward the rubbish skip. For the third day in a row, a small, mangy mongrel dog lurked there. It wagged halfheartedly at Lauren, clearly poised for flight if she reacted aggressively, but too hungry to run off. Lauren liked dogs and recognized a fellow troubled soul when she saw one. She crouched down and spoke in a nonthreatening tone to the animal. He was a mixture of brown and black, with lighter patches that might once have been white, but as his wiry coat was caked with dirt, it was difficult to tell. He looked at Lauren and cocked one ear inquisitively, the other remaining flat against his head, his wide soulful eyes reminding her a bit of a frog.

"Hey, Kermit," she said, thinking that the name suited him. "Are you hungry, boy?"

She rummaged amongst the leftovers and found a chop bone and half a sausage. She threw both to the dog, and he downed them in two swallows without involving his teeth in the process, licked his lips, and looked up at her hopefully. Laughing, Lauren found him something else.

Kermit appeared the next day and the next. On the fourth, he tried to keep up with the bus when she boarded it. On the fifth, she thought he'd taken himself off somewhere else, and was a bit downcast when he didn't appear, only to discover him sitting in the trees next to the place where she chained her bike up before boarding the bus, patiently waiting. He wagged his stubby tail in recognition when she approached, and Lauren's heavy heart lifted. She had no idea how he'd found her bike, but when for the first time he allowed her to pet him, Lauren accepted that, like it or not, she was about to share the shack with this eager-to-please little stray.

"Come on then, Kermit," she said, wheeling the bike away from the trees. "I suppose we'd better go and buy something for your dinner." She sniffed the gloved hand she'd just stroked him with and wrinkled her nose. "And something to give you a bath with as well, I guess."

If Kermit's frantic wagging was anything to go by, he was in complete agreement. At least with the bit about dinner.

That had been a week ago, and Kermit was now a firm fixture in the shack. He accompanied Lauren each morning as far as the bus stop and then sat guard over her bike until she returned, wagging furiously when he heard the bus approaching. He was proving to be a good companion, and Lauren found a little optimism filtering into her mood as a consequence. The weather gradually improved, and since the clocks had recently gone forward, the days were getting longer. She and Kermit took advantage of that and embarked upon long, exploratory walks in the forest, watching it slowly come to life again. A bit like her, she supposed. They made the acquaintance of some of the shaggy ponies who resided there, roaming free, and became intimately acquainted with the topography of the region. Lauren returned from these rambles physically exhausted and sometimes even hungry, wondering if that was a good sign.

Monday was her day off, but it proved impossible to lie in because something caused Kermit to start barking frantically at an early hour. It was, of all things, the postman.

"Well," she said, ruffling his spiky head. "I suppose dogs are meant to bark at postmen, so I can't really tell you off, can I?"

Kermit wagged in full agreement and resumed his place on Lauren's bed, as close to her as he could get. Duty done, he immediately closed his eyes again and was soon snoring. But she was awake now, even though it was still before seven o'clock, and went downstairs to see what the postman had brought for her.

Probably junk mail.

But it wasn't junk. It was a letter addressed to her that her mother had forwarded on. The postmark was too smudged for her to make out where the letter had originated, but she had a strange premonition that she wasn't going to like whatever it said. She almost threw it unopened into the dying embers of last night's fire, but curiosity eventually got the better of her, and she ripped it open. The note was typewritten and unsigned. Her correspondent claimed to know where she was living and wanted what was due to him.

Have one hundred thousand pounds in cash ready, and I'll be in touch, it said.

Lauren's first reaction was to laugh. One hundred thousand! Where the hell was she supposed to get that sort of money? And who'd want to threaten her like this, anyway? Jeff Williams sprang to mind, but he was the last person alive whom she'd voluntarily give money to. It ought to be the other way round if there was any justice in this world, but Lauren could now categorically state that there wasn't. Anyway, if her unnamed, cowardly correspondent knew where she lived, if he'd seen the shack even from the outside, then he must realize that even one hundred pounds would be beyond her right now. Not that he could really know where she lived, or presumably he would have delivered the letter personally. That thought made her feel a little better, and she tried to put the incident out of her mind.

In spite of her best endeavours to find displacement activities, she couldn't stop thinking about it, becoming increasingly certain that Williams wouldn't be behind such an unsophisticated threat. He was a meticulous planner and never took unnecessary risks any more than he did things without a reason. She fully expected him to try and see her at some point, but why demand money from a bloodless stone? Perhaps the letter's author was one of the many people who'd written to her whilst she was banged up—strangers offering to befriend her, men offering to marry her. At first she was bemused by their behaviour, until it occurred to her that they probably thought she knew where the money she'd stolen had finished up and wanted part of it.

Even though she tried to convince herself it was just some crank playing mind games with her, the letter unnerved Lauren, and she was continuously on edge for the next few days. She jumped at shadows, saw things that weren't there, and took great comfort from Kermit's presence. In her bleaker moments, she wondered if the shack was a little too remote, even for her, and whether she ought to stop trying to hide from a world that didn't particularly give a toss about her anyway.

Perhaps she'd become paranoid since receiving the letter, but she was convinced she was being watched. She'd seen the same shifty bloke hanging around outside the café three days running. He didn't ever come inside, and it was difficult to imagine why anyone would want to stop in what was little more than an oversized lay-by unless they were hungry or had been caught short. She hadn't seen him for the past couple of days, but if his intention had been to unnerve her, then he'd done a first-rate job.

Then she came home from work one day and was equally convinced that the shack had been searched during her absence. Everything had been put back as it was—almost, but not quite. Her nerves were stretched to breaking point by the discovery, and the noises in the forest, once so calming, now seemed threatening. For the first time she wished she had a radio or something. Anything that would drown out the sounds of nature and stop her straining to hear the slightest unfamiliar noise. Her fledgling feelings of optimism deserted her, and she was thrown back into the dark hole of despair she'd inhabited for the past three years. This time there didn't seem to be any point in trying to climb out of it.

She took one of her long afternoon rambles with Kermit a few days after the break-in, during which she'd tried to concentrate on the positive aspects of her life. There was only one, and it never varied. It was the day when she would revenge herself upon Williams.

"I'm coming for you, Jeff, never fear," she shouted aloud, frightening birds out of a nearby tree and laughing aloud, wondering if she was cracking up.

As she approached the shack, she saw a strange man sitting on her doorstep, reading a book like he had every right in the world to be there. She slowed her pace, her heart hammering in her ears, and did a quick mental revision of the rules. Which one had she infringed this time? Being incarcerated at Her Majesty's pleasure did that to a person.

Then the anger kicked in. She was free to do as she bloody well pleased, and having strangers foisted upon her did not please her one little bit.

"Who the hell are you," she demanded belligerently, "and what are you doing on my property?"

The man stood up. He was tall, probably over six foot and well put together with thick brown hair falling across his face, a half-day's growth of stubble on his chin and intelligent grey eyes. The sort of man a woman would look at twice. Well, any woman except Lauren, perhaps.

"Hi there," he said, speaking in a soft American drawl. "You must be Lauren."

Lauren froze. How had an American fetched up in her isolated spot in the forest, and more to the point, how did he know who she was?

"Not that it's any of your business, but my name's Louise," she said shortly, playing for time whilst she tried to decide what to do.

"Hi, I'm Nate Black." He took a step toward her and held out his hand, but she ignored it.

"Don't come any closer." She could hear the panic in her own voice. He obviously could, too, because he backed off, palms spread outward in a non-hostile gesture. "Right now, just get out of here before I set my dog on you." Kermit obligingly growled but didn't move from Lauren's side.

"Hey, I don't wanna bother you. I just hoped that we could have a chat. I tried to come and see you inside, but you wouldn't send me a V.O."

"I don't know what you're talking about." But Lauren could see that she wasn't fooling him. This guy knew who she was, and she instinctively trusted him. But then she'd instinctively trusted a man before, and look where that had landed her. When it came to men, her instincts weren't worth diddly-squat. She needed to shut herself away in the shack until this particular one got fed up with being blanked and legged it. Unfortunately, it didn't look as though it was going to happen any time soon since he was still blocking her path to the door. "Just leave me alone, okay," she said, trying to sidestep him.

"Look, I'm an investigative journalist, writing a book about miscarriages of justice, and I'd like to talk to you about what happened to you."

It was pointless continuing to deny her identity, but that didn't mean she had to talk to him. "There was no miscarriage of justice in my case. I was guilty. I've served my time," she said, thinking that sounded like a line from a bad movie and, against all the odds, feeling a wild giggle building inside her. "I just want to be left alone."

"I think there was more to it than that." He smiled at her, and for the first time, Lauren actually considered talking to him. There was just something about him. Something in his expression that made her think he might understand what she'd been through. But no! She had nothing to say to him and made a fresh attempt to reach her door. Once again he blocked her path. "Part of my book will concentrate on women who commit crimes that are out of character, and the forces in their lives that compelled them to do it."

Lauren stared at him. "Got your insurance up to date, have you?"

He blinked. "Sorry, I'm not with you."

"Unsubstantiated written allegations are known as libel in the legal world, in case you didn't know it, and people tend to get sued for that sort of thing."

"They told me you were smart."

"Don't patronise me."

"Hey, that's not what I'm doing." He smiled in an infuriatingly lazy manner that she found strangely disquieting. "And I don't intend to publish anything that's libelous. The book's been commissioned by one of the big American publishing houses, and their legal team will make sure I don't get carried away and cross that particular line. But, about your situation, you can't substantiate your allegations about Williams on your own, but perhaps together we could—"

"How did you know I made any allegations about him?" she asked, her suspicions on high alert. "It was never made public."

"I'm an investigative journalist," he said, flashing a set of perfect white teeth, his air of total confidence almost, but not quite, compelling, "and I have sources you can only dream about."

"This might upset your delicate male ego, but I really don't give a damn."

"You can't fight powerful institutions on your own, Lauren," he said. "But with the might of the press behind you, anything's possible."

"Just go away," she said wearily, aware that she'd already said more than she'd intended to.

"Come on, Lauren, what have you got to lose by just chatting to me? I promise I won't use anything you say without your prior knowledge and consent."

Lauren rolled her eyes. "And when a man gives me his word, that's supposed to make me feel better?"

"He really hurt you, didn't he?"

The compassion in Nate's eyes almost floored her. She could cope with just about anything life threw at her, expect sympathy.

"Just leave me alone."

"If it's any consolation, I know what you're going through. My mom was thrown in jail back in the States for something she didn't do. That's why I gave up my column on the *Sunday Inquirer* to go and help her out."

Lauren nodded without realizing she was doing so. She thought he looked vaguely familiar, and now she understood why. He'd written a popular column in the *Inquirer* for some years, doing exposés on the rich and famous, his picture accompanying his byline. "Did you get her off?" she asked, regretting showing any interest as soon as the words left her mouth.

"Yeah, eventually. The police thought she was an easy target so didn't bother to look any further." He paused to cock one eyebrow. "Sound familiar, does it?"

"Just go away and don't come back. I've got nothing to say to you."

When he didn't budge, Lauren lost it and told Kermit to attack. The dog charged up to Nate willingly enough and barred his teeth. Then he ruined it all by pausing to sniff his outstretched hand. He appeared to approve of whatever scent he picked up from it, rolled on his back, and let Nate tickle his stomach. Lauren sighed. *There's loyalty for you, but then Kermit was a male, so what else could she have expected?*

"Nice dog," Nate said, smiling up at her.

"Just go," she said again, taking the opportunity to sneak past him. Before he could turn round and work more of his charm on her, she had unlocked the door and took considerable satisfaction in slamming it in his face.

Nate must have got the hint because when she looked again, he was gone, but she was on edge for days afterward, lonely in spite of Kermit's presence. Nate had unlocked something inside her, but she couldn't begin to put a name to her feelings. Hope would be an exaggeration. There was no cause for optimism in her life, and she knew all his talk about journalistic resources was just that—talk. Or, more accurately, a means of getting her to talk to him.

Whatever, she was sure she'd seen the last of him and so was astonished when he appeared at the café just before the end of her shift, four days later. Her usually bleary-eyed and non-talkative fellow waitress perked up no end at the sight of him. He seemed perfectly relaxed even though it was obvious he didn't belong in such a dive. He was wearing jeans and a leather bomber jacket but still looked several cuts above the rest of the clientele.

"Will you look at that," said Cindy, Lauren's colleague. "What the hell's that hunk doing in a place like this?"

"Not staying long," muttered Lauren, wiping the counter as though she bore it a grudge and pointedly ignoring his friendly smile.

"Just my luck," complained Cindy, "he's taken one of your tables."

"He's all yours."

"Do you mean that?" Lauren nodded. "Gee, thanks!"

And she sashayed off to smile at Nate and take forever with his order.

He appeared three mornings in succession, but Lauren refused to relent. She didn't speak a single word to him, somehow trusting that he wouldn't let on to Cindy and the others who she really was, not if he still entertained any hope of getting her to talk to him, which he obviously did.

She left for work the next day, wondering how long it would take Nate to realize she was one of the few women on the planet who was immune to his quicksilver charm. Aware that he was no quitter, she was confident that he'd still be around today and took a perverse sort of comfort from that knowledge. She was equally disturbed by the degree of disappointment she felt at the prospect of his eventually giving up and moving on. She'd sort of got used to him sitting where he could keep her in his line of vision, watching over her like some sort of brooding guardian angel.

The turbulent nature of her thoughts made her less alert than usual, and she didn't notice a strange man lurking outside the shack as she wheeled her bike out. Kermit's growl alerted her to his presence just in time, and she was able to prevent him from grabbing her from behind by pushing the bike between them.

"You've been expecting me," he said, scowling at Kermit and slowly backing off.

"How can I have been expecting you if I don't know who you are?"

Lauren spoke belligerently, trying not to let her fear show. Prison had taught her never to reveal her weaknesses, especially when being threatened by mindless bullies, and that the best form of defence was always attack. She assessed the man as she spoke. He was short, probably no taller than her own height of five-eight, but stocky, twice her weight, and he looked as though he was well able to handle himself. He had a nose that had been broken, perhaps more than once, the lifeless eyes of a dead fish, and large hands that were fisted at his sides, as though he was impatient to put them to use on her.

"What do you want?" she asked when he showed no sign of leaving.

"What I want is the hundred grand you owe me."

Lauren actually laughed at that one. "Ah, so you're the anonymous letter writer."

"Yeah. I had a bit of bother finding you so thought I'd let you know I was on my way, before you got too cosy like and forgot about yer debts."

"Well, I'm sorry to disappoint you, but you're wasting your time. Look around you." She swept one arm in a wide arc. "Where would I get that sort of money?"

"Not my problem, sweetheart. In my world, you pay your debts or take the consequences."

"I don't owe you anything. You've got the wrong address. Now, get out of my way." She tried to wheel the bike past him, but he blocked her path with his bulk. Kermit's growling went up a level.

"Look, darling, I don't wanna hurt you, but if you don't play ball, then I won't hesitate to inflict serious pain, and that scrawny mutt of yours ain't gonna stop me. My name's Reg Fowler." Lauren seriously doubted it was his real name but didn't intend to get into a discussion on the matter and just shrugged. "Does that mean anything to you?"

"Should it?"

"Doesn't matter, you won't forget it. Now, you and me are gonna go back inside your sumptuous accommodation, and you're gonna tell me where I can get me hands on me money."

"For the last time, I don't have any money." She noticed the vicious glint of determination in his eye and clutched her hands together to prevent them from shaking. She'd seen that look in the eyes of more than one hard woman inside and knew he meant business. She tamped down her fear, aware that it was essential to maintain her aggressive stance. "And even if I was in funds, why would I give them to you?"

"Don't play games. I know you have to put up a front until you've done your probation, but you're loaded, and I want what's mine."

He lunged forward with surprising dexterity for such a heavy man and grabbed her arm. At the same time Kermit sprang and sank his teeth into his shin. The man howled and shook Kermit off, knocking Lauren and her bike to the ground in the process. Her head made firm contact with the handlebars and just for a moment she was too dazed to move. She quickly realized that she couldn't stay where she was, vulnerable to his next attack, and grabbed her bicycle pump, more than ready to use it as a weapon. But Fowler, or whatever his name was, was already limping away, leaning over every so often to clutch at his bleeding shin.

"One more week, that's all I'll give you. Meet me one week today, I'll let you know when and where, and have my money with you."

"But I—"

"Meet me where I say, or I'll be back," he warned her, "and the next time I won't play so nice."

He hobbled toward a car he'd left farther down the track. Lauren, quaking now there was no need to disguise her fear, watched him drive away and waited until she was sure he was gone. Then she went back inside, washed the side of her face where it was bleeding, her hands trembling so badly that the dressing she stuck over the wound finished up at right-angles. She made a big fuss of Kermit, who had undoubtedly saved the day. Her hands still trembled, and she wished that she had some medicinal brandy to help her with the shock. It wasn't so much what the man had said that bothered her. She had no money and could easily prove it by showing him the inside of the shack—except she was sure now that it had been searched, and by him, so he must already know that. He must really believe that she had the stolen funds hidden somewhere and was serving out her probation before she touched them. But the question remained. Who was he, and who did he work for?

Whatever, she didn't doubt that he would be back if she ignored his next letter, and this time Kermit would get hurt if he tried to defend her. Worse, her precious privacy had been invaded, and she would never have a moment's peace at the shack ever again.

Lauren cycled to the bus stop on wobbly legs, only just catching the bus that would get her to work on time, her head spinning from the exertion. All the while she was thinking hard. She needed help and could no longer afford to be picky. Under the circumstances, there was only one person she was prepared to put her trust in.

Well, some of it, anyway, and he'd be sitting at Cindy's table when she arrived at work, staring at her through those remarkable grey eyes that appeared to see so much.

The only problem was, when she arrived, Nate was nowhere in sight.

Chapter Three

The intrusively shrill sound of the alarm pierced Nate's subconscious. With a groan, he slammed it off and buried his head under the pillow, attempting to chase the tail end of an erotic dream. Damn, it was gone, his recollection of its content flimsy and incomplete. He sat up, grouchy and discomposed, ran a hand through his hair, and wondered why he was still bothering with Lauren Miller. There had to be more productive ways of spending his time. Dragging himself out of his warm hotel bed at the crack of dawn every damned day, just to be ignored by Lauren in that god-awful café she worked in, wasn't exactly his idea of a good time.

Women usually warmed to Nate, but this one appeared singularly unimpressed by his charm offensive. Her frosty attitude hadn't thawed one iota in all the days he'd been going to the café, but he enjoyed a challenge and refused to be discouraged. His journalistic antennae were on high alert, and something told him there was a lot more to her story than had ever reached the public domain. If he could somehow win her trust and persuade her to open up to him, what she had to say could well prove to be the elusive unique selling point he'd been seeking, to give his book that all important edge.

So he carried on going to the café, which at least gave him an excuse to look at Lauren. And Nate enjoyed looking at her. Even after the ordeal of prison, she was still a traffic stopper. According to Peter Read, she'd once been voluptuous but had obviously shed a couple of stone whilst inside and was now too thin. All the pictures he'd seen of her before she was arrested showed a confident young woman with thick dark hair hanging halfway down her back and big blue eyes that dominated a heart-shaped face, screaming confidence and vulnerability both at the same time. The sort of woman that men instinctively went that extra mile for.

That face was now gaunt. Hollow cheekbones drew his eye, as did a strained, wary expression, and eyes as dead as her emotions. Her short, spiky hairstyle suited her face, adding to her appearance of fragility. Nate knew that to have survived three years in the tough environment of a women's prison, Lauren had to be anything but fragile. That only added to his curiosity about her determination to bury herself away from the world without any apparent need for anything from anyone.

That was bull, of course. Everyone needed people, but working in that dump of a café couldn't be doing much for her self-esteem. Some of the drivers who frequented the place were the dregs, and Nate felt uncomfortable about her continuous exposure to their crude language and questionable standards of hygiene. By dragging her true history out of her, he hoped to open up the emotional floodgates. Pouring it all out to a sympathetic listener might restore her zest for life. He had contacts, knew people who'd be prepared to look past her criminal record and see her for what she really was. In short, he could help her, but she didn't seem to want his help.

She deliberately blanked him whenever he was in the café, but over the last couple of days he'd caught her glancing at him a couple of times when she thought he was busy fending off Cindy. He got the impression that she was trying to decide what it was that he really wanted from her. If she'd been used and then left in the lurch by some bastard, it was little wonder that she suspected his motives, and he needed to handle her with kid gloves. But how the hell was he supposed to do that when she wouldn't even talk to him?

He dropped his head back on the pillows, thinking it through. Perhaps if he disappeared for a day or two? She'd got used to him being there, even if she didn't deign to speak to him. Women, in his extensive experience, were the most contrary creatures on the planet.

If he didn't show for a while, played hard ball, maybe she'd actually be pleased to see him again when he reappeared. He wasn't too optimistic, but his present tactics weren't working, so anything was worth a try.

Having made the decision to give the café a miss that morning, Nate treated himself to a well-earned lie in, reconstructing his day in his head. Perhaps he should approach this story from a different angle. Lauren wasn't the only person with a tale to tell, and this being Thursday, he knew where to find the next person on his list who might shed a little light on matter. All he had to do now was to arrange an accidental meeting with her.

Nate had the inside track on all the major players and knew that Gloria Williams attended a spinning class at a high-end Wimbledon gym every Thursday, without fail. When the class finished, she and a couple of girlfriends always hit the pool, flaunting toned bodies in front of the lifeguard and any other men whom they considered deserving of their attention. Hopefully Nate would qualify.

By the time he reached the gym, the spinning class was nearing its end. He paid a small fortune for a day's membership and headed for the locker room. The pool was almost deserted. Nate, a strong swimmer, got rid of the frustration that had accrued from weeks of celibate living by doing several lengths of flat-out crawl. He was breathing heavily when the sound of feminine chatter warned him it was show time.

Nate ignored the three women as they stepped into the pool at the shallow end. They started on slow lengths of breast stroke, keeping their heads well clear of the water, presumably to protect their hairdos. He recognized Gloria at once from the pictures he'd seen of her. She was now on the wrong side of forty, and there wasn't an ounce of fat on her perfectly proportioned body. That just wasn't natural, and Nate suspected that she'd received a little artificial help to stay in shape. Her blonde hair was piled artistically on top of her head, diamonds twinkled on fingers, ears, and in her tummy button, and her fingernails and toes were painted bloodred. She didn't immediately start swimming with her friends but instead stood on the steps and did a quick take of the pool. Her gaze fell upon Nate, and she was slow to look away. He groaned, opened his mouth at the wrong moment, and swallowed a mouthful of chlorinated water. He recognized the predatory look and wondered if he'd bitten off more than he could chew in targeting her, but he was here now, so what the hell.

Keeping his head down, Nate swam directly into Gloria's path, colliding with her just as she pushed off from the steps.

"Hey, sorry," he said, placing one hand on the side of the pool and treading water. "I didn't see you there. Are you okay?"

"No damage done." Gloria pushed hair away from her pale blue eyes and regarded him with open interest. "Say, are you American?"

Nate flashed a conciliatory smile. "Guilty as charged."

"I thought so. We don't get many Americans here. Are you just passing through?"

"I haven't decided yet." He turned up the heat behind his smile. "Depends if I find anything worth hanging around for."

"A bit of a free spirit then, are you?" She, too, was treading water, its pressure causing her breasts to spill over the top of her bikini. Nate wasn't a fan of silicone, but he wasn't about to let that stand in his way. He concentrated his eyes on them, just as he was supposed to. "That must make for an interesting life."

"You have no idea." He held out a hand to her. "I'm Nate."

"Gloria." She took his hand and locked his fingers in a surprisingly tight squeeze.

"Well, it was nice meeting you, Gloria, but I guess I'd best be getting along. I'm done here and feel the lure of decent coffee calling. Is there a cafeteria here?"

"Oh yes, just follow the aroma of fresh coffee beans."

"Gotcha!"

And he knew that he had. He wasn't the slightest bit surprised when, less than a quarter of an hour later, minus her girlfriends, Gloria sashayed into the café. She was dressed in tight-fitting jeans and a low-cut top, and her hair was still damp. Presumably she hadn't spent the time to dry it properly for fear that he would leave. His suspicions were confirmed when he noticed that her makeup looked hastily applied. He suppressed a smile, doubting whether she'd ever got ready so quickly in her life before.

"Hey, Gloria, isn't it?" Nate stood up, affecting surprise.

"Oh, I thought you'd be long gone," she said unconvincingly. "The coffee must be good today."

"I've tasted worse. Can I get you one?"

Of course she said yes. He ordered another for himself and spent a moment appraising her over the rim of his mug.

"At the risk of sounding corny," he said, smiling, "do you come here often?"

She laughed. "Only all the time."

That was his cue to say that he could tell as much from her figure. He duly obliged, causing Gloria to let out a coquettish giggle that had no place in the repertoire of a woman her age.

"What does your husband do?" he asked, nodding toward the rings on her left hand.

"Oh." She fiddled with a diamond solitaire the size of a small duck egg, as though annoyed with herself for not having removed it. "He does something boring in the city."

"Sorry, I didn't mean to pry. You obviously don't want to talk about him."

"No, it's not that." She paused, and Nate allowed the silence to lengthen, pretty sure she wouldn't be able to resist breaking it or boasting about her husband's high-flying position. Once again she didn't disappoint. "Jeff's a partner with a major stockbroking firm. He works very long hours, and I don't see much of him during the week," she said with a significant smile. "He has a flat in town and often stays over so that he's on hand for breakfast meetings."

"He must be an idiot if he leaves you all alone." Gloria preened. "Do you have children?"

"Yes, a boy of twelve and a girl of ten, going on twenty-five."

"You don't look old enough."

More fluttering eyelashes. "If I didn't know better, I'd say you were trying to chat me up, Nate."

"If you weren't married, then you wouldn't be left in any doubt about that."

"You're not married yourself then?" Gloria's eyes drifted toward his fingers.

"Nope, not anymore."

"What happened to your—"

"Say, don't I know you from somewhere?"

"I don't think so. I'm sure I'd remember if we'd met."

"No, I've seen your picture somewhere." He tilted his head to one side, deliberately allowing long strands of hair to fall across his face. He'd been told by more than one woman that whenever he did that, the desire to reach across and push it aside was compulsive. He glanced at Gloria's hands. She'd clasped them together on the table in front of her so tightly that her knuckles turned white. Suppressing a smile, he regarded her closely, as though still trying to place her. "In a society magazine, perhaps?" he suggested.

"Not likely."

"I never forget a beautiful face." He flashed another high-voltage smile. "Come on, give me a clue."

"I think you've got me mixed up with someone else." Her voice turned icy. "The only time my picture was plastered over the front pages was under circumstances I'd much rather forget."

"Sorry, this obviously makes you uncomfortable, so let's talk about something else." Nate suspected that she felt flattered to have made the front pages, however distasteful the reason for it. Suggesting a change of subject was the surest way to keep her talking about it.

"No, it's okay. It's just that a few years back a girl that worked for my husband's firm stole a load of money. It hit all the headlines, and Jeff and I were besieged by reporters." She shuddered. "It was a horrendous time for us."

"Ah yes, I remember something about it now."

"And I wish I could forget. That's not the sort of thing you want to be associated with."

"No, I understand that, but surely it was nothing to do with your husband?"

"No, of course not, but the girl worked for him, so her behaviour was ultimately his responsibility."

"I remember that she was a good-looking girl from a decent background, and no one could think what made her do such a thing."

Gloria snorted. "Good-looking? Well, how else could she have wheedled her way into a position of trust so early on? People like her always know how to manipulate men."

Pots and kettles sprang to mind. Nate held the thought and summoned up a sympathetic smile instead. "You mean she was involved with your husband?"

"No, don't be ridiculous! Jeff doesn't need women like her when he has me to come home to."

"Of course he doesn't. That's not what I meant. It's just that you said—"

Gloria sighed. "It never made the papers, but when she was first caught, Lauren tried to say that she was romantically involved with Jeff and that he'd persuaded her to steal the money." She dismissed the possibility with an airy wave of her hand. "That's nonsense, of course, and she soon gave up on that story when she couldn't produce any evidence to back it up."

"I would imagine that she did." Nate drained his coffee and signalled to the waiter for a refill. "But it must have been difficult for you." He briefly covered her hand with his, and she made no attempt to move it away. "What with you and Jeff being so compatible."

"Oh, we understand each other perfectly."

Nate feigned disappointment. "Ah well, there goes my hopes. No way can I compete with a successful stockbroker. Well, it's been nice chatting to you, Gloria," he said, getting to his feet, "but I guess I'd better leave you to—"

"Do you have to go?"

He met her gaze and held it, conveying a blatant message without the need for words. "I think it would be best."

"Don't worry about Jeff. I told you, we have an understanding. I don't ask him what he gets up to in London, and he doesn't cross-question me about my life down here." She leaned toward him, giving him a perfect view of her enhanced cleavage, and finally reached up to move his hair away from his eyes. "It's an arrangement that suits us both."

"Damn, I've got an appointment today that I can't break." She pouted. "Tell you what, give me your number, and if I'm still around next week, I'll give you a call." He paused, treating her to another full-on smile. "Once hubby's safely tucked away in the city, of course."

She returned his smile, reminding Nate of a cat within pouncing distance of the cream. "Naturally."

Nate left the gym, retrieved his car from the multi-storey and headed back toward the New Forest. He had made some progress at last. Gloria had just confirmed a number of his growing suspicions. Jeff Williams was not quite the upstanding pillar of society that Peter Read had suggested. He and Gloria had an open marriage, and under such circumstances, it was very difficult to imagine him ignoring the likes of Lauren Miller when she was working right under his nose and beholden to him for her advancement in the company.

Nate returned to the café the following morning and was encouraged when, instead of blanking him as usual, Lauren's face briefly lit up when he pushed the door open. He took his usual table and sat back, crossing one leg across his opposite knee. He admired the economic elegance of her movements as she cleared the table next to his and felt elated when instead of leaving him to Cindy's not-so-subtle ministrations, she headed toward him herself.

"Morning, Louise. Did you miss me?"

"Why do you ask? Have you been somewhere?"

Nate chuckled. "Say, what happened to your face?" He frowned when he noticed a plaster stuck awkwardly over what looked like a cut or bruise.

"Nothing." She shrugged. "I fell off my bike."

"You ought to be more careful."

"What are you, my mother?"

God, she was spikier than her hair. "Just a concerned customer."

"I'm touched."

"I can see that," he said, taking in her scathing expression.

"Do you still want to talk?" she asked abruptly.

"No, love, I come here for the excellent cuisine and the opportunity to flirt with Cindy."

He was pretty sure Lauren almost smiled at that, but she'd realigned her features into her more customary belligerent expression before he could be certain.

"Meet me at the cottage this afternoon," she said, walking away without giving him the chance to respond.

* * * *

"It doesn't matter." Sandra ran a hand through his hair and kissed his temple. "Don't worry about it. You're just feeling tired, that's all."

Infuriated, Jeff delivered a vicious slap to the side of her face. She cried out and looked at him with abject shock, tears forming in the corners of her eyes. Why did women think that telling a man it didn't matter when he couldn't rise to the occasion would make him feel better? It did just the opposite, highlighting his inadequacies and making him feel ten times worse. It had never happened to Jeff before, and to give Sandra her due, she'd always accommodated his eclectic tastes without complaint, ensuring that he didn't need the little blue pill.

That was before Lauren was released from prison. Since then his mind had been full of her, and he'd had trouble getting it up. She'd been out for over three weeks now, but she'd not gotten in touch with him, and his investigator hadn't been able to find out where she was. She was hiding from him, which both surprised and infuriated Jeff. Lauren had been besotted with him, just as Sandra now was. She'd served a prison sentence for his sake, and he'd been absolutely convinced that she'd contact him the moment she was released. She'd be angry, of course she would, but Jeff would soon talk her round. She must see that there hadn't been any point in them both going down. She would forgive him eventually and then tell him what she'd done with the money. At least she'd kept her wits about her and moved it before the police had a chance to freeze the accounts. That was one of the many things he admired about Lauren. She possessed the ability to remain cool under pressure. It was just a pity she hadn't chosen to share the money's whereabouts with him before she took the fall.

He'd been so sure of her dedication that it hadn't even crossed his mind that she might abscond with the funds herself. Perhaps he should have risked getting a message to her, just to keep her sweet, but what with the police being all over Drake's murder and her having been the last person to see him alive, it had been too dangerous. He'd convinced himself that she'd understand but could see now that she was exacting revenge by keeping him dangling and making him sweat. Jeff had made the mistake of taking Lauren for granted, and it was playing havoc with his love life.

"What did you do that for?" Sandra clutched her cheek and looked at him with confusion rather than condemnation in her eyes.

Jeff looked straight through her, disgusted by her willingness to take whatever he dished out, without complaint. Where was her self-respect? She'd been useful to him whilst he and Lauren had been running their little scam, and he'd actively pursued her for that reason. As company accountant responsible for his area of the operation, her cooperation was vital. He charmed her into not looking too closely at certain aspects of his portfolio and, more crucially, into keeping the auditors off his back. How much she actually knew about his nefarious activities he couldn't have said, but from the few subtle threats she'd issued when his attentions waned, Jeff couldn't risk finishing their relationship. A woman scorned, with access to damaging information, was something he definitely didn't need. But now that Lauren was out, there was nothing else Sandra could do to safeguard his interests, so it was time to move on. Or rather, to move back.

To Lauren.

Jeff's phone rang. It was his investigator, with another negative report, but just hearing Lauren's name on someone else's lips was enough to do what Sandra had been unable to achieve. He was rock hard. He grabbed Sandra's hand, forced her to her knees, and pushed her head toward his groin. She didn't hesitate to take him in her mouth.

"Still haven't been able to track her down," said the man, his tone apologetic. "Can't understand it. None of my contacts in the police know where she is."

"They don't know or aren't saying?" Jeff suppressed a groan and pushed Sandra's head down more firmly.

"I'm pretty sure they don't know. I pay them too well for them to hold out on me."

"Strange." Jeff thrust himself deeper into Sandra's mouth. She gagged but gamely kept working on him.

"Can't understand why they're protecting her new identity so well. And she must have a new identity. If she was living anywhere under her real name, or working under her own National Insurance Number, I'd have found her by now."

Jeff knew why but didn't choose to share that information with his investigator. The police suspected that she had the money and wanted to find it before she disappeared with it.

"Keep looking," he said. "Spend whatever it takes but find her."

"I'm on it."

Jeff cut the connection seconds before exploding at the back of Sandra's throat, holding her head in place so that she was forced to swallow. He threw his own head backward as he climaxed, calling out her name. Except the name that actually escaped his lips wasn't Sandra's.

It was Lauren's.

Chapter Four

Lauren finished her shift on autopilot. She avoided Nate's table, keeping her back turned toward him as much as possible. She was out of practise at handling men—not that she'd exactly excelled in that department in the first place. Still, she didn't want to give the impression that she'd thawed toward him or that there was any possibility of their becoming friends. She'd talk to him to get him out of her life, and that would be that.

She already regretted inviting him to the shack and ceding some of her hard-won privacy. Nate was obviously intelligent, and half truths and vague explanations for her actions wouldn't satisfy him. She'd have to be very convincing to stand any hope of getting rid of him. Damn! She should have ridden out the panic occasioned by Reg Fowler's thuggish threats and forged ahead with her plans. Those plans didn't involve persistent, annoyingly self-assured American hunks. There was nothing Nate could do for her, except draw the attention of the world to the fact that she was out of prison—a situation she particularly wished to avoid. Stupid, stupid, stupid!

"Stop beating yourself up, Lauren," she muttered to herself, aware that the damage was already done. Nate was at least as determined as she was. He had to be. Why else would he turn up in this dump day after day and plonk himself down at one of her tables, following her every movement with eyes like lasers. His mere presence made her feel that he knew something she didn't about her own situation, piquing her curiosity and weakening her resolve. That presumably was his intention, and fool that she was, she'd played straight into his hands.

The cup Lauren held slipped through her fingers and smashed into tiny pieces on the tiled kitchen floor, as splintered as her nerves. She jumped clear of the mess, squealing as hot coffee splattered all over her feet. She barely felt it. What the hell had she been thinking, inviting Nate to the shack? She didn't know anything about the man and only had his word for it that he actually was a journalist. She conveniently forgot that she'd recognised him for his byline picture. Lauren rolled her eyes. Just like everyone else, he probably thought she knew where the money was and reckoned he could persuade her to share.

She wiped up the mess from the kitchen floor and fetched a fresh cup of coffee for her customer, still wondering what had made her behave so rashly. She thought prison had knocked all impulsiveness out of her. In jail, impulsive behaviour brought you to the attention of people whose interest it was far better to avoid.

It was all Nate's fault. Instead of being relieved that he'd got tired of bugging her, Lauren had been disappointed by his non-appearance the previous day. He was a pain in the neck, but she'd got used to him being around and, loath though she was to admit it, took some sort of comfort from his determination to befriend her. Did that mean she felt she could actually trust him? She frowned, her senses rebelling at the mere thought of ever completely trusting any men ever again. A better reason for her knee-jerk reaction would be that Reg Fowler's visit had spooked her badly enough to make her hanker after company. It was a trite explanation, but if she worked at it, she might almost convince herself that it was true.

She ignored Nate as he got up from his table, extracted himself from Cindy's extended farewells, waved to her, and left. The place seemed empty without him, even though every table was occupied. She glanced at the clock. Still another hour and a half left of her shift. It seemed more like an eternity.

Lauren hadn't told Nate to arrive at any particular time. It didn't make much odds because no matter when he came, she wouldn't be ready for him. She couldn't decide whether she wanted him to arrive early and get the torture over with or if she'd prefer to delay the moment indefinitely. In the end she took Kermit for one of their long rambles so that she wouldn't be stuck at home, nerves jangling, waiting on his pleasure. She arrived back at the shack by midafternoon, still undecided how much to tell him, and found Nate once again occupying her doorstep.

"Hi." He stood when he saw her approaching. "Hope I'm not too early. I wasn't sure when you wanted me."

There was nothing she could say to that which wouldn't sound clichéd, so she made do with moving round him and unlocking the door. He followed her inside, looking about with interest.

"Nice place you've got here. Cosy." She raised a brow, convinced that he was being facetious. "Blimey," he said, appearing exasperated as he ran a hand through his hair, "but you're a hard person to compliment."

"Sorry." He was being polite, looking for ways to break the ice, and she regretted her defensiveness. "It's just that where I've been residing for the past few years, you quickly learn to treat all compliments with extreme scepticism. The person doing the complimenting invariably wants something you're unprepared to give up."

She eyed him with caution, uncomfortably aware that within the close confines of the shack he was even more lethally attractive. And dangerous. Yes, the word fitted him well. There was something about this man that spelled danger, and excitement, too. A potent masculinity she was struggling to ignore ignited the air between them, causing something dormant to stir deep within her. She shook her head, but the feeling refused to budge. Hell, what was happening to her?

"I guess you're no different," she said.

"Yeah, I am." He looked her straight in the eye and held her gaze. "You can trust me, Lauren."

She snorted. "Can I?"

"I won't hurt you or ask you for anything you're not willing to give up." Lauren forced herself to look away from him, unsure whether he was being sincere or simply trying to soften her up with *double entendres*. "On that you have my word."

"Perhaps." She shrugged. "We'll see." She turned her attention toward the fire, just to avoid his laser eyes, and raked away the remnants of last night's ashes.

"Here, let me." His hand brushed against hers, and she snatched it away.

"I can manage, thanks." She screwed up newspaper and laid kindling on top of it. "It gets cold in here pretty quickly," she explained, just for something to say to fill the heavy silence. "There's no other heating."

"Come on, I'll do that." He hunkered down beside her.

"Do you ever take *no* for an answer?" she asked, scowling at him as she stood up and let him take over.

"Not often." He flashed a puerile grin. "I didn't know if you'd have had lunch, or supper, or whatever it is you have in this country at this time of day, so I brought something with me." He indicated a couple of carrier bags on the floor by the door. "You dish it up, and I'll start the fire."

Lauren wasn't sure how she felt about having her space taken over but got the feeling that if she didn't do as he asked, then he'd simply do it for her. Besides, she was ravenous. Her nerves had played havoc with her since inviting him here, and she'd had virtually nothing to eat all day. She took the bags into the kitchen and examined their contents. He'd brought enough Chinese food to feed a small army.

"I didn't know what you liked so I brought a little of most things," he shouted through the doorway.

She didn't bother to respond, wondering how he could have known that she adored Chinese food. He couldn't have. It must just be a coincidence. There were a couple of bottles of decent red wine, as well. She examined the labels and was impressed, not having thought that Americans knew much about wine. Lauren hadn't had any alcohol since before they locked her up and wasn't sure that now was the best time to fall off the wagon. Everyone knows that booze loosens tongues. But she could already imagine the taste of the rich red liquid warming her insides, helping to ease the tension that had gripped her ever since Fowler's visit. Just one glass, two at the most, couldn't possibly hurt. She laid plates and cutlery on the kitchen table that was barely large enough for two and certainly not big enough to accommodate all the containers of food. She left some on the work surface and went to see how he was doing with the fire. Annoyingly, he already had flames dancing up the chimney. Kermit was rolling on his back in front of heat, Nate tickling his tummy.

"Seems to be going okay," he said, following her into the kitchen. "Have you got a bottle opener?"

"I've no idea," she said, unable to resist picking up a spare rib and nibbling at it, licking the sauce from her fingers with the tip of her tongue. "Try that drawer over there. I expect my mother thought to bring one over. It's not the sort of thing she'd forget."

He rummaged in the drawer, produced the corkscrew, and brandished it triumphantly above his head. His hand stilled when he saw her licking her fingers.

"Got any glasses?" he asked, his voice a degree or two thicker.

Lauren barely noticed that she ate twice as much as he did, nor did she wonder why he refilled her glass so frequently. All she knew was that food had never tasted more delicious, and if the wine made her feel a little fuzzy…well, that was only to be expected after all this time. It was nothing. She could handle it. Nate kept up a constant stream of conversation about inconsequential matters, forcing responses from her that gradually became less and less guarded. She knew what he was doing, of course. He was trying to make her relax and place her trust in him, and there was no harm in letting him think he was succeeding. That way, if she chose not to be completely honest when they got down to the real reason for his visit, he was less likely to notice the prevarication. Lauren had learned a thing or two about men the hard way, and it amused her to think that she now had this one dancing to her tune.

They moved back to the sitting room with their glasses, and Lauren curled up in the only chair, her feet tucked beneath her. Kermit leapt up and joined her, squashing himself into the space between her and the arm of the chair, his head resting on her thigh. She absently stroked his spiky head, feeling a sense of well-being that had evaded her for over three years. It no longer seemed so important to remain on her guard. Even if she told this man the absolute and complete truth—like she'd tried to tell her parents and the prison councillor—he wouldn't believe her any more than they had. Besides, if he thought she was an out-and-out liar, there'd be no mileage in her story as far as his book was concerned, and he'd clear off to bug someone else.

"You look like you wanna fall asleep."

Lauren jolted back to awareness. Two people in this small room, especially when one of them was as large as Nate, made it seem like the walls were closing in on her. He was opposite her on the settee with wonky springs, the space between them so tight that if her legs hadn't been curled up they'd have probably been touching knees. She felt the beginnings of a smile tugging at her lips and for once didn't attempt to suppress it. Nate had brought her decent wine and her favourite food, so the least she could do was be a little less uptight with him.

"I'm not used to rich food." She rubbed a hand across her stomach and sighed with contentment. "Haven't had any for a while."

He chuckled. "You seemed to be making up for lost time out there."

"I expect I'll live to regret it."

He regarded her without smiling, and if Lauren hadn't known better, she'd have said his features were etched with concern.

But, of course, she knew better. Much better.

"So cynical." He flashed a brief smile before standing to throw another log on the fire, pushing it into place with the heel of his shoe and hastily removing his foot to avoid the shooting sparks. "There, that oughta do it."

"You look comfortable with log fires."

He smiled. "I should be. I was brought up in Colorado, and that equates to log cabins and below-freezing winters. I only moved to New York when I started to make it as a journalist, but I still go back to Colorado whenever I can. The skiing's to die for."

"I know. I skied in Breckenridge once, in another life."

"Yeah, it's a good town. Less pretentious than some of its neighbours."

"What did your mother do?" Lauren asked on impulse.

"Beg your pardon?"

"Your mother. What did she do to finish up in prison?"

"Oh, the usual story. She and my dad are divorced, and she got involved with another guy. What we'd call a redneck back home. I didn't like him much, but then I didn't see much of them, and if he made Mom happy, then who was I to complain." He picked up his glass and took a long swig of his wine, his expression fierce and remote. "What I didn't know was that he was into armed robbery and used Mom's place to stash some of the stuff his stole. We think one of the neighbours suspected something and tipped off the police. Mom lived in an up-market area where her guy was very obviously out of place. Anyway, the police raided, found the gear, and Mom was charged with handling stolen goods. She was given five years—"

"That seems extreme."

"It was, but then I always thought the jury was hard on her because of who she was. She wasn't short of money, you see. She had what most of them didn't, so they couldn't excuse what she'd supposedly done as readily as they would if she'd been down on her luck."

"How long was she inside before you were able to appeal her case?"

He grimaced, his long fingers twisted so tightly round the stem of his glass that she thought it might snap. "Over a year."

"That must have been tough on you all."

"Yeah well, she's out now and has got herself a job helping with administration in the office of a lawyer who deals with cases like hers, pro bono." Nate shrugged. "She's giving something back, and that makes her feel better about herself."

"I'm sure it does."

Nate brushed her fingers as he reached forward to refill her glass. Lauren snatched her hand away as though it had been scalded, realized she'd overreacted when she caught the lazy amusement in his expression, and felt her cheeks flood with colour. This was not going the way she'd intended, and she strove to regain her composure.

"Thanks."

He flashed a glamorous smile. "You're welcome." He stretched his legs sideways. It was the only space available for him to park them in, and shifted his position. "Ouch! This couch feels like it bears me a grudge," he said, grimacing.

She smiled at his discomfort. "I guess it's seen better days."

She couldn't think of anything else to say and didn't bother to try. Nor did he, and for a protracted moment, an emotionally charged silence stretched between them. The only sound in the room was the crackling of the fire and Kermit's soft snores. Even so, Lauren knew that the time had come to pay for her dinner, and suddenly she was anxious to get it over with.

"So, what do you want to know?" she asked.

"Anything you're prepared to tell me that doesn't make you uncomfortable." He took a sip of his wine and placed the glass carefully on the edge of the fireplace. "Why not start at the beginning? Tell me how you got into stockbroking in the first place."

"Actually, my original intention was to go into law." She shrugged. "Perhaps I should have done, but then hindsight's a wonderful thing." He nodded, perhaps in agreement or possibly because he wanted her to cut to the chase. "My mother didn't particularly want children, but my father desperately wanted a son to follow in his footsteps, and his father's before him, and take over what used to be the family solicitor's practise in Southampton."

"Hasn't he heard that women are allowed into the law as well nowadays?"

She dredged up a brief smile. "That snippet of news must have passed him by."

"Sounds like a bit of a dinosaur, if you don't mind my saying so."

"I don't mind at all. You're only telling it the way most people see it."

"Including you?"

"Perhaps."

Nate shifted his weight, more cautiously this time, in a renewed effort to find a comfortable position. "Anyway, you were saying?"

"When he found out he had a daughter, he lost all interest in being a dad. Mum had no intention of having more kids, so I was it. I had everything a child could wish for in terms of material possessions but no real home life. They weren't interested in me, and so I was dead set on getting my dad to notice me and be proud of my achievements."

"You did well at school?"

"Yeah, I liked studying, but no matter how well I did, unless I came top, it was never good enough, and that's what decided me against the law. It's no longer a family firm. Dad sold out some years ago, and it's now a four-man partnership. I'd never be able to eclipse his partners, who are all brilliant, so I figured I'd try some other way to gain Dad's approval."

Lauren lapsed into silence.

"Stockbroking?" Nate reached across to refill her glass. Mildly surprised to find that it was empty again, she didn't object.

"Yep. Money is my father's god. I got a First in economics from Cambridge, so I figured the money market was as good a place as any to make my mark. I worked for a year with a smaller firm than Whytelake's, heard they had an opening for a junior trader, got interviewed by Jeff Williams, and the rest, as they say, is history."

"And was he impressed, your father, I mean?"

Lauren couldn't disguise her surprise. "That's where you're supposed to ask why I stole all that money."

He smiled. "I guess you'll tell me if you want me to know."

"I haven't spoken to many people about this, but you're the first one not to jump right in and ask that question."

"Perhaps I understand that these things are never quite that cut and dried."

"Because of your mother?"

"Yeah, it was so easy to look upon her as being guilty. She lived in that house, all that stolen stuff was there, so she *had* to have known something about it. But she didn't, and that's the God's honest truth."

"Yes, but I *did* steal that money. I admitted it, and now I feel like a goldfish in a bowl, aware that half the world's watching me, or would be if they knew where I was, wondering where it is now."

"Is that why you work in that café?"

"Yes, I suppose." She lifted her shoulders. "The powers that be created a new identity for me so that only they would know where I was, but I don't delude myself about that. They didn't do it out of the kindness of their hearts. It's more a case of watching me and hoping that I'll lead them to the money."

"You're probably right."

"Every time a stranger comes into the café, I wonder if it's someone working undercover, hoping to get close to me."

"No wonder you were so suspicious about me."

She shrugged. "Yeah, well."

"So no one else knows where you live?"

"No!" Lauren spoke a little too decisively. She took another large mouthful of wine, hoping it would cover the gaff, cursing beneath her breath when she became aware of Nate's intelligent eyes boring into her profile. He hadn't missed the lie. "But you found me, so I guess anyone else can if they really want to." She frowned. "How did you find me, by the way?"

He laughed. "I sweet-talked someone in the Probation Office."

She glowered at him. "That's illegal."

"So sue me."

"I just might."

He stood up, and she thought for an unsettling moment that he was going to leave. "Let me use your john whilst you think about that."

"It's off the kitchen," she said, baffled by the relief she felt because he intended to stay for awhile longer.

He returned after a couple of minutes, the second bottle of wine, minus cork, in his hand. Lauren decided that she really shouldn't drink any more.

"That boiler makes a hell of a racket," he said, nodding toward the bathroom. "Does it work?"

"Only when it feels like it. I need to get it fixed sometime. No, not for me," she said, covering her glass with her hand. "I've had enough."

"A drop more won't hurt you, and it'll only go to waste otherwise because I have to drive." She wasn't aware of removing her fingers from the glass but must have done because when she looked again, it was full. "I'll look at it for you, if you like."

Lauren didn't know what he was talking about. Her brain seemed to have ground to a halt. "The wine?" she asked, frowning.

"No, idiot, the boiler."

"I thought you were a journalist, not a plumber."

"Hey, I'm just a country boy at heart and can turn my hand to just about anything."

"I'm sure you can." Lauren forgot about her decision to quit drinking and took a long swallow. "I stole the money because Jeff asked me to," she said into the silence.

"I figured as much."

"You believe me?" Lauren was so astonished that she spilt several drops of wine over Kermit's head. She hastily put the glass down, pulled a tissue from her pocket to wipe Kermit clean, and then gaped at Nate in disbelief.

"Yeah, I believe you."

She was aware of a slow, involuntary smile breaking across her features. "You're the first one that has," she said, shaking her head, still not entirely convinced.

"Tell me about it," he said.

"Where to start?" She paused, playing with her lower lip with her forefinger as she formulated her words. "Jeff was like no one I'd ever met before, and I was dazzled by him, trusting idiot that I was. Older than me, he took me under his wing and showed the sort of interest in me that I'd always hoped my father would."

"Didn't that seem a bit odd?"

"Not really. He was my boss and my mentor. He seemed to like me and went that extra mile to help me because he said I showed a natural aptitude for the business." She spread her hands, staring not at Nate but at the flames flicking round a new log he'd just thrown on the fire. "I was naïve enough to believe him."

"No reason why you shouldn't have."

"He helped me, praised me when I went with my intuition, took risks, and got things right. He promoted me, in retrospect perhaps sooner than he should have, and introduced me to some of our more prestigious clients. That involved some travelling and long lunches and dinners. After one such, when he'd drunk a little too much, he got all maudlin, started talking about his home life and what a mess it all was. How he only stayed for the sake of the children. Yes, I know," she said, seeing the sceptical expression on Nate's face. "It's the oldest line in the book. *My wife doesn't understand me.*" She rolled her eyes. "In my own defence, I thought that, too, at first. I mean, if you'd met his wife, you'd understand. She's gorgeous, entertaining, fun to be with, and…well, rich."

"Rich?" Lauren was left with the impression that that was the first thing she'd said that truly surprised him.

"Yeah, she married Jeff before he established himself and brought her family money to the marriage. She has a trust fund, and if Jeff were to divorce her, he'd be left with very little. Even their house in Wimbledon is in her name."

"I didn't know that."

"There's no reason why you should. It's not something either of them shouts about. Anyway, the vicious things he said about her gradually convinced me that there really was no love lost between them. No one would talk about someone they care about in such disparaging terms, even if they were playing a part."

"You'd be surprised."

"Not anymore I wouldn't," she said, shaking her head. "Nothing anyone says or does would take me in now."

"That's hardly to be wondered at, given where you've been residing."

"Jeff apologised for laying it all on me, said I was easy to talk to but that he shouldn't have burdened me with his problems and offered to get me a taxi. He'd had too much to drink and was going to spend the night in the hotel."

"Doesn't he have a flat in town?"

Lauren nodded. "Yes, but I didn't know that at the time."

"But you didn't go home in a taxi?"

"No, he suggested another drink first. He apologised again for bleating about his marriage and promised not to mention it again. He wanted to talk about the clients we'd just met and said he was considering letting me handle one of their smaller accounts to show he had faith in me. So even when he suggested having that drink in his room, I still didn't smell a rat." She stared off into the distance. "Well, that's not quite true. I probably did, but Jeff was good-looking and sophisticated and all those other things that turn women on." Lauren shuddered. "God, that must have sounded so shallow."

"No, sweetheart, it didn't. Your reaction was exactly the one he was hoping for. He played you and knew precisely what he was doing."

She dredged up a brief smile. "Thank you for saying that."

He offered her a courtly bow that made her laugh. Lauren couldn't remember the last time she'd laughed spontaneously or laughed at all, for that matter. If felt good, even if she held the wine responsible. "You're welcome."

"Jeff seemed lonely," she said, bringing herself under control again. "He obviously enjoyed my company. I felt flattered because of that and was happy to go with the flow."

"You wanted to impress your surrogate father."

"You make it sound rather incestuous, but yes, in retrospect I suppose I did." She retrieved her glass and took another healthy swig. To talk about the next part definitely required Dutch courage. "We finished up in bed, I stayed the night in the hotel with him, and that's how it started."

"He was going to leave his wife for you?"

"Yes, but we needed money for that. We, or rather he, created a bogus client account, fed me insider information he was gaining from various sources I knew nothing about, and I played the futures market accordingly, sequestering the profits into offshore accounts only he and I knew about."

"How long did this go on for?"

"Two years. And then finally it was time for the big one. One final big trade and we'd have enough to get away. The information was advance notice of a Rights Issue from an electronics conglomerate.

The guy passing the information wasn't prepared to do so over the phone. It was too sensitive for that. Jeff was going to meet him in a hotel, get the information, and pay him for it, but at the last minute a client conference came up, so he asked me to go in his place."

"Oh Jesus!"

"Yep, nothing like a trusting fool in love, is there?" She sighed. "I went to that hotel room, met Drake, got the information, paid him, and left. Went back to work, made a killing on the info, and was metaphorically packing my bags, ready to head off into the sunset with the love of my life."

"But Drake fetched up murdered?"

"Yep, with my name and company phone number in his pocket and my fingerprints all over the room."

"Which is why you told the police what you were really doing there?"

"Too right! No way was I going to be accused of murder. The police didn't really suspect me, but I didn't know that at the time and was terrified. Drake was stabbed, which is apparently not a woman's preferred method of committing murder. I could prove I went straight back to work. Fortunately I was seen on the CCTV in reception wearing the same clothes I'd gone out in, no blood stains in sight. I was never really in the frame for the murder, but by the time I realized that, I'd already told them about the bogus accounts, my involvement with Jeff, the whole thing."

"But Jeff denied it, and the accounts were empty."

"Yes, and it was only then that I realized I had no way of proving my involvement with Jeff. We'd never been seen together anywhere expect in a business setting, he'd been very careful about that. I'd never been to his flat because he said Gloria sometimes came up to use it without telling him. What's more, he'd never sent me cards or presents or anything that would lend credence to my claim." She inhaled sharply. "Even his client meeting that afternoon had been booked for several days, so he'd obviously never intended to meet

Drake." She turned away from Nate. "I was set up but had no way of proving it. Gloria and Jeff are the golden couple and completely untouchable. No one would ever believe my version of events."

"I do."

Her head shot up, and she regarded him intently. "Yes, I think you probably do," she said slowly. "But why?

"Because Gloria Williams propositioned me yesterday."

Chapter Five

"What!"

A kaleidoscope of conflicting emotions chased one another across Lauren's face. Shock, suspicion, disbelief. Nate could identify them all. She looked directly at him, asking a thousand questions with her luminous eyes, but he was in no rush to answer them. She needed time to absorb what he'd said, first. Jolted out of her attitude of guarded self-containment, her eyes slowly widened, her features illuminated by an expression of dazed incomprehension. For the first time he was catching a glimpse of the vibrant person she'd once been and hoped he'd done enough to persuade her to be completely honest with him. He'd spent enough time coaxing secrets out of people to know when someone was holding out on him, and Lauren Miller sure as hell qualified in that respect. She'd told him the truth, as far as it went, but there was still a bunch of stuff she *wasn't* telling him.

"But I don't understand." Her breath shook. "Gloria wears her fidelity like a mantle." She scowled, nibbled at the end of her index finger, and then shook her head emphatically. The gesture lacked conviction, and he suspected that his revelation had answered a lot of questions she'd spent hours mulling over in jail. "You must have misunderstood," she said. "What happened? Tell me everything."

"Well," he said easily, crossing one leg across his opposite knee and wincing when his rear was aggressively attacked by a rogue spring. "I was getting a little tired of being blanked by you, so yesterday I went off to see if I could approach this story from a different angle."

"You deliberately went in search of Gloria?"

He shrugged. “Sure, it seemed like the most logical step.”

When his words trailed to a tantalising halt, she folded her arms beneath her breasts and glared at him. “And are you planning to share your experiences with me before I die of old age?”

“I guess it can’t do any harm,” he said, shrugging. “Seems only fair since you’ve been so frank with me.” He grinned across the narrow space that divided them, but she chose not to meet his gaze. “I’ll spare you all the lurid details, but suffice it to say that the lovely Gloria was anxious to get to know me better.”

“I don’t believe it!”

Nate affected surprise. “What, you think I’m that repulsive to women?”

“What I think about you is probably best kept to myself.”

“Perhaps,” he said, winking at her, “but I’d still give a lot to know.”

“You’ve got Gloria drooling all over you,” she said crossly. “Isn’t that enough?”

“Spoilsport!”

“Nate!”

“Okay.” He threw his hands up, still grinning. “Gloria and Jeff don’t have the perfect marriage that they make the world believe. And in case you feel inclined to argue her corner—”

“Why would I do that?” she asked impatiently. “I’m the one that had a long relationship with her husband, remember, so I *know* that not everything is perfect in paradise.”

“Sure, but the image the Williams’s project to the rest of the world is one of marital bliss, right?”

“Yes, but Jeff’s the only one who’s acting,” she said, absently stroking Kermit’s ears. “Gloria’s totally faithful to Jeff, the epitome of the perfect wife. I think Jeff always rather resented that aspect of her character because he never felt he could live up to her expectations, hence seeking solace elsewhere. Anyway, if she even suspected that he’d strayed, then she’d cut him off without a penny.”

"That what he told you?"

Lauren scowled. "Yes, and Gloria's family are the ones with all the connections, remember. If they split, then her pride would be hurt, she'd turn vindictive, get him blackballed at the golf club and all the other places that matter to him. Jeff's social image is very important to him."

"He was playing you, love, and I can prove it." Nate paused to take a sip of wine. "I only spoke with Gloria for about twenty minutes, but before I left her, she'd given me her mobile number and e-mail address." Lauren merely raised a brow, her stunned expression doing all the talking for her. Nate, aware that the surest way to get her to open up was to ignite her desire for revenge, didn't spare her feelings. "She told me quite blatantly that they have an open marriage. She doesn't ask Jeff what he gets up to in town, and he leaves her to her own devices in Wimbledon."

"You found out an awful lot in a very short space of time," she said suspiciously.

"I'm a reporter. It's what I do."

Lauren shot him a look that told him precisely what she thought of his profession. "Yes, I suppose it is."

"I thought you'd be pleased."

"Oh, I'm delirious." Lauren shook her head and then lifted her glass to her lips, looking surprised when she found that it was empty. Nate leaned forward to refill it. He'd barely done so before she snatched it up and drained almost half of it. She'd have the mother of all hangovers tomorrow. "Did she say anything about me?"

"Sure. I brought the subject round to the case, and she was adamant that you and Jeff weren't romantically involved."

"But if they have an open marriage, how could she be so sure?"

"Oh, she knew all right. I could tell from her defensive body language. I guess it's one thing to have a private agreement with your spouse but entirely another if it's gonna be plastered all over the papers. Gloria Williams is a vain individual, and the thought of being publicly cuckolded by a younger, prettier woman doesn't sit comfortably with her."

Lauren didn't acknowledge the compliment. Nate wasn't sure that she'd even registered it. "But I don't see how this proves I was telling the truth to Inspector Read," she said, frowning.

"It won't, not on its own, but it's a small step in the right direction. Finding the money in Jeff Williams's possession is the only way to prove his involvement beyond any doubt."

The light that had briefly flared in her eyes dulled before he'd even finished speaking. "And that'll be next to impossible," she said, withdrawing in on herself.

"Why do you think he set you up, Lauren?" he asked, finally posing the question that had been uppermost in his mind. "You must have thought about it."

She drilled him with a look. "What do you think? Sorry," she added with a placating wave, "I didn't mean to be short with you. It's just that I've spent more hours than is healthy mulling it over, and I still don't know."

"That must be one hell of a frustration."

"Trust me," she said, meeting his gaze. "You have no idea." She toyed with the stem of her glass before readdressing his earlier question. "It was a fairly fail-safe operation, but I guess he just wanted to be sure that if anyone *did* get caught, then it wouldn't be him."

"But you only got caught because Drake was killed and he had your name in his pocket. Who do you suppose killed him?"

Lauren shook her head helplessly. "I don't know that either."

"But I gather it was the following day before Drake's body was found."

"Yes, he had the *Do Not Disturb* notice on the door, and the chambermaid only went in the next day when he was overdue to check out."

"And it was another day still before the police got round to you."

"Hmm, and when I showed them the account with the money in it, or tried to, to prove I was telling the truth. But the money had been moved, and no one's been able to trace it."

"But the bogus client account and the fact that the money had been there was enough to get you prosecuted."

Lauren rolled her eyes. "Well, obviously!"

"Okay, okay, don't shoot the messenger. I'm just trying to get my head round the sequence of events." He stretched his legs cautiously to one side, prepared for the spring that stabbed his backside when he shifted his weight, but still wincing when it did. "It can only have been Williams who arranged for Drake to be killed. Surely you've reached the same conclusion."

"Well, yes, if his death was connected to our business. He might have been engaged in criminal activities with other people who wanted him done away with."

"That seems like a reach."

"Jeff couldn't have killed him anyway. He was in a room full of people at the time of his death."

"Doesn't mean he didn't arrange it."

Lauren sat up a little straighter. Nate wondered what exactly he'd said to make her come back to life but didn't push it. She'd tell him if and when she felt the need. "And we'd prove that how?"

Nate grinned. "Glad to hear you talking in the plural."

"It was just a figure of speech." She sat forward, elbow resting on her knees. "Nate, I survived my time inside by plotting increasingly bizarre revenge ploys against Jeff Williams. It helped me to get through the ordeal, but at the end of the day, no matter what Jeff did to persuade me, I'm still guilty of stealing that money. I've never tried to deny that but—"

"You've only done what a lot of city people do. Insider trading is not that rare."

"Yes, possibly." She half smiled. "It's a national pastime, like forgetting to declare income to the taxman or MPs fiddling their expenses. People sort of assume it's okay to do things like that and it's only a crime if you're caught." She met his gaze and held it. "And I was caught. Jeff talked me into it, but I'm a big girl, I knew it was wrong and could have said *no*. At the end of the day I can't prove Jeff's involvement and nor can you, so you can't write anything about it."

"Oh, I don't know." Nate stretched his arms above his head and smiled at her.

"Sorry you've had a wasted trip." She stifled a yawn. "But now, if you'll excuse me, some of us have to work in the morning."

"How much money did you deliver to Drake?"

If she was surprised by the question, she gave no sign and answered it without hesitation. "One hundred thousand."

Nate let out a low whistle. "In cash?"

"Obviously. He was hardly likely to take a cheque."

"But I gather he was nothing to do with the electronics company that was planning the rights issue."

"No, he was some small-time crook, probably hired by the real whistle-blower."

"And said whistle-blower could have been the murderer."

Lauren conceded the point with a nod. "Possibly, but I don't see why."

"To tie up loose ends and keep his identity safe. He was obviously a cautious guy. Otherwise he would have delivered the information in person."

"True, but I still don't see how—"

"What happened to the money?"

Lauren focused her eyes on his face. It was obvious that she hadn't picked up on the significance of his question straight away. He blamed the wine for slowing her thought process. "What do you mean?"

"Well, it wasn't found in the hotel room. Peter said—"

"How do you know that? Nothing was ever said about it." Nate silently cursed his stupidity. Her suspicions about him had gradually given way during the course of the evening, but in one unguarded moment, he'd blown all the advantages he'd created. "Who have you been talking to?"

"No one, I just felt that—"

"Peter, you said Peter." She pounced on his slip of the tongue, not quite so wasted as he'd thought. "That's Inspector's Read's name." Her eyes narrowed to icy slits as she struggled to extract herself from her chair. "I might have known that beneath that charming exterior you'd be just like all the others." She threw her head back, abandoned the attempt to stand since it appeared to be beyond her capabilities, and made do with blowing a long stream of air through tightly-pursed lips instead. "Why else would you persevere at the café day after day? You'd have to be a masochist or someone with a very specific agenda. A book about female prisoners!" Her expression told him exactly what she thought of that possibility. "You think I know where the money is, don't you?"

"No, Lauren, on my life, I—"

"Don't lie to me!" she cried. "You know Inspector Read, and he told you where to find me, hoping I'd open up to you because he couldn't get anywhere."

"No, no he didn't. You've got it all wrong." He stood up just as she made a renewed attempt to do so herself. She swayed drunkenly as her feet hit the floor, almost toppling into the fire.

"Whoa!" Nate caught her arm just before she fell. "I think the wine's gone to your head," he said, stating the obvious. He slipped an arm round her waist and steered her toward the stairs. "Come on, I'll help you up. And tomorrow, when you're sober, we'll talk some more. But I promise you, on my mother's life, that no one put me up to this."

"Do you even have a mother?"

"Doesn't everyone?"

"In your case, I have severe doubts."

He chuckled as he attempted to guide her toward the stairs. She put up one hell of a struggle, but no way was he letting her go.

"I can manage on my own."

"Like hell you can!"

Nate picked her up and carried her up the rickety stairs, Kermit following closely at his heels. She fought him every inch of the way, kicking, hurling verbal abuse, and scratching his face.

"Ouch, quit that, will you. I'm not your enemy!"

"You could have fooled me."

He kicked open the door to her bedroom and deposited her on the bed. Suddenly all the fight left her, and the moment her head hit the pillow, she appeared to pass out. Nate wondered if he ought to undress her but decided against it. She already felt that he'd deceived her. If he tried to make her more comfortable, there was no telling what conclusions she'd draw when she woke up. Telling her that he preferred his women to be conscious probably wouldn't cut it. Nate pulled the covers over her, fetched a pint glass of water, and placed it where she'd be able to reach it if she woke, and left her to sleep it off.

"Come on, mate," he said to Kermit, "I bet you need to go out."

Kermit yapped, which Nate took as an affirmative. He followed the little dog down the stairs and let him out the front door. As he waited for him to do his business, he stared up at the starry sky, wondering what his next move ought to be, cursing himself for letting slip that he knew Peter Read. All the work he'd done to gain this damaged woman's trust was now history, and he'd have to start all over again. Which meant staying the night in the shack. If he left, she'd never invite him back again. Hell, she'd probably never speak to him again! Nate could only hope that between now and the cold light of sobriety he'd have thought of a way to talk her round.

He found a duvet in the cupboard in the bathroom and, resigned to sleeping on the spring-defective sofa, rolled himself in the thick comforter and struggled to find the least painful position. Then he closed his eyes and waited for sleep. Something told him it would be a long time coming.

When the shower stubbornly refused to produce any hot water the following morning, Nate tried to locate the problem. If nothing else, fixing the defective boiler might persuade Lauren to look upon him with a little less hostility. He collected some tools from the trunk of his car, stripped the boiler down, and took a closer look. It just needed a decent servicing. All the pipes were fuzzed up. He tried to work quietly, closing the bathroom door to prevent the noise reverberating through Lauren's delicate brain, but some sound escaping was unavoidable.

He'd almost finished, pleased with himself for managing so well with so few tools, when the bathroom door crashed open and a banshee wielding a baseball bat took a wild swing at him. Nate grabbed Lauren's wrist seconds before the bat made contact with his skull and extracted it from her grasp.

"Hey, easy there, it's only me."

She blinked, groggy and disorientated. "What the hell are you still doing here?"

"Fixing your boiler." He replaced the outer casing and turned on the hot tap. Steaming water gushed out in a steady flow. "There you go. It should be fine now."

Lauren, still wearing the clothes he'd put her to bed in, slumped onto the edge of the bath, rubbed her forehead, and groaned. "Have you been here all night?"

"Yeah, I'd had too much wine to drive," he lied.

"Well, you should be sober enough now, so what's keeping you?"

"What, no thanks for being your plumber?"

She shot him a look. "Get lost!" She opened the door wide, inviting him to leave the bathroom, and glanced out of the window at the bright morning, the sun already high in the sky. "What time is it?"

"Almost ten."

"What! Hell, I have to be at work."

"No, you don't. I called in for you and said you were sick."

"Great, just great!"

"What's wrong?" He flashed a perplexed smile. "I thought you'd be grateful. You put some away last night. No way were you ever going to make it to work this morning."

"And now everyone at the café will know that an American man spent the night with me. They aren't exactly rocket scientists, but even they ought to be able to figure it out."

"No, they won't." Nate put on an upper-class English voice. "*Hello, is that the greasy spoon. Ah good, this is Louise's father speaking. I'm afraid she's eaten something that disagreed with her and won't be at work today.*"

He watched her struggle to maintain her fierce expression. She couldn't manage it and burst out laughing. "You're full of surprises."

"And you ought to laugh more often," he said softly. "It suits you."

"I haven't exactly had a lot to laugh about recently."

"True." He packed up his tools. "Anyway, you need a shower, so I'll leave you to it. Kermit and I will go and get some stuff for breakfast, and by the time you're done, I'll have it all ready for you."

"I don't want anything to eat. I just want you to leave."

"Yes, you do, and no, you don't." He patted her shoulder. "Trust your Uncle Nate to know what's best for you. There's nothing like a massive fry up, American style, to fix a hangover. No arguments," he said, pushing a hand forward to fend off the protest he could sense her formulating. "I'll feed you and tell you everything I know about your case, and then, if you still want me to bugger off, I will." He flashed his most disarming smile. "Can't say fairer than that, can I?"

"Well," she said ungraciously, "if that's the only way that I'm going to get rid of you, then I suppose it will have to do."

"Attagirl!"

Good as his word, by the time she emerged from the bathroom, the food was ready. She was wearing clean jeans, a thick sweatshirt that disguised her shape, and her hair was still wet from the shower. She looked distinctly hungover but tucked into the food he placed in front of her, disdainfully at first and then, abandoning all attempts at disinterest, with increasing gusto. He sat opposite her, eating in silence, watching her all the time.

"Come on then," he said as soon as she'd finished. "A good long walk is the final step in the rehabilitation process."

"God, you're so bossy!"

But she picked up her jacket and followed him from the shack without further protest. Nate threw sticks for Kermit to chase but made no attempt to talk to the sullen figure walking beside him, giving her time to gather her thoughts.

"Better?" he asked after some time.

"A little."

He found a convenient log and steered her toward it, all but forcing her to sit down.

"God, but I can see why you like this forest." She didn't deign to answer him, so they sat in uneasy silence until he spoke again. "Lauren, I know what you're thinking, and you're dead wrong."

"Am I?" She stared at Kermit as he barked at the base of a tree, in a vain attempt to entice the squirrels out of it. She sounded weary rather than annoyed.

"Dead wrong," he rcpeated emphatically. "I know Peter Read, and we've been friends for awhile." He briefly explained how their friendship had come about. "I am writing a book, and I really did try to come and see you inside but not because I thought you know where the money is. I wanted to hear your side of the story. Peter told me you were out. I figured you'd be in this part of the world somewhere and looked for you through the Probation Service."

She plucked a blade of grass, twisted it round her finger, and then threw it aside. "It doesn't matter," she said.

"It does matter. Why do you think Peter told me you were out?"

She shrugged. "How the hell would I know?"

"He told me because he isn't entirely convinced that you acted alone."

Lauren stared at him as though he was speaking in Swahili. "I don't believe you."

"Well, you should because it's true. He doesn't think any more of Williams than I do, and he hates getting things wrong."

"He didn't get it wrong. He got his woman."

"Yeah, but not the man who manipulated her."

Lauren sighed. "And he never will."

"Don't you want your revenge? Didn't you say that was what got you through your time inside?"

"True, but now that I'm out, I realize how unrealistic that is. How does an ex-con with a grudge get anywhere near a man who's protected from the common herd by about three layers of lackeys?"

"There are ways, especially if you're not acting alone."

"I'm not dragging anyone else into this."

"I'm not asking you to. I'm volunteering."

She turned to face him. "Why?"

"For the story, of course."

"Oh, of course, how could I have forgotten?" Lauren got to her feet and turned in the direction of the shack. "I appreciate what you're trying to do, even if you are only doing it so that you can write something about the case that won't get you sued, but it's a non-starter, and all I want now is to be left alone."

"You don't have a very high opinion of me, do you?"

"Don't take it personally. I feel like that about the whole world right now."

"That's hardly surprising."

She didn't respond, and they walked in silence back to the shack. He'd give her a few days and then put a suggestion to her. He had a way of getting back at Williams incubating in his brain. No way was she going to fester here, hidden away in this bloody forest because an avaricious man exploited her and ruined her life. In spite of what she'd implied, she'd never be able to put it behind her until she could exorcise all traces of that man from her psyche.

"I'll just get my laptop, and then I'll leave you in peace," he said. "I left it in your lounge."

She nodded, unlocked the door, and then turned away to see what Kermit was doing. He'd gone haring off into the trees, chasing something, and Lauren went after him. Nate suspected she'd only done so to avoid clumsy good-byes.

He entered the living room and only saw it at the last minute. The postman had been whilst they'd been out, and a single envelope lay on the mat. He frowned. She'd told him that no one knew where she was, but she'd obviously lied about that. He wondered what else she hadn't told him. As soon as he picked up the envelope, he realized that the postman wasn't responsible for its appearance. It had been hand delivered, and the envelope wasn't sealed.

Nate was an investigative journalist. There was never any question of him not opening it.

Chapter Six

"Kermit, where are you?"

He eventually emerged from the trees. Lauren picked him up and tucked under his arm to prevent him from dashing off again. By then Nate was striding away. He waved over his shoulder as he approached his car parked farther down the lane, slammed the door, put it into gear, and moved off without once turning back. Lauren didn't quite know what to make of his abrupt exit. She'd expected him to linger, inventing excuses to spend the rest of the day with her. She absolutely hadn't wanted him to do that but now felt peeved by his obvious anxiety to be shot of her.

With a shrug, she wandered into the shack. She put her reaction down to a hormonal imbalance, still feeling irritated and unsettled. A cholesterol-fuelled breakfast followed by a walk in the forest had done little to alleviate Lauren's hangover and much to promote indigestion. She swallowed down two antacid tablets, wondering if her grouchiness had something to do with having another person invade her personal domain.

The desire to crawl back into bed was seductive, but Nate's abrupt departure had unsettled her, and she'd never be able to sleep. The shack felt overwarm. Nate had got the fire blazing again before they went for their walk, and she noticed that he'd even hauled a load more logs in, saving her the trouble. Right now she couldn't decide if the man was too good to be true or if it was just a ploy to get what he wanted from her.

She moved restlessly from the lounge to the kitchen and back again, with no clear plan in her head. The shack seemed empty without him, and for the first time since leaving prison, she felt lonely. Lauren balled her fists and cursed beneath her breath. This embryonic dependency upon someone else wasn't part of her master plan, and she needed to nip it in the bud. She absolutely didn't need Mr. America worming his way any further under her skin with his sympathetic smile, softly persuasive voice, and those probing grey eyes that saw far more than they were supposed to.

She glanced round the sitting room, trying to decide what to do with the rest of the day. That's when she saw it. A letter addressed to her propped neatly in the centre of the mantelpiece. Her heart skipped a beat. Nate must have put it there when he came in to get his laptop. He was telling her, in his own not so subtle manner, that he knew she'd lied to him and someone else knew where she lived. Someone who delivered their post by hand. That explained his abrupt departure and solved another of her problems, too. If she'd lied about something as insignificant as anyone else knowing where she was, then her account of what happened between her and Williams must be suspect in his mind. Well, at least he'd stop bugging her, and she'd be free to get on with her life. That was a good thing, wasn't it?

Lauren dismissed thoughts of Nate's disenchantment and turned her attention to the letter. Her whole body shook as she glared at it, willing it to go away. She had no idea how long she stood there, simply staring at the envelope before she reached for it, her hands trembling so much that she almost dropped it into the fire. She'd been trying not to think about how the man calling himself Reg Fowler would contact her, but now she had her answer. At least they'd been out walking when he chose to make his delivery, which was something. Fielding Nate's inevitable questions about the man when she didn't know the answers herself would have been one intrusion too far.

The envelope wasn't sealed. She tapped it against her teeth, delaying perusing its contents because she didn't really want to know what it said, wondering whether Nate would have got there before her. Would a man with his innate sense of curiosity have resisted taking a peek?

Well, of course he bloody wouldn't! Of all the damnable luck. She *never* had visitors, and yet Fowler chose to call on the one occasion when she did. She muttered for a little longer, feeling she had every right to be aggrieved, and then ripped the envelope open so forcefully that she almost tore the letter itself in half.

Tomorrow, 2 o'clock in The King's Arms. Leave the dog at home and bring the money.

That was it. Once again the message was typewritten and there was no signature. Lauren fell into the chair she'd occupied the previous evening and thought it through. Should she go, confront the guy and see if she could find out a bit more about him, or should she ignore his letter? It didn't take her long to realize she only had one choice. At least he'd opted for a public place, so she'd be relatively safe. If she didn't go, he'd only turn up here, where there was no one other than Kermit to help her out. It did briefly cross her mind to contact Inspector Read and explain her problem. If Nate was right and he half believed her account, then perhaps this Fowler guy could help make sense of things.

Lauren quickly dismissed the idea of involving the police. She only had Nate's word for it that Inspector Read was sympathetic, and he probably only said that to win her trust. Besides, after some of the things she'd heard about police tactics whilst serving her sentence, any trust she would have once placed in them was as dead as her emotions. Lauren stood up and stretched, recovered from her temporary weakness. By the time she met with Fowler, she'd have thought of a way to make him open up about why he thought she owed him a huge sum of money. Then perhaps she'd involve others.

She was clumsy and short-tempered in the café the following night. Nate didn't appear, but then she hadn't expected him to. She still couldn't decide whether he'd actually read her letter. Snooping in other people's private mail wasn't the sort of tacky behaviour she thought him capable of, even if he was a journalist. Well, she thought, hanging up her apron and heading for the door, she'd know soon enough. If Nate had read it, then wild horses wouldn't keep him away from The King's Arms.

Lauren just had time to drop Kermit back at the shack before she headed for her meeting, deliberately arriving fifteen minutes late. As she made her way there, she thought some more about Fowler's request to meet her in a public place. He could hardly bully her in a pub full of people, so he presumably really did believe that she'd arrive with an envelope full of cash. If so, when she pushed through the door with nothing on her except a few quid shoved in the back pocket of her jeans, then he was in for a disappointment. She paused at the door to the pub, taking in the *No Dogs* sign displayed prominently in several places. Could that have been why he'd chosen the location? He was obviously scared of dogs—that much had been apparent from his reaction to Kermit during their first meeting—and felt safer when he only had an eight-stone woman to bully.

She scanned the pub. It was emptying out after the lunchtime rush, but there were still enough people dotted about to make her feel relatively safe. Fowler sat at a quiet corner table with a half-drunk pint in front of him. There was no sign of Nate, and she didn't know whether to be relieved or disappointed about that. Fowler signalled to her, but she detoured via the bar first and bought herself an orange juice, using the time to harness her nerves before walking toward his table.

"You're late," Fowler said, scowling.

"Some of us have to work for a living." She took the chair as far away from his as possible. "Well, what do you want?"

"Did you bring it with you?"

"Did I bring what?"

His scowl deepened. "Don't play games with me, darlin'. I want the money you owe me."

"Look, I don't even know who you are." She picked up her glass and took a small sip, trying not to make it obvious that she was looking round for Nate, annoyed because she felt the need to do so. "We've never met in our lives before, so how can I owe you money?"

He didn't say a word. Instead, he reached inside his jacket pocket, and Lauren instinctively flinched. Surely he wasn't insane enough to reach for a weapon here in the middle of a busy pub? Before she could decide what to do, he withdrew his hand and placed a small Dictaphone on the table between them. He pressed play, and her voice, sounding small and tinny but definitely hers, echoed from the speaker. Evidently she was talking to someone on the phone. Lauren was totally unable to hide her shock when she heard herself promise the person on the other end of the conversation £100,000 in cash when the deal was done. Fowler turned the machine off and simply stared at her, but Lauren was too stunned to speak, and it was Fowler who eventually broke the silence.

"Well?" he asked, draining the rest of his drink in one swallow.

"I didn't make that call," she said, knowing how pathetic that must have sounded.

Fowler rolled his eyes. "Give me a break," he said.

"All right, I agree that's my voice. But that could have been about anything. Anything at all. In a previous life I dealt with those sorts of sums as a matter of course. I could have been talking to a client," she said, feeling a little more in control now that she'd come up with a plausible explanation.

"That's taken from my answer-phone," he told her, with something approaching a smug smile. "I ain't no client of yours, so why would you be leaving me messages?"

"Wrong number?" she suggested.

"Don't get smart with me." He pulled a packet of cigarettes from his pocket, glanced at the prominent no-smoking signs, shrugged, and put them away again. Lauren couldn't decide if it was a good or bad thing that he missed his nicotine fix. "We have a deal. I've waited six years, and now I want what's mine. I ain't even asking for interest on the dosh 'cos it ain't your fault that you weren't around to pay up before now. There, I can't say fairer than that, can I? All I want is what's owed to me, and I'm running out of patience."

Lauren's mind went into overdrive. It was true, she *had* conducted telephone conversations like the one she'd just heard all the time. But not exactly like that. She'd never promised cash sums to anyone. It wasn't the way they worked. The only explanation she could come up with was that Jeff had recorded several of her calls, spliced them together, and planted this message on Fowler's phone. But why? Who was he, and what did he have to do with it all?

"I'm sorry, but I don't know what you're talking about, and I certainly don't have that sort of money to throw about." She shrugged. "You've seen where I live, and I bet you know where I work, as well. Why would I subject myself to that sort of lifestyle if I had money to burn?"

"Because the filth think you know where the money is and are waiting for you to lead them to it," he said with exaggerated patience. "It's bloody obvious. You're being clever all right, seeing out your probation and keeping yer head down until the heat's off and you're free to travel. Trouble is, if I wait for that to happen, I'll never see what's mine."

"Even if what you say is true and I did have the money, which I don't by the way, then by getting some for you, I'd lead the police straight to it."

He sneered at her. "I've seen where your folks live. Your old man'll lend you it if you ask him. That'll get me out of your hair and leave you with all your limbs intact." He picked up his glass, scowled when he noticed that it was empty, and replaced it on the table with a loud thud. "Well, what's it to be?"

"I'm sorry," she said. "I know you don't believe me, but I don't have a clue where that message came from or why it should be on your answer-phone." He merely snorted. "But you're obviously something to do with the information from that electronics company that finished up with Drake being killed."

"Here, you're not pinning that on me," he said, startled out of his aggressive stance and darting nervous glances round the pub.

Lauren took a flyer. "Look, you're right about my dad. Not only is he loaded, but he also feels guilty because he kind of disowned me when I went to prison. If I asked him, he'd give me that money and as much again. It's all yours," she plunged on recklessly, "if you'll tell me where you fit in to all this." She saw greed and calculation in his eyes and knew she had him hooked. The fact that she'd just doubled his fiscal expectations was neither here nor there. Right now the need for information, some answers to the questions that had been plaguing her for six years, transcended all other considerations. "Let me get you a refill," she said, standing and picking up his glass, "whilst you think about it."

When she returned to the table with new drinks for them both, she could see that he'd made up his mind. But he took his time saying so, swilling beer round his mouth and further frazzling her nerves. "Do you work for Caldan Electronics then, Mr. Fowler?"

"Yeah, since I left school."

"Some time then."

"Twenty years," he said.

"You must have worked your way up to a position of some responsibility in that time." She frowned, convinced that she was still missing something. "Why risk it all by giving away the company's secrets?"

He snorted into his beer. "I'm a janitor," he said, resentment pouring off him in waves. "In other words, I'm invisible. I know a lot about computers, went on several courses early on, and found I had an aptitude for them, but all the qualifications I got were of no interest to the company. Just because I didn't go to a posh school, don't talk right, and don't always know which knife and fork to use in a fancy restaurant." He blew air through his lips. "Like anyone cares about that sort of stuff nowadays."

"And you saw lesser men being put into positions that you could have held down with your eyes closed," Lauren said, injecting a level of sympathy into her tone.

"Yeah, and most of them don't give me the time of day, the snooty bastards."

"So you decided to get your revenge?"

"I'm in the offices alone at night. Some of the lazy sods don't even turn their computers off, but even those that do, getting round their passwords is a doddle, and I soon had more than enough information to make myself some money." He sneered and took a long draught of his beer. "It was the best fun I'd had in ages when the news broke prematurely and I saw management chasing their tails, trying to figure out who'd blown the whistle. I left a few obvious clues on the terminals of those who'd been particularly unpleasant to me and watched them squirm. That's when being invisible came in handy. They all protested their innocence, started blaming one another, but not once was the finger of suspicion pointed toward me."

"How did you know who to pass the information on to?"

He tapped the side of his nose. "I know a few people who know a few people."

"And the arrangement you made with my boss was that he'd meet Drake at that hotel and pay him for the information." Lauren held her breath whilst he took forever to answer the question that would irrefutably prove Williams was involved. He eyed her askance for so long without speaking that she was unable to stop herself from giving him a prod. "Is that the way it went down?"

"Nah, Williams said you'd meet me and—"

The elation that Lauren felt at having Williams's involvement confirmed by a third party was short-lived. Fowler would never admit it to the authorities in a million years, so she was not really any further forward. “Why did you send Drake instead of going to the meeting yourself?”

His expression was insufferably smug. “I’ve already told you, I ain’t as daft as I look, and I haven’t survived this long by taking unnecessary risks. I knew that when the news of the leak broke, everyone would be under the spotlight, and anyone not at work when they ought to be would become a suspect.” He paused to rub his chin, still looking thoroughly pleased to have got one over on his employers. “I doubt they would have looked my way, but even so, I wasn’t about to take the risk.”

“So you recruited Drake?”

“Yeah, I’ve done stuff with him before and knew I could trust him.”

“You told him what you were doing?” Lauren’s scepticism must have been apparent in her expression.

“Don’t be daft.” He waved the suggestion aside. “All Drake knew was that he had to pass the information I gave him to you and take payment in return. I knew he wouldn’t understand what it was and wouldn’t have thanked me if I’d been daft enough to tell him. He was being well paid to do an easy job, and that was all he cared about. I knew he wouldn’t double-cross me, but I didn’t expect him to get killed.”

“Well, I certainly didn’t kill him, Mr. Fowler, but I did pay him.”

He eyed her suspiciously, clearly not believing her. “Where’s the money then? It wasn’t found in his room.”

“Presumably in the pocket of the killer.” Lauren picked up the Dictaphone that still lay on the table between them and shuffled it idly between her fingers as she thought about a situation she’d already worried to death a thousand times before. “If he was sent there specifically to kill Drake, then he’d know about the payoff and would hardly leave that sort of cash behind.” Lauren frowned. “Either that or it found its way into the pocket of one of the policemen called to the scene.”

"So cynical," Fowler remarked, chuckling.

"Have you ever been inside?"

"Point taken." He drained his beer. "So what about my money then?"

"You'll get it," she promised. "But it'll take me a couple of weeks to get it together."

"Don't even think about double-crossing—"

"Who do you think killed Drake, Mr. Fowler?"

"Dunno, do I? Your boss, perhaps."

"Possibly, but he was in a meeting at the time."

"I didn't mean he did it himself." Fowler screwed up his features into an ugly scowl. "His type never do their own dirty work."

"But he didn't know Drake would be there, did he? He thought you'd be going yourself. Do you think he was trying to tie up loose ends?"

"I ain't never met him, so I wouldn't know how ruthless he is. I can probably guess though." He appeared to lose himself in thought, as though debating whether or not to say anything else. "I rang him after Drake was killed, and he said he knew nothing about it, but then he would, wouldn't he. Then I asked him when I could get my money, and he put me onto you."

"Why am I not surprised?" Lauren asked, her temper boiling over at the lengths Williams had gone to pin everything on her.

"He told me you'd emptied all the accounts of the money you'd stolen and that I'd have to get it from you when you came out. He even phoned me and told me you'd been released."

"Did you tell him that you'd found out where I was living?" Lauren asked, trying to keep the panic out of her voice.

"I didn't tell him anything. I don't trust the bastard." Fowler stood up and grabbed the Dictaphone back from her. "Meet me here, same time two weeks today and have the money with you, or it'll be the worse for you."

He shoved his way through the closely packed tables and was gone.

Lauren sipped at the remnants of her drink and waited five minutes more before leaving herself.

She mulled over all she'd just learned and, in particular, the one conclusion that stood out a mile. Nate had found her, this Fowler character had found her, so if Jeff Williams was looking for her, he'd also know by now where she was. She needed to be prepared. Abandoning her unfinished drink, she left the pub, avoiding eye contact with other customers.

Lauren now had independent collaboration that Williams had deliberately set her up, but having the fact that he was a conniving, ruthless bastard confirmed by a third party didn't get her anywhere. All she'd done was place herself further in debt by promising Fowler two hundred grand that she didn't have a hope in hell of raising.

That problem paled into insignificance when, the following afternoon, someone rapped hard on the door to the shack, producing a volley of barks from Kermit. Supposing it to be Nate, she considered not answering, but the knock was repeated almost immediately, this time for an elongated period that told her he wasn't going away. With her head still full of her problems, she pulled the door open and spoke without looking up.

"What do you want this time?" she demanded.

"Good afternoon, Miss Miller."

"Inspector?"

Lauren's insides roiled. Inspector Read stood on the threshold, looking exceedingly grim, and he wasn't alone. Two other plain-clothes detectives, a man and a woman, stood at his shoulder, and two policemen in uniforms stood directly behind them. This wasn't good.

"We have a warrant to search these premises, Miss Miller." He waved a piece of paper under her nose. "Mind if we come in?" Kermit was at her side, barking like crazy. "Perhaps you'd put the dog somewhere else so we can do our work."

"What's this all about?" she asked, not moving from the open doorway.

"Perhaps we could discuss it inside."

Lauren's mind reeled. She'd recovered from her initial shock and knew she had no choice but to let them in if they really did have a warrant. She took the paper that the inspector offered her and scanned it without taking in all the words. It was enough to see her name and the address of the shack in bold type at the top of the document. She picked Kermit up and stood back to let the police troop into the front room. It wasn't large enough to accommodate them all, so she moved into the kitchen, followed by Inspector Read.

"I suppose you're hoping to find hidden funds secreted beneath my bed, Inspector," she said coldly. "Sorry to disappoint you, but you're all out of luck today."

"This is a little more serious than that," he said blandly, his demeanour giving nothing away.

"Well, what is it about then?"

She listened as what sounded like a dozen pairs of feet trampled above them, rampaging through the privacy of her bedroom and, she was willing to bet, not taking too much care about putting things back the way they found them. She tried not to let him see how much this invasion affected her.

"All in good time."

He picked up one of the empty wine bottles waiting to be taken to the recycling bin and examined the label. A slight inclination of one eyebrow was his only reaction, but she could tell he knew it was expensive, lending a lie to her supposedly impoverished existence. She roundly cursed Nate Black for his ill-timed generosity but refrained from explaining his presence to the inspector. She'd learned inside that it was better not to volunteer information because things inevitably became twisted. It was a bit like the childhood game of Chinese whispers, she supposed. By the time an innocent statement reached the third of fourth person, it was already distorted out of all recognition.

Lauren turned away, Kermit still squirming beneath her arm, and stared out of the window. She'd listened to enough tales of police coercion whilst inside to know how they operated. They'd got some tame magistrate to sign a warrant so they could come here and harass her, not really expecting to find anything but hoping to unsettle her. Well, they were doing a first-rate job, but she was damned if she'd let them know it.

Lauren and the inspector waited out the search in silence. When the uniforms came back down the stairs, shaking their heads, Lauren and her shadow moved into the lounge so that the plods could search the kitchen. The sound of drawers slamming and pots and pans being moved about made it clear that they were being thorough, but Lauren wasn't worried. There was nothing here that they could possibly take exception to. She cocked her head to one side, listening to their cursory conversation, curious to know precisely what it was that they hoped to find. They appeared to be sifting through her mishmash of cutlery and utensils with particular care.

The female detective joined them, clutching what Lauren recognized to be a transparent evidence bag containing the mobile phone her mother had given her.

"We'll need to take this away for analysis," she told Lauren coldly. "You'll be given a receipt."

"If you're hoping to find it programmed with the numbers of Cayman Island banks stuffed full of embezzled money, then you're in for a disappointment," she said, addressing the remark to the inspector. "My mother gave me that phone, but I've never used it."

"Just doing our job, madam," he said blandly.

"Okay, you've done it. Now get out."

"Sorry, miss, but we need to ask you to come with us."

She glared at him. "What the hell for?"

"We have some questions we'd like you to answer down at the station."

Lauren put Kermit down, not caring if he went for their ankles, which he immediately attempted to do. He took a particular dislike to the female detective who squealed and tried to kick him away. Lauren folded her arms beneath her breasts and left Kermit to do his worst.

"I'm not going anywhere until you tell me what this is about," she said.

"How well do you know a gentleman named Ronald Fowlds?"

"Never heard of him," she said, not even needing to think about it.

"Strange, because you were seen in deep conversation with him in a pub yesterday afternoon."

"But that wasn't..." Lauren bit her lip, her mind in overdrive. "I did have a drink with someone yesterday, but his name wasn't Fowlds."

"Is this your drinking companion?"

Read produced a picture from inside his jacket and flashed it beneath her nose. Her sharp intake of breath when she recognized the man she knew as Reg Fowler was clearly all the confirmation he required. Nevertheless, she felt obliged to explain.

"But he told me his name was Fowler," she said lamely.

"No doubt there's a simple explanation, but we do need to ask you some official questions."

"But why?"

"Oh, didn't I say?" Read flashed a smile that could have been apologetic, spiteful, or merely designed to unsettle her. "He's dead."

Chapter Seven

"What!" Lauren's legs gave way beneath her, and she fell into her chair by the fireside, almost causing the woman detective to topple over as she barged her out of the way. She dropped her head into her splayed hands and shook it from side to side. "Does it never end?" she muttered.

"He was murdered sometime yesterday, and as far as we've been able to ascertain, you were the last person to be seen with him."

"Am I a suspect then?" Lauren asked, raising her eyes to Read's.

"At this time we're merely trying to establish the nature of your relationship with the man."

"Come along then, Miss Miller." The woman detective took her arm, all but dragging her to her feet and frog marching her toward the door. Kermit took exception to this and growled, making a fresh assault on the officer's ankles, which was when Lauren pulled herself together.

"It's okay," she said, shaking herself free of the woman's grasp, ushering the dog into the kitchen and giving him a rawhide bone to keep him occupied. "All right," she said to Read, reaching for her jacket but ignoring the woman detective—DS Taylor she thought she'd been told her name was—whose officious attitude was seriously starting to irritate her. "I'm as ready as I'll ever be. Do I need to have a lawyer present?"

"That's your right, of course, but at this particular time you're not being charged with anything."

"I see."

And she did—all too clearly. She allowed herself to be led to the first of two cars parked in the lane and slid into the back seat. Read sat in front next to the driver. Lauren used the time it took to drive to the police station in Southampton to try and figure out what had happened to Fowler, who had killed him and why. The silence in the car was broken only by the static and occasional bursts of activity from the police radio. She stared at the back of Inspector Read's head, trying to view the situation from his perspective.

He must know by now where Fowler had worked and made the connection to the insider trading that had landed her in prison in the first place. Taken with the fact that she was seen in a pub in close conversation with the man the day before, would anyone really believe she wasn't in cahoots with him? In Read's position, she would probably have arrested herself. Perhaps he thought that Fowler was looking after the money for her. The police had never attempted to disguise their displeasure at her lenient sentence. By all accounts, they were even less thrilled when she served barely half of it and downright pissed off because they'd never been able to find the missing funds. If ever there was a time for revenge, this one had been handed to them on a silver platter. Did they really think she was stupid enough to put herself in that position? Probably, because she knew from bitter experience that desperate people did the stupidest things.

They arrived at the station, and she was placed in a dreary interview room. The walls were painted gunmetal grey, and the one small window, covered with mesh, was too grimy to let in much natural light. There was a metal table bolted down and three incredibly uncomfortable chairs, a tape machine, a video camera fixed high up in one corner, and nothing else. As she'd walked beside DS Taylor to reach this room, people stopped what they were doing and stared. She sensed their hostility. The innocent-until-proven-guilty maxim had obviously passed this lot by. Asked if she'd like tea, she refused, not entirely sure that whoever fetched it wouldn't spit in it.

They left her alone after she declined tea, saying someone would be with her soon. She knew they'd keep her waiting, probably for as long as half an hour so that she could think about the gravity of her situation. The girls inside had told her that was a favourite ploy. They'd be watching her from somewhere outside the room, probably via that camera, trying to detect from her body language just how uptight she actually was. Like anyone, even an innocent person, could appear relaxed under such intimidating circumstances. She adopted a bored attitude, tapping her fingers impatiently on the table, looking nowhere except straight in front of her. Lauren put the patience she'd learned inside to good use by playing them at their own game but didn't delude herself. She was deeply in the mire and had no one to turn to for help.

* * * *

Nate watched, grim-faced, from the other side of the one-way glass as Peter and the female detective entered the room, offering perfunctory apologies to Lauren for keeping her waiting. He introduced himself and his colleague DS Taylor and asked Lauren if she minded the interview being recorded. She shook her head but was asked to give verbal agreement for the benefit of the tape. She did so, and Peter then asked if she required legal representation.

"Am I being charged with something?" she asked.

"Not at present. You're merely helping with our enquires."

She folded her arms and glanced directly at the mirror, as though she knew he was watching her.

"Then I don't," she said.

She injected mild impatience into her tone, but Nate could see fear in her eyes and thought she was being foolish. She really did need someone in there, fighting her corner.

"Tell me about your relationship with Ronald Fowlds," Peter said.

She sat ramrod straight and looked him directly in the eye. "I don't know anyone by that name."

Peter produced a post-mortem picture of Fowlds and placed it on the table in front of her. "For the benefit of the tape, I'm showing Ms. Miller a picture of Ronald Fowlds."

"I know this man as Reg Fowler, and I've met him precisely twice in my entire life."

Once again she made direct eye contact with Peter as she spoke. She completely ignored DS Taylor, who was making a poor job of concealing her impatience, champing at the bit to get into her role as bad cop.

"When and under what circumstances?"

"The first time was over a week ago. He accosted me outside my cottage first thing in the morning when I was about to go to work and took me by surprise."

"What did he want?"

"Money. He said I owed him, and he wanted paying."

"How much money?"

She paused for so long that Peter was obliged to repeat the question.

"A hundred grand," she muttered with transparent reluctance. She must know how that would sound to the detectives and what they would now think. Damn, Nate was half thinking the same thing himself, and he didn't think she'd murdered anyone.

"Speak up for the tape please. Did you say a hundred thousand pounds?"

"Yes."

Peter quirked a brow. "That's a lot of money. Why did you owe him so much?"

"Inspector," she said, laying both hands on the table and leaning toward him. "I'd never laid eyes on the man in my life before that morning."

"That's not what I asked you."

"I didn't owe him a bean," she said, with a heavy sigh. "And even if I did, I couldn't have paid him because I don't have it. When will you people start believing that?"

"Then why do you think he accosted you?"

She shrugged, starting to lose her cool. "How should I know? Half the population seem to think I know where that money is, including you lot. He tracked me down and obviously thought he could scare me into parting with some of it."

"How do you suppose he tracked you down?" DS Taylor asked.

Lauren glared at her. "You tell me."

"Only the police and probation services know where you are."

"Precisely!"

"If a man twice your weight threatened you, Miss Miller, how do you account for the fact that you got away unscathed?"

"My dog bit his calf quite badly," she said, apparently in control of herself again and sticking to the bald facts.

Peter and his cohort exchanged a glance. Nate knew why. The victim had a stitched gash on his calf, and the medical examiner thought the injury was caused by a dog bite. They were trying to find out which hospital had treated him so they could get this confirmed, but Lauren had scored a point by telling the truth about that one.

"And that's how you escaped injury?"

"Yes. He pushed me to the ground, and I hit my head on the handlebars of my bike. If you ask my coworkers, they'll tell you that I had a cut above my eye. You can still see where it was." She moved her fringe aside and indicated the place in question, the remnants of the cut still visible.

"And when did you next see Fowlds?"

"You know that."

"Yes, but I'd like you to tell us."

She sighed. "Yesterday afternoon in The King's Arms pub in Brockenhurst."

"Why did you agree to meet him?"

"When he came to the cottage that morning, he said he'd be back and that this time he wouldn't take no for an answer. He delivered a note telling me to meet him in the pub, and I knew that if I didn't go, he'd come to the cottage again, where I'd be unprotected."

"Where's the note now?"

"I threw it in the fire."

"How convenient," remarked DS Taylor, rolling her eyes.

"What's hard for me to understand, Ms. Miller," Peter said, "is that this man could hardly threaten you in a pub full of people or put pressure on you in any way whilst in that establishment, so why ask to meet you there?"

"You'd have to ask him that one."

"Unfortunately we can't," Taylor said caustically.

"I did wonder about that, and I think he was really scared of my dog—"

"What, that little thing?" Peter's expression was openly disbelieving.

"Of any dog. Some people are. And just because Kermit's small, that doesn't make him any less dangerous or brave. After all, he did try to take you lot on," Lauren reminded him, looking directly at Taylor as she spoke, "and he bit Fowler quite badly."

Peter conceded the point with a nod and moved on. "What did you talk about in the pub?"

"I wanted to know why he was demanding money from me. He said he worked for the company and supplied the insider information about the rights issue—"

"And you didn't know that already?"

Peter quietened his partner with a quelling glance.

"No, I didn't know, but it made sense."

"But the man was a janitor."

"So he told me. A janitor with computer skills and a grudge to bear."

"But you'd never so much as spoken to him before and hadn't cooked up the insider trading scam with him?"

Lauren hesitated for a beat too long. "No."

"Then how do you account for this?" Peter produced a Dictaphone. Nate noticed Lauren pale when she saw it, but when her voice echoed out of the machine offering money to Fowler, she stared Peter straight in the eye and didn't blink. He looked away first and switched off the machine.

"Care to explain?"

"I can't. That's my voice, but I didn't make that call to Fowler. I don't mention him by name, so I could have been talking to anyone." She shrugged. "There's nothing else I can tell you, and why would I lie about it? I've been to prison for committing that fraud, so if Fowler was my partner, why wouldn't I tell you?"

"Because you killed him to stop him from demanding money," Taylor suggested.

"You'll have a hard time proving it because I didn't kill anyone."

"What did you do when you left the pub?"

"Cycled back home and stayed there, alone, all the evening."

"So you have no alibi."

"I've no idea since I don't know what time Fowler was killed."

Good answer, thought Nate, but the odds were still heavily stacked against her. Fowler's body was found on the edge of the forest, not that far from the track leading to Lauren's cottage. He'd been stabbed in the stomach and left there to bleed to death. Lauren could hardly have thrown him across the handlebars of her bike and cycled there with him. Unless he followed her there of his own free will because she told him she had the cash for him at the shack, or unless the police could prove she had access to a car, they couldn't place her at the scene. Forensics would have a go, of course, but so far they'd turned up nothing of an incriminating nature. She'd met the man in the pub that afternoon, and her fingerprints were on the Dictaphone. It was circumstantial stuff but still pretty damning.

Peter and his sidekick kept on at her for another half an hour, but her story didn't waiver. In the end she stood up and said that unless she was being charged with something then she intended to go home. Peter asked her to wait, turned off the tape, and he and Taylor left the room. She remained at the horrible metal table, a forlorn figure doing her best to fight officialdom. Nate still didn't know what to make of her story—she hadn't told him everything, he was pretty sure of that—but his heart still went out to her. However desperate she was, he was convinced that she was no murderer.

"Well," Peter said, materialising at Nate's side, "it's a good job you're a nosy bastard who opens other people's mail and can confirm she received that letter. Otherwise I might be tempted to keep her in overnight."

"You haven't got enough."

"Oh, haven't I! Motive and opportunity for starters."

"Yeah, but our old friend *means* has got your stumped."

"Temporarily. You'd be surprised what forensics and good old-fashioned police work can turn up between them. If she was at that scene and shed so much as one hair from her head, then we'll find it. If she had access to any sort of vehicle other than that bike, we'll find out. And if she was seen talking to Fowlds outside that pub, we'll find out about that, too. Then we'll have her."

"You really think she used her feminine wiles to lure the man to a quiet spot in the forest, calmly stabbed him in the stomach, and left him there to die. Come on, Peter, he was twice her weight and not stupid, apparently. Even if he thought she was gonna pay him off, he'd still have been wary, especially as he appears to have a phobia about dogs."

"Perhaps that's it. Thanks, Nate. She met him there, the dog distracted him, and she did the rest."

"Yeah, right, good luck proving it."

"Okay, so that's a reach." Peter rubbed his chin. "But she's holding out about something."

"Perhaps she doesn't trust the police for some reason."

"She claims to be on the breadline but has a taste for fine wine."

"A 2006 Shiraz?" Peter nodded. "Blame yours truly."

"Ah." The policeman nodded. "I should have guessed."

"Find any bloody knives or blood-stained clothing at her cottage?"

"You know we didn't, but then she wouldn't be stupid enough to leave it there, would she." Peter grinned. "Well, I'm going to let her go, for now. Why don't you do your knight-in-shining-armour bit and drive her home. Perhaps she'll open up to you, especially if you have any more of that wine knocking about."

"Ah, so that's why you called me in on this right at the start. I did wonder. You think it's all a bit too contrived, too convenient, and reckon she'll tell me whatever it is that she won't tell you."

"Pillow talk?" suggested Peter, grinning.

"We haven't got that far."

He raised a bushy brow. "Losing your touch?"

"Don't count on it."

Lauren walked into the reception area of the police station ten minutes later looking tired and dispirited. Nate stepped forward, but her eyes were trained on the ground, and she almost walked into him before she realized he was there.

"What do you want?" she asked ungraciously.

"I thought you might need a ride home."

* * * *

Lauren stared suspiciously at Nate for a prolonged moment, wondering how the hell he'd got to hear about her problems so quickly. The answer was obvious. He was in cahoots with his old pal, the inspector. Her natural reaction was to tell him to get lost, but it occurred to her that the police hadn't offered her a lift. Her only alternative was a long wait for the bus and an even longer trudge through the dark forest when she reached the other end. She was still reeling with the shock of learning that the man she'd met with the previous afternoon had been murdered virtually on her doorstep. She sighed, physically and mentally drained after the grilling she'd just undergone, and with ill grace asked Nate where his car was parked.

He led her to a midrange BMW in the station car park, which he unlocked with a remote as they approached it. He opened the passenger door for her and then slid into the driving seat. In spite of herself, she was interested in his wheels. The interior of a car often revealed a lot about its owner. The soft, worn nature of the leather seats suggested that it wasn't new, but it did appear to be cared for. Better yet, it was tidy. There were no fast-food wrappers, empty drinks cans, or newspapers littering the back seat, and for that she was grateful. She'd always been intolerant about sloppiness.

He appeared to respect her requirement for a little space and, putting the car into gear, moved off without saying a word. The radio was tuned to a classical music station, the sound masking the soft rumble of the car's engine and the noise of the tyres as they sped across the tarmac. Lauren felt lulled by an almost hypnotic sense of well-being, which was ridiculous given her current predicament. It forced her to speak.

"So what *were* you doing at the police station? Somehow I doubt you just happened to be passing."

"Peter rang me before he picked you up."

Her suspicions intensified. "And why would he do that?"

Nate briefly took his eyes off the road and glanced at her. "That's what I've been wondering myself." He returned his attention to overtaking a slow-moving van. "Presumably he had his reasons."

"Were you on the other side of that glass when they grilled me?"

"Yes."

"Yes!" She glowered at him, infuriated that he could remain so calm, but he was still in the process of overtaking, so the gesture was wasted on him. "I'm being framed for the murder of a man I barely know, and all you can say is *yes*."

"What would you have me say, Lauren?" His voice was irritatingly calm at a time when she wanted to get rid of some aggression by picking a blazing row with him. "If it's any consolation, I don't think you did it, and I told Peter so."

"Thanks," she said gruffly.

"You're welcome."

"But they think I did it, and that's what counts." Lauren's anger drained away as the reality of her predicament struck home. "If I were in their position, I'd probably think I was guilty, too," she said glumly.

"Perhaps it's all just a little too convenient," he said.

"What do you mean?"

"Well, you met the man in a public place, and he then fetched up dead, virtually on your doorstep." Nate shook his head. "Even if you had a reason to kill him, you'd have to be extremely stupid to do it in a location that led straight back to you. Plus, you'd have had to lure him there in the first place."

"Yes, you heard me try to tell the inspector that, but it means less work for them if they think they've got their woman."

"Detectives like Taylor probably think like that, but fortunately for you, Peter likes to be sure he's got a watertight case."

"That must be why they let me go," she said pensively. "If they think I have access to that money, then I must be a flight risk, so I really didn't expect to be free tonight. You can have no idea how much I dreaded being locked up, even overnight."

He removed one hand from the steering wheel and covered her own with it. "Let's hope it doesn't come to that," he said gently.

"It probably will. I wasn't able to prove that Fowler had invited me to join him at that pub because I destroyed that letter. Just imagine how that looked. Anyway, even if I hadn't, it was typewritten and anyone could have sent it."

"Good job I'm a snoopy journalist then."

"You read it?"

He shrugged. "Couldn't help myself. Sorry."

"Well, under the circumstances, I guess I should be grateful."

"I was mad at you because I thought you were holding out on me. You said no one knew where you were, and yet someone hand delivered a letter addressed to you." He sighed. "I needed to know."

"And Inspector Read believed you?"

"When Fowlds was found and you were seen on the pub CCTV with him, the case got referred to him in London because of you."

"Of course. This isn't the inspector's patch, is it?"

"No, the locals had to get onto him because the money's still missing and anything to do with you goes through them."

"Very comforting!"

"It ought to be. Left to the locals, you'd have been locked up and they'd have already stopped looking for anyone else."

"I take it DS Taylor is a local."

"Yeah, and she's not happy to have Peter overriding her instincts."

"Are you going to tell me what you told him to make him let me go?" she asked when Nate paused for a little too long, concentrating on a snarl-up in the traffic flow ahead.

"Sure, I mentioned that I'd been to the cottage but that you didn't see anyone as a rule and had only given in to me because I was making a pest of myself. That about covers it, doesn't it?" he asked, flashing her a brief sideways smile.

"More than," she agreed. "But how did that help?"

"I gave you a character reference."

Lauren snorted.

"Look, his body was found not two miles from your cottage. That in itself would be enough to sound warning bells because all the local plod know where you live." She nodded. "He worked for *that* electronics company, so even the thickest copper would put two and two together and think to come asking questions."

"Yes, all right," she said grudgingly. "I know they're just looking for a reason to pull me back in. I guess I should thank you."

"It's a small town," he said. "They don't get a lot of murders here, so it's big news. Even if you hadn't been caught on CCTV, someone would have remembered him going to that pub, and they'd sure as hell remember you. You're not so easy to forget, in case you didn't know."

"Is that supposed to be a compliment?"

"I guess it is." He turned toward her, and even in the dim interior of the car, she caught a brief flash of white teeth. If this display of admiration was supposed to make her feel better, it wasn't working, but she was too weary to tell him so. "Anyway, I told Peter word for word what the letter said, so he had independent collaboration before you told him about it, which I guess took some of the heat off you."

"Temporarily," she said gloomily. "But thanks."

"For being a snoop." She could hear the smile in his voice. "It's my job."

By the time they pulled up outside the shack, darkness had descended upon the forest. She didn't invite him in but knew he'd follow her anyway. In view of what he'd done for her, she couldn't really say that she wanted to be on her own. Besides, she didn't. The shack had been invaded, and she was strangely reluctant to face it again for the first time, alone. He released Kermit from the kitchen, and they both received a rapturous welcome. Lauren took one look at the devastation wreaked by the malicious local constabulary and groaned.

"I don't think I can handle this," she said. "Not again."

That's when Nate took control. He steered her back into the sitting room and deposited her in her chair. This room had come through almost unscathed. It was so small and there was so little in it of a personal nature that it took less than a minute for him to put it back the way it was. He got the fire going in an annoyingly short space of time, even though the evening was warm and she didn't think it was necessary. Nate waved away her arguments.

"You've had a shock and need to keep warm," he said.

She didn't have the strength to argue and closed her eyes instead, weariness seeping through her bones. With flames leaping up the chimney, Nate went his car and returned clutching a bottle of something. He forced a glass into her hand and made her drink. Fiery liquid hit the back of her throat, and she choked. It had been so long since she'd had spirits of any kind that it took a moment for her to identify it as brandy.

"Every time I see you I finish up with a hangover," she said, taking another swig. Alcoholic oblivion had never seemed so attractive.

"It's medicinal," he told her with a wink. "Right, stay where you are, both you," he added, scratching a delirious Kermit's ears. "I'll have this place straight in a jiffy."

"But you really don't need to—"

"Yeah, I really do."

She heard him in the kitchen, washing things, straightening drawers, putting stuff away. She forced her mind to go blank. The brandy helped. Just for an hour or two she'd let someone else take the strain. Then she'd send him on his way and see this thing through on her own. She *hadn't* killed anyone, so they wouldn't be able to prove that she had.

"What are you doing?" she called out to Nate, whom she could now hear moving about upstairs in her bedroom.

"Just changing your linen," he called back. "They turned your bed over, so I figured you'd like to start fresh." He reappeared, a bundle of sheets tucked under his arm. "Right, where's your washing machine?"

"In Brockenhurst. It's called a launderette."

"Ah, I see. I'll just put these in the linen basket, and then you're all set. Everything's as good as new."

"Thanks."

"Hungry?" he asked her.

"No."

"Still, you gotta eat."

It would be useless to protest, so she let him get on with it. A short time later he reappeared from the kitchen with cheese on toast and a pot of coffee. She nibbled a corner of the toast, wondering if she'd be able to swallow it past the lump in her throat. She managed to and took a second tentative bite. Before she knew it, she'd finished her own and started on his. When she realized what she'd done, she covered her mouth with her hand and apologised.

"Forget it. I've already eaten today." He nodded toward her empty plate. "Judging by the way you just demolished that lot, it's more than can be said for you."

"Strange as this might sound to you, I've had more important things on my mind."

He settled on the settee across from her, a glass of brandy in his hand.

"So," he said easily, "wanna tell me about it?"

She puffed out her cheeks. "So this is where I pay for being rescued."

"Same rules as before. You only need to tell me what you feel like telling me."

"Then there's nothing to tell. If you listened to my third-degree by your friend Inspector Read, then you know it all anyway."

"I don't think so."

She glowered at him. "Are you saying that I lied?"

"No, you didn't lie, but you didn't tell him everything you know either."

"What makes you say that?" she snapped.

He stretched his arms above his head and took his time responding. "I think you told the truth when you said that you'd never met Fowlds before he accosted you here outside the cottage. I also think that you went to that meeting because you thought he might be able to shed some light on the things that have happened to you." He quirked a brow at her. "Am I right?"

She reluctantly nodded.

"I mean, anyone would be curious. I know I wouldn't have been able to resist finding out a bit more, but you told Peter he couldn't enlighten you. Why did you lie?"

"I didn't lie, I—"

"Lauren!"

"Oh, all right." Lauren didn't see any point in holding back. He'd only peg away at her until he got to the truth, and anyway, it felt good to share it all with someone who might actually believe her. Slowly at first, and then without recourse to caution, she told him everything that Fowler had told her.

"Why didn't you tell Peter all this?"

She rolled her eyes. "They didn't believe me about Jeff the first time round, and I still have no proof. It died with Fowlds, or Fowler, or whatever the hell his name is."

"Which is all the more reason for you not to want him dead."

"They'd only say I was making it up to give myself a reason not to kill him."

Nate considered the point. "Okay, so at least you know now that Williams was pulling his strings."

"Yes, but even if Fowler was still alive, he'd hardly confess to what he'd done. I've been put away for it, but I guess there's still a cosy cell waiting for him with his name over the door."

"Still, you ought to have told Peter. He's more receptive to information about Williams than you give him credit for."

"But I have no proof!" she screeched. "And then there's that telephone message in my voice, which is pretty damning."

"You think Williams recorded you speaking to someone else."

"Well, of course I bloody do! How else could it have got there?"

"So," Nate said, stretching his legs out in front of him and colliding with her knees. "Sorry." He moved his legs to the side, looking awkward and uncomfortable. She suddenly felt very hot but put it down to the effects of a roaring fire in a small room on a warm night. "We know you didn't murder Fowler, so the next question is, who did? Your mate Williams gets my vote."

"How would he have known that Fowler was here yesterday, meeting with me?"

"Fowler told him?"

"I don't think so. He said he didn't trust him."

"Yeah, but Williams made a point of ringing Fowler and telling him you were out. He also managed to convince him that he didn't have the money and that he'd have to wait until you got out to get paid, so there must be an element of trust between them."

Lauren nodded slowly. She hadn't considered that. "But I still don't think he'd have told Jeff he was meeting me."

"Maybe not, but why did Jeff tell Fowler you were out?"

"I suppose because he wanted him to find me."

"Smart girl! My bet is that Williams had someone watching Fowler and reported back to him when he discovered you here at the shack."

"Yes," she said slowly, "that's just the sort of thing he would do. But if he knows where I am, why hasn't he made contact?"

She'd pushed the thought of him being aware of her location to the back of her mind. Being forced to face it made her go from hot to cold again, and her whole body was rocked by a virulent series of shivers.

"Are you cold?" She shook her head. "Shall I bank up the fire?"

"No, don't bother."

He reached out and covered her hand with his. "Don't worry. He won't risk coming after you himself."

"I wish I shared your optimism."

She glanced up at him from beneath lowered lashes. The light from the flickering flames licking round a wide log highlighted his hair, streaking it with bronze. It played across his profile, alternatively shading it and then bringing it back into focus as he contemplated her dilemma. He looked up and smiled, his eyes soft and compelling. Drawn toward him, aware, in spite of everything, of the sexual tension lurking just below the surface, Lauren quickly averted her gaze.

"He's a control freak," Nate said. "He must be worried about what action you're planning to take against him now you're out."

"I'm not planning anything."

He held her gaze, his grey eyes full of unsettling intelligence. "Aren't you?"

"What can I possibly do to him?"

"You'd just been banged up for three years with nothing to think about but revenge, and he'd be an idiot if he wasn't worried about what you might do."

"So you're saying that Jeff Williams deliberately let Fowler know I was out so that he could trace me." She propped one elbow on the arm of her chair and rested her head in her splayed hand. "Then, when he found out we were in a pub together, he somehow got someone to follow Fowler when he left, lure him to the bottom of this lane, and calmly stuck a knife in him. And he managed to set it all up within the hour that we were inside the pub." Her voice rang with scepticism. "If I don't think it's possible, what chance do we have of convincing Inspector Read?"

"I guess you're right. My theory was a bit far fetched, but I still think Williams is behind it all."

"I can see that he'd want to tidy away any loose ends," Lauren said speculatively. "Perhaps that's why Drake was killed. Fowler said no one knew he wasn't going to that meeting himself, and as he'd never met Jeff in person, Drake was probably killed by mistake." She furled her brow, feeling another headache coming on, which was hardly surprising after the day she'd had. "But if Jeff wanted Fowler done away with, why wait so long? He could have arranged for him to meet with any number of accidents over the past few years."

Nate took a moment to think about that one. It was the first time he'd shown any hesitation, even if some of the theories he voiced were wildly improbable. He still had doubts about her. She could sense that from the way that he looked at her so intently, as though trying to see inside her head. Well, that was okay. She didn't trust him either and certainly didn't intend to share her plans for the future with him.

"He was being careful," he eventually said. "Killing two birds with one stone, if you'll pardon the pun. With Fowler murdered on your doorstep, suspicion was bound to fall upon you. If you came out of prison, made your accusations about Williams public in order to exact revenge...well, he couldn't risk that. No one would believe it, but mud sticks, and his reputation matters to him. So he got in first and has neatly done away with all his problems." Nate paused. "Or thinks he has."

"Thanks," she said, shuddering.

"Sorry, just thinking out loud. It's a bad habit."

"It's okay." She fell silent for a moment, mulling it all over. "Is that why you think he won't come here?"

"Yes, he can't afford to risk being seen anywhere near you."

"They'll come for me again, won't they, Nate?" she said, aware of the tremor in her voice. "They think I did it and won't let up on me until I say something to incriminate myself. I know how they work."

He leapt from his seat and knelt beside her chair, solid and reassuring even when he was on his knees. "They can't make it stick, Lauren, because you didn't do it, always remember that."

She noticed that he didn't deny the possibility of her being arrested and formally charged, and her heart sank. "Since when has that stopped them?"

He removed the glass she was still holding and took both of her hands between his own, rubbing them as though attempting to stimulate her circulation. "I won't let anything bad happen to you, Lauren. You have my word on that." His gaze, eyes blazing with determination, was fastened on her face. She felt too full of emotion to bear his scrutiny and, afraid of what he might read in her expression, looked away. "If they do come for you again, call me, and I'll get you the best legal representation money can buy."

"And why would you do that?"

"Because you're being unjustly accused. Remember what happened to my mom."

"I don't buy that."

"And," he added, grinning sheepishly, "because you're gonna be overcome with gratitude when I get you out of this thing. We'll prove Williams guilty, of course, and then you'll give me your exclusive story for my book, and we'll make a killing."

In spite of the gravity of her situation, Lauren found herself laughing, something she'd thought she'd never do again.

"You're incorrigible, Mr. Black," she said, pulling her hands out of his grasp. It was far too comfortable being consoled by him, and it wasn't a habit she couldn't afford to indulge.

"That's me," he said, getting to his feet and resuming his seat. "One thing I don't understand though—"

"Only one?" She rolled her eyes. "Lucky you."

"Yeah well, only one that's been bugging me for a while anyway. If Williams has got all that money stashed away, why is he still here playing happy families?"

"I've wondered about that, too, but I reckon it was never really his intention to go anywhere. I think he just wanted financial independence from Gloria for his own peace of mind. He hated being beholden to her for his material possessions and for the help that her money gave him to establish himself in the places that matter to him."

"Yeah, that makes sense I guess."

"He also loves being a partner at Whytelake's, and I can see now that he'd never give that up easily. He loves the power and respect the position affords him, you see." She paused, absently pulling at her lower lip as she articulated her thoughts. "I can't believe now that he convinced me he'd ever want anything more than he's already got, other than independent means, of course." She shrugged. "Just goes to show how naïve I was back then."

"So we're dealing with a power-hungry misogynist?"

"Oh no, Jeff doesn't hate women," she said, surprised by the suggestion. "Just the opposite, in fact. He just hated being under Gloria's fiscal control. I guess he's more of an old-fashioned chauvinist who doesn't think the power in a relationship should lie with the woman."

"I disagree. I think his dislike of Gloria and all she stands for dates back to before his marriage." Nate tilted his head to one side, thinking it through. His hair, too long by most people's standards but Lauren thought it suited him, fell to one side like a thick curtain, shading his face. "Probably something to do with a controlling and manipulative mother."

"Do you Yanks always have to psychoanalyse everything?" she asked. Her sharpness was intended to disguise the sudden spark of desire she felt as she observed him, relaxed and contemplative, mere feet away from her as he worried away at her problems with a single-minded determination.

"Comes with the territory, I'm afraid," he said, grinning. "Kids as young of four or five are routinely put into therapy back home nowadays."

"God help them."

"Yeah well, I have a feeling that God isn't going to be much help with your problems, so I guess we'd better not rely too heavily on his intervention. We'll just have to dream up a way of proving Williams's involvement for ourselves."

Chapter Eight

There was just one small lamp and the dwindling fire illuminating the room, so Lauren's features were largely in shadow. Even so, Nate observed her expression undergo several changes as his words sunk in. Her situation was every bit as parlous as she herself had pointed out. It could only be a matter of time before Peter's team found some little thing to incriminate her. If that happened, any doubts that Peter harboured about her guilt would be discarded by his superiors, and he would be forced to arrest her. Just one piece of solid evidence was all they needed. Something linking her to the scene of the crime, however tenuously, added to all the circumstantial evidence they'd already amassed would be enough to close the circle.

He wouldn't let it happen but was at a loss to know how to help her all the time she continued to hold out on him. She *had* to have plans for revenge. She wasn't the type to just let this go, when the bastard had ruined her life. Even so, now wasn't the time to push it.

"You need my help, Laurcn," he said softly.

"I appreciate the offer, Nate, but I can't think about it now." She stretched her arms above her head and yawned. "I'm beat."

"Sure you are, but you *will* have to do something soon. Or we will. You must see that." He stood up, looming over her. "Why won't you trust me?"

She stood, too, mere inches away from him. Their gazes locked, and neither one of them spoke. He forced himself not to reach for her. Even though he could sense an awakening of her interest in him, the first move was hers. He didn't want his rampant libido to scare her off and undo all his good work.

"Kermit needs to go out," she said, snatching her eyes away from his.

"I'll take him."

"Thanks."

She fell back into her chair, curled her feet beneath her, and crossed her arms over her torso. Nate wandered down the path with Kermit. He sniffed the air as he waited for the dog to reappear from the bushes. Rain threatened or a storm perhaps. It would be quite spectacular to see, out here in the wilds with no artificial streetlights to diminish the show, but he wasn't about to endure another night's torture on that bloody sofa, and he'd already decided not to take advantage of Lauren's vulnerable condition.

When he returned to the shack, she stood at the open door, leaning against it, arms folded against the cool night air.

"Go back in," he said. "You'll get cold."

"I'm fine."

But she didn't look fine. Her features were drawn, etched with tiredness, and she appeared susceptible and very scared. She shouldn't be alone, but he didn't trust himself to stay with her.

"I'll be off then."

But he didn't move. Instead he watched her, arms still folded defensively as she stared at the ground in front of her. There was something she wanted to say but was having trouble finding the words. He moved a step closer but didn't touch her.

"What is it?" he asked softly.

"I don't want you to go," she said so quietly that he thought he must have misheard her. She was still looking at the ground and not at him. "I hate feeling dependent, but I don't want to be alone. Not tonight."

"You'll be okay," he said. "No one will try to get at you here, not now. You're quite safe, except for the fact that there's a storm on the way." He ignored the hurt in her eye. His noble intentions had been misinterpreted, and she thought he was rejecting her. Much she knew!

Desire surged through him, but he tried to pretend it wasn't there. "The storm will keep everyone with sense indoors," he said, trying to make light of the situation but only making matters worse.

At last she lifted her eyes and looked directly at him. Her shoulders shook with emotion. "I just don't think I can stand—"

Her tears proved to be his undoing. He'd never thought to see her cry, not under any circumstances. She seemed too tough for displays of girly emotion. That she'd given way to it now, in front of him, indicated just how close to the edge she actually was.

There was now no question of Nate leaving her alone.

He steered her back into the shack, closed the door behind them and, without hesitation, pulled her into his arms.

"Hey," he said, stroking her spiky hair as she sobbed against his shoulder. "It's okay, we'll sort it."

"I can't stand…I don't think I can—" She was crying too hard for her words to be articulate.

"Don't talk," he said, his hands travelling the length of her back in a slow, rhythmic sweeping motion. "Just let it all out. You'll feel better."

The floodgates opened. Nate lost all track of time and simply held her trembling body until her emotion was eventually spent. When she lifted her head from his shoulder and looked up at him, tears still sparkling on her lashes, instinct took over. Muttering curses beneath his breath, he lowered his head and brushed her lips with his own, just to reassure, but Lauren had other ideas. With a strength that surprised him, her hand came to rest on the nape of his neck and forced his head back toward hers in a gesture he was powerless to resist. This time it was she who initiated the kiss, not gently but with purpose and aggression. Her lips were demanding as they hardened against his, making it plain that she didn't require cosseting. Nate guessed that after three years of prison and all the crap that had been thrown at her since, she needed to feel alive and desirable. She wanted to blot out the horror that her life had become and lose herself in sensual pleasures that deprived her of the ability to think about anything else.

All this Nate instinctively understood, probably better than she did, and it would take a more disciplined man than he'd ever be to refuse her. She'd regret it tomorrow, probably blame him for it happening in the first place, and he'd have the devil's own job getting her to trust him again. Still, he'd cross that bridge when he came to it. Right now he had other priorities.

He took control, deepening the kiss as he held her hard against his aroused body. His tongue worked its way into her mouth, and she instinctively accommodated it, sucking its tip deep, only to release it and then search it out again. Nate, who hadn't anticipated anything like this happening tonight of all nights, was totally unprepared for the depth of her passion. He wasn't too sure how well equipped he was to deal with it, but he'd sure as hell give it his best shot. He broke the kiss, determined to make sure she understood what she was getting into before they took this any further. Nate was already almost at the point of no return.

"Sure?" He watched her closely as he posed the question.

Instead of answering him, she simply turned toward the stairs and started climbing. Nate followed directly behind her, his mind a deliberate void. Sometimes it was a curse, having the sort of brain that went for in-depth analysis at the most inappropriate times, and he made a deliberate effort to switch off.

As soon as they entered her bedroom, they fell into one another's arms, panting, touching, urgently kissing, and simultaneously stripping one another of their clothes. They were naked in seconds, and their passion was fast and brutal. Nate barely had the time to search his wallet for a condom before Lauren cried out, clawing at his back as she closed about him and climaxed. He thrust deeper into her, delirious with anticipation, and felt her come a second time as he shot his load into the thin layer of latex sheathing his penis.

Afterward they lay together, bodies sticky with sweat. They were both breathless and, in Nate's case at least, only temporarily satiated. He already knew that once would never be enough for him.

"Thanks," she said, curling up catlike on her side and resting her head on his chest. "I needed that."

He chuckled. "So I gathered."

"Don't get any ideas," she said, frowning up at him. "These were exceptional circumstances, and you just happened to be here."

"Glad to be of service," he said, lazily tracing the outline of her breast with his forefinger.

The second time round he made it last, forcing her to remain docile whilst he investigated every inch of her body. It was no easy task because she wasn't the passive type. He familiarised himself with the taste and smell of her, revelling in her enjoyment as she squirmed and wriggled beneath him, always demanding more, never holding back. When their time came, they climaxed in unison, the prolonged sensation reverberating through them both louder than the thunder that was now cracking directly above the shack.

She fell asleep in his arms almost immediately afterward, and he watched over her as she finally found some peace. Nate was now wide awake, his mind still in full working order. There were elements of Lauren's case that didn't add up—something she wasn't telling him. He just couldn't figure why Williams had waited so long to kill Fowlds and deliberately frame Lauren for his murder. There was nothing Lauren could do to implicate him. He had nothing to fear from her, only from Fowlds, so why risk keeping him alive so long?

* * * *

Jeff Williams glanced at his watch, bored with the proceedings but too pleased with the way things were going in his life to let it show. Gloria adored entertaining and did it with understated style and great panache. He raised his glass across the table to her in a silent toast, unaffected by her beauty, any feelings he'd once had for her long since dead.

He poured dessert wine for those that wanted it and exchanged flirtatious banter with a couple of the women. He toed the line here in Wimbledon and restricted his interaction with the females to flirtation, even though he could have had any one of them whenever he wanted to. It amused him to speculate, but he had no intention of letting the hard-won respect he'd earned on home turf become tarnished by rumours of tawdry affairs.

He sat back in his chair and allowed the dinner-table chatter to pass over his head. It was Friday night, and he wondered if Lauren had been arrested for Fowlds murder yet. He knew she'd been questioned the previous day and then released, which was immensely satisfying. The poor darling must be petrified of going back inside, but then, if she'd come straight to him as soon as they'd released her, none of this would have been necessary. He hated to think of her living in that shed in the forest. She deserved a lot better than that. He'd been curious about her accommodation and so took a big risk one morning when she was safely at work and had a quick look at the place. He was appalled by what he'd seen. And as for that café she worked in? Jeff shuddered. Her standards had slipped. No way would the Lauren he'd once known have put up with that sort of rig for long.

Once he found her, he could have gone to her, of course, but that would put him at a disadvantage. No, this had to be done on his terms, and he was pleased with himself for managing to arrange things so quickly. That fool Fowlds had been easy to manipulate, and Jeff was glad now that he'd risked keeping him around for so long. Once his man told Jeff that Fowlds was meeting Lauren in that pub, it was easy to put his plan into action. There was just enough evidence to incriminate Lauren but not enough to hang the crime on her. He wanted her docile and reliant upon him, not banged up again where he couldn't get at her.

Jeff had made sure he'd been seen in the office on Wednesday afternoon until well after the murder went down. Gloria came up to town because by chance they had a Director's dinner at the Mansion House that evening, a full white-tie affair with wives in attendance, which made it all feel like it was meant to be. Gloria stayed the night at the flat, and Jeff could account for every moment of the whole day, and the night, too. Not that he'd been questioned, nor did he expect to be, but he hadn't got where he was without paying excessive attention to detail.

One thing did bother him. His man had reported that some guy was hanging round Lauren's place of work. His car had also been seen near her shack, but a trace on the number pinpointed it as a fleet car. Probably just some horny salesman sensing a good thing, keen to get his end away. Jeff frowned. He didn't think she'd be looking for a man so soon after her release because Lauren simply wasn't the promiscuous type. He felt a moment's jealousy at the thought of someone else getting their hands on her before he did, but it soon passed. Right now Lauren would have more urgent things on her mind than kick-starting any sort of social life.

Jeff's resources had taken a hammering in dealing first with Drake and now Fowlds. Murders-for-hire didn't come cheap. Nothing in life worth having ever did. That was part of his problem. Still, at least the one he'd used on both occasions was professional and discreet. He'd never met Jeff, nor Jeff him, which suited them both. He'd paid him off by wire transfer and didn't anticipate the need to call upon his services ever again. He didn't even have anyone watching Lauren now, confident that she'd soon come to heel.

"Did he reappear?"

Jeff returned his attention to the discussion between some of the women.

"How would I know?"

Gloria sounded a little too casual. One of her friends was probably referring to some guy she had the hots for. Gloria wasn't quite as discreet about these things as she liked to suppose. Just for the hell of it, Jeff asked who they were talking about.

"Oh, just some guy who appeared at the pool."

"Some guy!" Her recently divorced friend stared at Gloria as though she'd lost her mind. "Darling, what's wrong with you? I know you're happily married, but that's never stopped you window-shopping before. The guy was drop-dead gorgeous, and you had coffee with him before the rest of us could get anywhere near him, you wretch!" Gloria glowered at her friend who, somewhat drunk, appeared to have forgotten about Jeff. "Oophs, sorry!" she said, giggling. But Jeff could tell from the malicious glint in her eye that her gaff had been deliberate. She resented Gloria's success with this mystery man and was out to cause trouble.

"Who was this Adonis, then?" Jeff asked. He didn't particularly care but thought it would look strange if he didn't ask.

"Oh, I don't know," Gloria said, flapping a dismissive hand. "I'd forgotten all about him."

"Nate something or other, wasn't it?" asked one of the women.

"Yes," Gloria agreed. "I think that was it, but I didn't take much notice. He was just passing through, apparently." Gloria glanced across at Jeff, her eyes sparkling with amusement. "Not jealous are you, darling?"

But Jeff didn't even hear her. He didn't know the full name of the guy hanging round Lauren, but his investigator, the official one as opposed to the one who made his problems permanently disappear, thought he heard him referred to as Nate.

* * * *

Lauren woke with a headache and someone in her bed who shouldn't be there, touching her body. The sensation wasn't unpleasant. She felt strangely unthreatened by it, which is why it took her a moment to force her eyes open. As soon as she did, memories came crashing in on her in a breathless rush, and she sat bolt upright, knocking Nate's hand from her breast. She remembered it all now and was overtaken with panic. The police had grilled her about Fowler's murder and really thought she'd done it. She'd let Nate drive her home afterward *and* allowed him to spend the night with her. She rubbed her face, unsure which circumstance bothered her more. A glance at the clock brought her to her senses. With a gasp, she threw back the covers and stood up.

"Hey," Nate drawled, "where's the fire?"

"I'm late for work."

He leaned up on one elbow, giving her an up-close view of an impressively muscular torso. Presumably she'd seen it all before but averted her eyes anyway, pushed aside the long, cool fingers that now rested on her thigh, and stood up. She turned her back to him, snatched up a T-shirt, and pulled it over her naked body.

"You're not seriously intending to go to work today?" he asked incredulously. "Not after all you've been through."

"Of course I am," she said, not looking at him. "I already took one sick day. If I pull that stunt again, I'll be out of work, and that will affect my parole."

"But surely you can explain."

She placed her hands on her hips. "Sorry, boss, can't come in today. I was interviewed by the police yesterday about a local murder, they have me pegged as the killer, and so, as you can imagine, I'm a bit upset about it." She rolled her eyes. "He knows who I really am, but there's a limit to his exploitation of the desperate."

"Yeah, okay, point taken. But can't you just—"

"Look, I don't have time for this. I have to go."

He got out of bed as well and didn't seem to care that he was totally naked. "Well, at least let me make you breakfast."

"No time for that. Besides, I'm not hungry. Let yourself out and…er, thanks for the lift home."

"Lauren!"

She made a dash for the bathroom, only to realize that all her clothes were still in the bedroom. She returned to retrieve them, pretending not to notice his perplexed expression. He was propped up in bed, still displaying that muscular chest, but at least the bedspread now covered him from the waist down.

"Let me drive you to work. You're in no condition to cycle to the bus stop."

"I'm fine." She could hear the agitation in her own voice and wasn't surprised when his frown deepened. "I just need to get back into my routine."

"What will you do about Fowler?"

She shrugged. "What can I do?"

"The police won't give up until they get answers, you know."

At last she looked at him. "Yes, I do know that," she said quietly, grabbing jeans, any old sweatshirt, and clean underwear. "Thanks again."

Ten minutes later she was cycling through the silent forest, Kermit scampering to keep up with her furious pace. At least Nate hadn't tried to follow her, but she wouldn't be surprised if he showed up at the café. She tried to examine her feelings as she pushed the pedals, puffing slightly from the exertion, annoyed by the deviation her plans had taken. She had thought it all through so meticulously, right down to the last detail. She just hadn't anticipated that she'd be suspected of murder not a month after getting out. That changed everything, of course.

She ought to feel totally deflated but couldn't seem to focus on her most immediate problem. Instead, her mind kept returning to Nate. She contemplated his robust performance in bed and the way it had made her feel. Alive, sensual, desirable…all of the above, and that definitely wasn't in the script. She was annoyed with herself for weakening and letting him stay, vowing that it was the first and only time it would happen. She wobbled over an uneven piece of ground, catching her inner thigh on the side of the saddle. It was sore, pleasantly so, and a mild climax rocked her sensitised body. Yea gods, what the hell had he done to her?

Lauren worked on autopilot. The café was busy, but thankfully Nate didn't put in an appearance. As she filled orders, cleared tables, and worked the cash register, she also focused her mind on her dilemma, squelching all thoughts of Nate if they happened to slip past her guard. He was right about one thing, though. The police had her firmly in the frame for Fowler's murder. Inspector Read wouldn't stay in this part of the world for long, and once that hostile female detective was left to her own devices, there was no telling what schemes she'd dream up to embarrass Lauren. Or what evidence she might invent to persuade the CPS to prosecute. Lauren hated being incautious, but she now had no alternative. She would just have to move her plans forward.

When she took her break, she made sure the passageway outside the toilets was clear and used the payphone on the wall. Her call was answered almost immediately.

"Hi," she said, recognising the voice at the other end. "It's me."

"Lauren, I'm so glad you called. How are you?"

"Not good. Something's happened."

The voice was full of concern. "What?"

"I can't tell you over the phone."

"I hadn't expected to hear from you so soon. Presumably this mystery development is the reason for that."

"Yes. Look, I have to see my probation officer in Southampton on Friday morning. Can we meet after that?"

"Of course. I'd love to see you. You know where to find me."

"Yes. Will you tell Sophie?"

"Leave it to me. We both look forward to seeing you on Friday."

Lauren hung up, just as a burly lorry driver emerged from the gents and leered at her. She ignored him and returned to her duties, feeling just a tad better about things now that she had a plan of sorts.

* * * *

Nate waited for Lauren to leave before he got out of bed. It was obvious that she needed space. It was equally obvious that she was exceedingly agitated, and he couldn't help wondering what she'd be forced into doing to help herself. Instinct told him that she would no longer bury her head in the sand and pretend that the rest of the world didn't exist. She was too intelligent to just hope for the best. Whatever plans she had—whatever it was that she wasn't telling him—would go down sooner than originally intended, and Nate would be there, helping her efforts along, whether she liked it or not.

He got up, showered, and scrabbled around for something to eat. When would she make her move? She wouldn't want to do anything out of the ordinary that would draw attention to herself, and the only time she stepped outside of her routine was when she saw her probation officer. She kept a few scraps of paper behind a jar on the mantelpiece. He looked through them and discovered that she had an appointment in Southampton this Friday. If she was going to do anything, it would be then.

Nate resisted the urge to visit the café and make sure she was all right. Aware that she wouldn't appreciate the intrusion, he thumped the kitchen surface in frustration. When she asked him to stay the night, he really thought he was getting through to her and that she would open up to him at last. She'd certainly enjoyed what they did between the sheets, shedding her inhibitions with a speed that both surprised and delighted him. But this morning she'd withdrawn into herself and couldn't even look at him. She was the weirdest, most compelling broad he'd met in quite a while, and she had as much chance of shaking him off the scent of a good story as he had of willing a Pulitzer.

Nate called Peter Read, not surprised to learn that he was on his way back to London.

"Your girl is prime suspect," he told Nate.

"Yeah, I gathered that much, but I'm pretty sure she didn't do it."

Peter's throaty chuckle echoed down the line. "Well, you would say that, wouldn't you?"

"Trust me, Peter, I'm never wrong about these things."

"Oh, known a lot of murderers in your time, have you?"

"I've interviewed a few during the course of my journalistic career, and I've also spoken to enough lying toe-rags to known when they're spinning me a line."

"Yes, perhaps but—"

"Come on, Peter, you don't think she did it either, do you?"

"What I *think* doesn't come into it. It's what the locals can prove that counts."

"Yeah, and WDC whatever her name was didn't like Lauren."

"She won't manufacture evidence, that's for sure."

"Let's hope not."

"They'll have to call me if they want to talk to her again. Orders from on high."

Good. "You'll give me some warning if that happens?"

"If I can. But in return, if you find out anything, you'll let me know first."

Nate paused, his mind whirling. He didn't intend to lie to Peter, but his first loyalty lay with Lauren. "What makes you think I'll be looking?" he asked, hedging.

Another chuckle. "I've seen the way you look at the girl."

"Ahh."

"And your car was outside her place all night."

"Nothing gets past you, does it?"

"That's why I'm a policeman."

"I knew there had to be a reason."

Nate was smiling as he cut the connection, even though he hadn't learned much to make him smile.

Now it was a waiting game.

Chapter Nine

On Friday morning, Nate stood across the street from the probation office and watched Lauren emerge. When she didn't head for the bus that would take her back to Brockenhurst but instead turned in the other direction, he knew it was game time. At first it was easy to follow her because the streets were busy, but as she made her way to a quiet part of town, it became trickier. Fortunately it didn't seem to occur to her that someone might be trailing her, and she kept moving at a brisk pace, not once looking over her shoulder. He almost lost her when she turned into a quiet side road of neat terraced houses. There was no one else walking that pavement and only a couple of vehicles moving in the street. She would hear his footsteps if he stayed to close. He fell back, watching from a distance, frustrated, as she turned into one of the houses and rang the bell.

Damn it, they all looked the same, and it was impossible to see which house she'd actually gone into. The door was opened almost immediately, and she disappeared inside. He couldn't see who'd opened it, and so Nate had no choice but to carry on down the road and see if he could identify the house in question. He thought he saw a flash of royal blue door but couldn't be absolutely certain. He passed the house he favoured, but the front window was covered by a thick net curtain. Two people were inside, and he was fairly certain that one of the silhouettes belonged to Lauren. After the things they got up to the other night, he was pretty well acquainted with all those curves. As he carried on walking, he noticed that the houses on either side showed no signs of life whatsoever. This appeared to be the sort of street where young professionals would live, so it was reasonable to assume that most inhabitants would be at work at this hour on a Friday.

Nate found a place to conceal himself farther down the street. Keeping a careful watch on the house, he pulled out his phone and called the *Inquirer.* He got himself put through to a female junior reporter he'd once had a brief fling with, and turned on the charm.

"Hey, Cindy, it's Nate. How you doing?"

"Nate." She sounded pleased to hear from him. "It's been awhile."

"Too long. We must have a drink sometime soon."

"But in the meantime," she said, sounding amused rather than annoyed when it must have been obvious that he was only calling because he wanted something.

"Could you just take a peek at the electoral register? I'm chasing a story and—"

"And you want to know who lives at a particular address."

"Got it." He reeled off the address in question. "It's probably a massive waste of time."

She laughed. "Which is what you'll be doing the next time you get round to calling, unless you do it soon."

"Hey, I already said I would. I've only just got back to England, and you were the first person I thought of calling."

"Of course I was!" A cynical snort echoed down the line. "Here we go. The house is rented to a Ms. Melanie Frost. Hum, nice name. Sounds just like your type."

"You're my type, angel." Someone else—another woman—approached the house. "Look, something's happening. Gotta go."

"Don't be a stranger, Nate."

The other woman also disappeared into the house, leaving Nate with a problem. He'd assumed that if Lauren met with anyone, it would be in a public place and he'd be able to somehow…somehow what? He realized now that he didn't have a brilliant master plan. Some investigative journalist he was! Lauren was meeting with two people. She wanted that meeting to be in private, specifically didn't want him to know anything about it, and would be less than impressed when he knocked at the door and demanded to know what was going on. Well, tough because that's exactly what he planned to do.

Nate waited five minutes, giving the three of them time to get reacquainted. It had started to drizzle, but he turned up his collar and barely noticed the discomfort. When he considered enough time had elapsed, he approached the blue front door. This time there was a long delay before it was answered. A petite, attractive blonde woman looked up at him, suspicion written all over his face.

"Ms. Frost?"

"Yes, who are you?"

"A friend of Lauren's. Is she here?"

The woman gasped but covered her reaction by turning it into a cough. "What…no, sorry, I don't know anyone of that name."

"We both know that isn't true. I watched her come in here not five minutes ago."

"You're mistaken. Please leave." The woman made to close the door, but in true salesman style, Nate jammed his foot in the opening. "Just tell her that Nate's here. If she doesn't want to see me, then I promise I'll go." He flashed a disarming smile. "You can close the door if you like. I'll wait out here in the rain."

To his astonishment, she did precisely that. So much for his lethal charm. Some time passed, and nothing happened. Nate was about to ring the bell again when the door opened.

"You'd better come in," Melanie Frost said ungraciously.

Nate stepped into a small entrance hall and glanced into the room on the left. The tall woman he'd seen approach the house was seated beside Lauren. What Nate hadn't realized about her was that she was exceptionally beautiful. Light coffee-coloured skin, thick black hair twisted into a knot at her nape, huge almond-shaped eyes, and a figure that would stop traffic. All of this Nate took in almost vicariously because his entire attention was focused on Lauren. She looked furious, her eyes shooting daggers at him, and her beautiful companion had to place a hand on her arm to stop her getting up and launching a physical attack on him.

"You followed me," she said furiously.

"Yeah." He flashed another lazy smile. "Mind if I sit down?"

"Like you'd take any notice if I said *yes.*"

"I just want to help you."

"I don't need your help."

She glared at him. He glared right back.

"Who is this?" Melanie asked, breaking the tension.

Nate, who still hadn't sat down, offered her his hand. "Hi, I'm Nate Black. Presumably Lauren hasn't gotten around to telling you about me?"

Melanie shook his outstretched hand. "Pleased to meet you," she said weakly. "Am I pleased to meet him?" she amended, turning toward Lauren.

Lauren shrugged. "It's a free country."

Nate turned toward the Amazonian beauty, hand once again outstretched. "Hi," he said. "I don't think I caught your name."

The woman glanced at Lauren. "You might as well tell him," she said, sighing. "He's clearly not going anywhere until he knows all my business."

"Sophie Rand," the woman said, standing up. With high heels, she was the same height as Nate's six two. "Are you a policeman?"

"No, nothing like that."

"Worse," said Lauren sullenly. "He's a journalist."

Sophie elevated her brows. "You'd better fill us in," she said, resuming her seat beside Lauren.

Lauren succinctly outlined their history, leaving out all mention of his overnight stay at the shack. When she got to the end, Nate sensed a lessening of tension amongst the other women.

"So you just want to help her?" Sophie asked, making it obvious that was all that mattered to her.

"Yeap, but she won't have it."

"So you followed her here?"

"I had a feeling she'd do something stupid to try and prove her innocence."

"Thanks for your high opinion of me," Lauren snarled.

"How did you ladies meet?" Nate asked.

Neither spoke, instead looking toward Lauren, who nodded. "Go ahead," she said, sighing.

Melanie spoke first. "I was her predecessor."

"Her what!"

"I worked at Whytelake's, too." She paused, meeting Nate's eye. "I was Williams's previous victim."

Nate couldn't have been more surprised. "You had an affair with him, too?"

"If that's what you'd care to call our sordid activities."

"Then why didn't you say something when Lauren was—"

"Because I wouldn't let her," chimed in Lauren. "She couldn't prove it any more than I could."

"But it would have leant credibility to your claim."

"No, without proof it would have looked like a disgruntled ex-employee with an axe to grind."

"Williams got fed up with me because I wouldn't play naughty with the company funds," explained Melanie. "I think by then he'd already targeted Lauren and wanted rid of me because he'd found someone younger and easier to manipulate. He got nasty, found a reason to dismiss me but said if I went quietly, there would be a bonus in it for me."

Lauren curled her lip. "A bonus but no reference, so she wasn't able to get another job in the industry."

"Nothing definite was known about my reason for leaving," Melanie said, taking up the tale, "but rumours got round, and I knew that I'd had it with finance."

"How do you get by?" Nate asked.

"I used my bonus to set up as a website designer. In a way, Williams did me a favour," she said speculatively, "because I'd always wanted to do something like that but didn't have the courage to branch out on my own. He forced me into it."

"She's a wiz with anything to do with computers," Sophie said.

"I wasn't very nice to Mel when she tried to warn me off Jeff," Lauren said. "At the time I was still enthralled with Williams and thought it was a case of spite." She threw back her head and sighed. "I wish I'd listened."

"I went to see her when she was arrested and offered to say what Williams had done to me," Melanie said, "but Lauren wouldn't let me." She shrugged. "She wouldn't let me visit her either because—"

"Because you have plans to get your revenge and didn't want anyone to get wind of that," Nate finished for her.

"Something like that," Lauren agreed.

"Why, Melanie?" Nate asked. "You got away comparatively unscathed and are now doing what you've always wanted to. You just admitted that, so why get involved?"

"Because he's a selfish bastard," Melanie said brutally. "And I'll bet he's doing it again to some other unsuspecting victim. It would be easy to turn a blind eye and get on with my life, but someone's got to stop him."

Nate was impressed by her determination, even if it did smack of a woman scorned. He was left with the impression that she'd actually fallen hard for Williams.

"Where do you fit into this, Sophie?" he asked, turning toward her.

"You don't have to tell him," Lauren said.

"No, it's all right. I'd like to." The woman turned her remarkable eyes on Nate. "Lauren saved my sister from a manslaughter wrap," she said quietly, her eyes misting.

Nate thought quickly, remembering something Peter had told him about Lauren's jail-house lawyering, and one case in particular. "The girl who was accused of killing her pimp?"

Sophie looked impressed. "You have done your homework." She reached for her water glass and took a sip. "Maisie and I are half-sisters, but I'm ten years older. Our mother was a tart and didn't know who either of our fathers were. When she died of an overdose, I brought Maisie up myself, trying to keep her on the straight and narrow. I was old enough to see what the life had done to my mother, and I didn't want that for either of us."

"That was a brave thing to do," Nate said quietly. "It can't have been easy."

"No, but I thought Maisie agreed with me, and I relaxed my guard. I blame myself now for not noticing that she'd got in with the wrong crowd. By the time I did, it was too late, and I'd lost her. Maisie woke up next to her dead pimp and had no idea what happened that night. She was out of it on drugs, which made her a soft target for the police."

"She was covered in his blood?"

Sophie shuddered. "Yes, but that was because she was asleep beside him when he was attacked. She just couldn't remember what happened. Anyway, her brief was useless, didn't look at the evidence properly."

"But Lauren did?"

Sophie smiled at her. "She sure did. She realized that, because of the angle of the stab wounds, the assailant had to have been taller than Maisie and left-handed. It's what got her off. She's now clean of drugs and working in a drop-out centre, helping others. Thanks to Lauren, her life has been turned completely around."

"And so you want to repay Lauren by helping her get revenge, too."

"Absolutely."

"What's the plan?"

It was Lauren who answered him. “Well, I don’t suppose we’ll ever prove that he was involved with the theft of the money and that it was his idea. He’s too well protected for us to get anywhere near that. But he has a weakness for beautiful women, Sophie more than qualifies, and she’s willing to try and entice him into an inappropriate situation. We’ll make sure she records what he says to her, and at least then the police will know that I didn’t lie about that.”

“And if they know that, then they have to believe that she’s no murderess either,” added Melanie.

Nate tried not to laugh. As plans went, it was weaker than bargain basement wine. She’d had three years to think about it, two willing accomplices to fall back on, and this was the best she could come up with.

“You’re willing to go to bed with the louse?” he said to Sophie in an even voice.

“No!” Lauren answered for her. “Just getting him talking intimately will be enough to prove a point.”

Nate leant back in his chair and stretched his arms above his head. “And do absolutely nothing to damage his power base.”

“What do you mean?” Three pairs of eyes regarded him intently.

Nate answered their question with one of his own. “What matters most in this world to Williams?”

“Power, influence, and respect,” Lauren said without thinking about it.

“Money,” added Melanie.

“His position at the golf club,” chimed in Sophie.

“And what are his weaknesses?”

“Women and greed,” Lauren supplied.

“Well then, I suggest that we use his weaknesses to destroy his power base.” Nate’s indolent smile encompassed them all. “What do you say, ladies? Are you game?”

Chapter Ten

The three women shared a prolonged glance, but it was Lauren who broke the ensuing silence.

"That's not possible," she said. "Jeff is too well protected."

"Think outside the box," Nate said.

"Perhaps he has a point," said Melanie tentatively. "We're not being very inventive."

"You said yourself that you'd like to do more to hurt him," Sophie added.

Lauren snapped. It was bad enough that Nate had followed her here. Now he was dolling out crazy suggestions like confetti and already had her friends eating out of his capable hands.

"This might come as a big surprise to you," she said, glowering at him. "But I've done nothing else but think about revenging myself on Jeff bloody Williams for three years. If there was any other way to get at him, don't you think it would have occurred to me by now? Contrary to what you obviously think of me, I'm not completely stupid."

Her scathing comments merely served to amuse him. "But you're not using that brain of yours."

"I beg your pardon!"

"Like I said, you're not looking at the bigger picture. If we play him right, then his greed will be his undoing."

"Feeding him insider information won't work, if that's what you're thinking," Lauren said. "They've tightened up their auditing procedures for some reason."

"Besides," added Sophie, "if he has all the money that he made Lauren steal, why would he want more?"

"People like him never have enough. Money is power. Besides, if he forked out to have two people murdered, that will have made a big dent in his little stash."

"But I still don't see how—"

"We create a situation that will tempt him," Nate said, talking over Lauren's interruption. "If he heard of a potentially good investment, how would he check it out?"

"The Internet," said Lauren and Melanie together.

"And the financial press, I should think," added Sophie.

"Right and I'm sitting in a room with a computer ace." All eyes turned toward Melanie. "And yours truly is not without contacts in the world of newspapers."

"What do you have in mind?" Lauren asked, her interest piqued in spite of her determination to remain detached.

"Well, we invent a situation. It could be anything. Perhaps a precious metal find on a remote piece of land in America. It's a big secret, but naturally we find a way to let Williams hear about it."

"How?"

"That's the easy part. Aren't beautiful women supposed to be his weakness?" He glanced at Lauren and Melanie and flashed a somnolent smile. "You won't get any arguments from me about his taste and," he continued, transferring that smile to Sophie, "we have a new model waiting in the wings to tempt him with. You got that bit dead right."

"Want do you want me to do?" she asked, leaning forward in her seat.

"Does Williams have a favourite watering hole at lunch times?" he asked.

"Unless he's changed his habits over the past three years, he used to frequent the gastro pub just round the corner from the office."

"Right, I'll check it out and see if he still does."

"He won't be there every day. Sometimes he entertains clients, and then he goes elsewhere. If it's just him and some of the guys from Whytelake's, he usually goes to the pub."

"I could find out his schedule," Melanie said. "I'm still friendly with his PA."

"Be careful," Nate said. "Don't make her suspicious."

"Oh, she won't suspect a thing. She often tells me what he's up to without my asking." Melanie shrugged. "She seems to think I'm still interested in the workings of the firm because that's what I want her to think."

"Smart girl!"

"How will knowing where he's lunching help us?" Lauren asked.

"If Sophie, a high-flying facilitator, just happens to walk into that gastro pub, I think it's safe to say that she'll attract his attention." Lauren and Melanie nodded in unison. "We'll pick a day when we know he's going to be there, and I'll use my contacts to ensure that a small piece appears in the *Inquirer's* financial pages, just rumour about a possible silver find in Colorado. It's known as the silver state, so that ought to fly. Sophie will be on the phone to the reporter who printed the innuendo, furious at him for leaking the information prematurely. She'll have the paper open in front of her and be talking loudly enough for Williams to overhear her."

"I get it," Melanie said, her eyes sparkling. "I create a website pertaining to you. Who will you be?"

"Oh, I don't know. How about Brad Frobisher of Frobisher Inc. We can create a whole family background and stick it on the website."

"I doubt that will be enough to fool him," Lauren said.

"No, but I'll arrange a whole heap of fake newspaper articles about the Frobisher family firm and their worked-out silver mine."

"Won't he know that they've been planted?"

"Not if he isn't computer literate, which he isn't," said Melanie with absolute confidence. "I can make it look as though they were posted months or even years back. What are the chances of him not taking that at face value?"

"Slim to non-existent," agreed Lauren, reluctantly impressed.

"Well, there you are then," Nate said.

"Okay, we've got Jeff to notice Sophie, and we've piqued his interest about your silver mine. How will that destroy his power base?"

"Why would an American businessman be in Europe when he's on the brink of a major breakthrough in his own country?"

"Because he's looking for investors," Melanie and Lauren said together.

"Yep." Nate stretched his long legs in front of him and winked at Lauren. The others noticed and sent her penetrating glances, loaded with questions. She tried to pretend indifference toward Nate and to ignore their curiosity but spoiled it all by blushing. "And Sophie will be railing at my journalist friend on the phone because his article had caused a potential investor to pull out at the eleventh hour."

"Ah, I see." Lauren nodded, only now starting to think that this harebrained scheme just might work. "But, hang on, we've already decided that he won't risk diverting company money and so—"

"And so he'll have to use the money that you and he stole," Melanie said, beaming at Nate. "It's brilliant!"

Nate's gaze was fastened steadily on Lauren's face. His unreadable expression made her feel uncomfortable. "What!" she snapped.

"He might do that, but if we're really clever, then I think he might risk speculating some of his client's dosh on the scheme. That's what he does, isn't it? He plays the futures game."

"Yes, but your fictitious company won't be publicly listed."

"Of course not, that would be illegal." Even Lauren joined in the laughter. "But if we're—that's to say Sophie and me—are convincing enough—"

"You plan to meet him?" Lauren asked.

"Sure, I'll be the main player."

"But won't that be risky? His wife knows who you are."

Nate shrugged. "You said yourself that she never comes up to town and doesn't get involved with his business dealings. By the time she gets to hear about it—if she does—it will all be over."

"She might not see you, but Jeff might recognize you. Your picture always accompanied your byline, don't forget." Lauren screwed up her nose. "Not that he'd ever admit to reading the *Inquirer,* but I'm betting that he does."

"No one ever admits to subscribing to our rag." Nate laughed. "Beats the hell out of me how it manages to sell so well."

"Glad to see you're taking this seriously," Lauren said, scowling.

"I appreciate your concern is all for me, and I love you for it—"

"Humph, don't kid yourself."

"Don't, worry, I'll change the way I look. He'll be too taken up with Sophie and the prospect of making easy money to recognize me."

"Yes, I suppose you're easily forgettable," Lauren agreed, offering him a saccharine-sweet smile. Quite why she felt so hostilely inclined toward him when he was making a far better stab at getting Williams than she'd ever have managed, she was unable to say.

"Anyway, we'll make it clear that I just need bridging funds for a couple of days. If we're convincing enough, then he'll be champing at the bit to get involved."

Lauren could see little wrong with his thinking and knew it was just the sort of scheme that Williams would want to get his grubby hands on.

"You'll need a whole heap of paperwork to back up your claims," Sophie said.

"Oh, don't worry about that. I'll produce enough geological reports, scientific surveys, rock samples, productivity estimates, and production timetables to baffle the keenest mind. He'll be convinced."

"And I'm convinced the sun's over the yardarm," Melanie said. "Red wine anyone?"

No one declined. Nate did the honours with the cork screw, and they soon each had a glass in their hand.

"Won't I need to have an office, or something?" Sophie asked. "After all, I'm supposed to be a high-flyer?"

"Let's not get into that. You're too exclusive to have your own website or any sort of entry on the local phone book. Your clients seek you out, not the other way round. In fact, why don't you work from home?"

"Not my real home?"

"God, no. We'll rent you a flat somewhere appropriate. *Canary Wharf* perhaps."

"That will cost a fortune."

"We're going to make a fortune if we pull this thing off. Doesn't do to skimp on the set-up costs."

"Okay," Lauren said. "Let's see if I've got this straight. Sophie and you are going to do all the face-to-face stuff with Williams."

"Well, you and Melanie can't for obvious reasons."

"Right, but Mel can do the websites and all the other online details, you'll be sorting all the background stuff with your newspaper contacts, Sophie can get herself settled in her new accommodation." She paused, hands spread in front of her. "What about me? What can I do?"

"Frustratingly for you, nothing."

"Nothing!" She sprang out of her seat. "Just a minute, I want to be—"

Nate stood, too, and placed his hands on her shoulders. "Think about it, Lauren. The police are watching you, just waiting for you to step out of line."

"I know that but still—"

"You have a job, and alarm bells will ring if you don't turn up."

"I could resign."

"And draw more attention to yourself?"

Annoyingly, she could see that he was right, but the prospect of ceding control to her friends and Nate still didn't sit comfortably with her.

"Couldn't I find another job here in Southampton?"

"Doing what?" he asked gently.

"I don't know." She waved her hands about in frustration. "Something. Anything."

"I could take on an assistant," Melanie suggested.

"I don't know enough about computers."

"And if anyone's watching you, which they probably are," Nate said, "it wouldn't take long to connect the two of you."

"Why should that matter to the police?"

"It wouldn't, but I should imagine it would be of great interest to Williams."

"You think he's watching me?" Lauren asked, unable to keep a note of panic out of her voice.

"I don't think we can afford to dismiss the possibility."

"Yes, but I could still—"

"The best way you can help this effort is to maintain your usual routine. I have a feeling that you didn't intend to go after Williams until things had settled down a bit. Am I right?" Reluctantly, Lauren nodded. "And you've only done so now because the police suspect you of murdering Fowler." Another grudging nod. "Well then, I rest my case."

"Even if we pull this off, we'll be no nearer to discovering who *did* murder Fowler," Lauren grumbled.

"Perhaps not, but the police will lose interest if they don't get any more leads." Nate pinioned her with a significant gaze. "And if you don't do anything out of the ordinary to engage their attention."

Lauren bit her lip so hard that she drew blood. "I suppose you're right."

"I am. Don't worry, we'll do this really soon, and then we'll all be rich and can retire to a life of luxury."

They spent a moment speculating upon the amount of money Williams's greed would compel him to part with and what they'd do with it when it was theirs. Returning it to its rightful owner, that was Whytelake's, and letting them know where it came from was Lauren's favourite suggestion.

"Minus our expenses, naturally," she said, grinning.

"How will we keep in touch?" Sophie asked. "Lauren doesn't have a phone."

"My mother brought me one, but the police still have it. Anyway, they know the number, so I wouldn't want to use that."

"It's a pay-as-you-go, so they wouldn't be able to trace the calls."

"Even so, it would feel contaminated."

"I'll get you another and give the girls your number," Nate said.

"Thanks," she said sullenly.

"Do you want to start giving me some background on Frobisher Inc. so I can get started on the website?" Melanie asked, flexing her fingers in anticipation.

"Sure thing." He stood again. "Excuse us, ladies," he said.

The two of them moved into the next room, where Melanie's computer was housed. Lauren could see them through the open door, heads together as they plotted their strategy. Sophie and Lauren were left alone. Both lost in thought, neither of them felt any immediate need to break the silence.

"You look well, Lauren," Sophie said eventually. "I'm glad you're not letting things get on top of you."

Lauren sighed. "The thought of seeing you and Mel kept me going."

"Maisie sends her love," Sophie said, smiling. "She begged to be allowed to come today, but I told her *no*."

"Yes, I'd have liked to see how she's doing." Lauren sighed. "But I'm not allowed to associate with anyone that I knew inside, including her, even though she was proved innocent."

"Never mind," Sophie said, her eyes twinkling. "You seem to have found someone else to take your mind off things."

Lauren quirked a brow. "Nate? Oh no, he only—"

"Honey," Sophie said, not attempting to hide her amusement. "Only you could bury yourself in the country and still find a hunk like that."

"He found me, and he's only helping because he wants the story."

Sophie chuckled. "Yes, sweetie, of course he does."

Lauren threw a cushion at her, refilled their glasses, and changed the subject. It was over an hour before Nate and Melanie rejoined them.

"Right," Nate said, reaching for his car keys. "I think we've got things going. Give me a number where I can reach you, Sophie. I'll look into the flat business tomorrow and let you know how I get on."

She tore a page from a notebook in her bag and jotted down a number. "Thanks," she said.

"No problem." He turned toward Lauren. "Lift home?"

"Thanks," she said grudgingly, aware that it would take forever to get the bus and that Kermit had been on his own all day.

* * * *

Friday afternoon and Jeff lingered at Sandra's, looking for reasons not to go home to Wimbledon. Gloria and he were due at a bash at the local golf club, but he couldn't raise much enthusiasm. It would be the usual crowd, the women done up in all their finery, flirting and competing to display the largest diamonds. The talk amongst the men would be of the latest deals closed and tomorrow's pairings for the handicap tournament.

Jeff usually excelled in such situations, but right now he couldn't concentrate on anything but Lauren. Who would have thought she'd have the strength to hold out against him for so long?

He couldn't find out what was happening in the police investigation into Fowlds's murder. He only knew that she'd been questioned and then released, which in itself ought to have been enough to send her running in his direction. He'd had Fowlds bumped off, partly to tidy up loose ends—he was still annoyed to have missed him the first time round—and partly to galvanise Lauren into contacting him. She'd be petrified to find herself under suspicion of murder for a second time, and who else could she turn to? Certainly not her stuffy parents.

Four days on and, much to his irritation, he hadn't heard a word from her.

Sandra, asleep beside him, woke with a start and reached for him. Her appeal had waned weeks ago, but thoughts of Lauren had made him rock hard and so he took her quickly and harshly. Pretending that she was Lauren ensured that he maintained an impressive erection for as long as it took, which wasn't that long, but Sandra didn't seem to mind.

"Glad you're feeling yourself again," she said, running a finger through the hairs on his chest. "Can you stay for dinner?"

Jeff slapped her hand away, got up, and headed for the shower without bothering to answer her. Even the local golf club held more appeal.

As he drove home, he made his mind up. If Mohammad wouldn't come to the mountain.

Tomorrow morning, instead of playing golf, he'd pay a little visit to a certain tumbledown shack in the New Forest and find out, once and for all, what the hell she thought she was playing at.

Chapter Eleven

Nate darted frequent sideways glances at Lauren as he drove her home, as though trying to second-guess her thoughts.

"Talk to me," he said.

"We've done nothing but talk all afternoon."

"You're pissed at me because I followed you, is that it?"

"How perceptive of you."

"I only want you to get your life back."

She snorted. "No, you only want a good story."

"I can understand why you're suspicious, especially after where you've been living."

"I doubt it."

"Journalists must have bugged the hell out of you and your family. Why should I be any different?"

"That's precisely what I've been asking myself."

"You have to trust me, Lauren. We're not all ambulance-chasers." She made a scoffing sound at the back of her throat. "Look, if you still feel bad about it, we'll call off the whole arrangement, and I'll leave you to do things your way."

"Stop being so bloody reasonable," she yelled. "I need you to argue with me."

He chuckled. "No, you don't. You just don't like feeling out of control."

Her lungs deflated with an extravagant whoosh. "I don't know what I feel," she said sullenly.

"Well, I've got a suggestion."

"This I must hear."

"When was the last time you had a night out?"

"Well now, let me see. That must have been three years, two months plus a week and a bit ago. Not that I'm counting."

"Then why don't we go and pick Kermit up and go for a pub meal somewhere?"

"I don't think so." She turned toward him, belatedly realising how sullen she must sound. Against all the odds, her instincts told her that he really was trying to help. But at what cost to her? "Thanks, Nate, I appreciate the offer, but I'm not good company right now."

"But you've still gotta eat and, if it makes you feel better, you're welcome to take cheap shots at me all the evening. I'm a big boy. I can take it."

Lauren knew all the about the dimensions of his body, especially the most intimate places, and had to agree that they were well proportioned.

"Okay," she said, making up her mind. "But…er—"

"Like I'd be insensitive enough to take you to The King's Arms," he said, recoiling. "I know a nice little watering hole on the…well, on the water. It's at Hamble."

"Sounds lovely."

They received an ecstatic welcome from Kermit. He'd occupied his time by overturning the kitchen bin and having a good rummage through the debris.

"The poor chap isn't used to being alone for so long," Lauren said, sweeping up the mess.

"Tell you what," Nate said. "I'll take him for a run whilst you hit the shower."

She wanted to make some cryptic comment about not needing a shower, but suddenly the desire to shed her old clothes and dress up for a night out was compelling. Nate must have known it because an annoyingly complacent smile graced his lips as he whistled to Kermit and disappeared out the front door.

"This is getting altogether too domestic," she muttered to herself as she stripped and hit the bathroom.

After her shower, Lauren automatically reached for a clean pair of jeans but changed her mind at the last minute. She hadn't worn a skirt since before she went inside. She rummaged through the clothes that her mother had brought to the shack and extracted a black pencil skirt that used to be a favourite. It would probably be a bit big on its own, but with a wide belt and a silky red blouse, it looked pretty good. She pulled on hold-up stockings and donned high heels, wondering if she would remember how to walk in them. Turned out it was a bit like riding a bike and one simply didn't forget.

"Might as well push the boat out," she mumbled, applying eyeliner and lip gloss.

She was in the lounge when Nate and Kermit returned. The former stopped in his tracks when he saw her and let out a low whistle.

"This is for my benefit, not yours," she said gruffly.

"I don't care what the reason for it is. I just appreciate the effort."

His smile was so infuriatingly smug that she wanted to hit him. Instead, she picked up her bag and treated him to a full-on glower.

"Ready?" she asked.

Kermit jumped into Nate's car as though he'd been travelling in it all his life. They made the drive to the pub he had in mind mostly in silence, classical music playing softly on the radio.

"Do you like the classics?" she asked at one point, galvanised into making small talk when the mellow concerto filling her ears caused her to relax. "Well, obviously you do," she said, not waiting for an answer. "I wouldn't have thought it."

"What, I'm a brash Yank, so I can't enjoy the finer things of life?"

She grinned across the distance that separated them, relaxed a little more.

"Something like that," she said.

"My mom always played classical music when I was a kid. I guess I just got kinda used to it."

They arrived at the pub and managed to grab one of the few remaining tables outside. Lauren could still feel the effects of the wine she'd had at Melanie's, but that didn't stop her from sharing another bottle with Nate. They ordered their food and sat back with their glasses as they waited for it to arrive.

"Since meeting you, I seem to be turning into an alcoholic," she said, taking a healthy swig.

"Nah, but you *are* in danger of losing that spiky attitude."

"Miracles take a little longer."

Their food arrived, and it tasted as good as it looked. Lauren cleared her plate, much to Kermit's disgust.

"Thanks," she said, pushing it away from her with a satisfied sigh.

"You're welcome. Glad you enjoyed it."

"Well, you can see that I did, so it's pointless denying it. It was a good idea of yours, Nate."

"I do have them occasionally."

"Like your way of getting at Jeff." She frowned. "Did you really think that up on the spur of the moment once you met my friends?"

"Pretty much, yeah."

"I hate to say it, but I'm impressed."

"I'm a journalist," he said, briefly touching her fingers. "It comes with the territory. You don't get far in my line of work unless you can think on your feet."

"Do you really reckon it will work?"

"Unless I read him all wrong, the combination of a beautiful woman and the prospect of easy cash will be impossible for him to resist. It all comes down to Sophie and me being convincing enough."

"I'm sure you will be."

"You don't look too delighted about it."

"No, because I want to be there to see it." She held up her hands when he made to interrupt her. "I know that's not possible, but I wouldn't be human if I didn't hanker after a front-row seat."

"You'll be able to read about the fallout in the papers."

"Only if he doesn't use his own money."

Nate looked at her so intently that she averted her gaze. "What?" she asked.

"Do you think he has the money to use?"

She bent down, pretending to pull imaginary specks from Kermit's coat, avoiding giving him a direct answer.

"He'll use company money," Nate said. "I'd stake my reputation on that."

"What made you follow me today?" she asked, twisting the stem of her glass between her fingers.

He shrugged. "Just a hunch. I reckoned you were planning your revenge against Williams but waiting for the dust following your release to settle first. When you were pulled in for questioning, it changed everything. I figured you had to try and get something on Williams before the police got something on you. Not," he added quickly, "that I believe there's anything for them to find. But still, if you were going to make a move, it had to be when you weren't in your usual routine."

"And you found out I was going to see my Probation Officer today."

"I did indeed." He smiled across at her. "Did he ask about your being questioned?"

"Didn't seem to know, and I certainly wasn't volunteering the information."

They finished their wine, and Nate settled the bill.

"Come on, I guess you have to be up early for work tomorrow, so I'd better get you back."

"Thanks," she said, sliding into the passenger seat of his car. "I didn't realize how much I needed to do something normal."

"My pleasure, ma'am."

They arrived back at the shack a short time later. Lauren was a bundle of nerves, wondering what he would expect when he got there. She was almost disappointed when he walked her to the door, pecked her on the cheek, and wished her good night.

She caught his gaze, and something in her expression must have alerted him to her thoughts. With a feral groan, he pulled her into his arms.

"I'm trying like hell to be a gentleman," he said. "You don't make it easy."

"What did I do?"

"You need to control your expressions," he said softly. "Right now I know precisely what you're thinking."

"Then I don't envy you."

He chuckled. "I'm only into reading positive vibes."

"Really, and what do they have to say then?"

"That you really, really want me to come in for a nightcap."

"Wrong," she said, her lips almost brushing his as she spoke in little above a whisper. "My wages from the café don't run to stocking alcohol."

"That's okay. We'll just have to think of something else to do instead," he said, bending his head to kiss her.

Nate stayed the night. She even let him drive her to work the following morning, making him drop her short of the café.

"Cindy will never speak to me again if she sees us together," she said, feeling happier than she had for years. And completely confused by what was happening to her.

"I'm gonna go up to town to sort Sophie's apartment," he said. "I'll buy your mobile whilst I'm up there and bring it down to you later. Is that all right?"

As far as Lauren was concerned, it was more than all right, but she forced herself to make a neutral response, scared of commitment.

* * * *

When Jeff woke up on Saturday, he'd decided against approaching Lauren. It would be madness, especially now she was under suspicion of murder. Damn it to hell and back, waiting to hear from her was playing havoc with his nerves. He changed his mind yet again, ignored the warning bells clanging inside his head, rang his golf partner, and made an excuse. There was absolutely no way he could chase a stupid ball round for hours, making small talk with other high flyers, when so much rode on Lauren coming through. Sensible or not, he'd go and see her and talk her round. He hardened at the prospect. Ever since he'd learned she was out, he hadn't been able to think about anything much except getting her between the sheets again. Once he did, he knew all the right buttons to push, and she'd soon be back under his control.

He hummed as he drove toward the New Forest, anticipating the moment. She worked until lunchtime, so he'd been told, and then caught the bus back to her cottage. Jeff headed for Brockenhurst and bought himself a pub lunch that he didn't eat, biding his time. When he estimated that it was safe, he drove to the lane where her cottage was, parked a short distance away, and completed his journey on foot. He was genuinely distressed by the downturn in her circumstances. Perhaps he had a conscience after all? The place where she lived looked as though it was held up by nothing more than fresh air and willpower. Poor Lauren, how she must be suffering!

Convinced now that she'd be delighted to see him, Jeff decided that she hadn't made contact, not because she didn't want to see him, but because she was being cautious. She wouldn't take any risks that would send her back to prison for breaking the terms of her parole.

Jeff approached the door to her cottage and listened. No sounds came from within, but there was smoke belching out the chimney, so he guessed she must be home. He knocked and was almost deafened by a volley of shrill barks. He swore. He'd forgotten that she had a dog.

The door was wrenched open, and for a protracted moment, they merely stared at one another. Jeff wouldn't have known her had his investigator not sent him photographs of her. She'd lost a ton of weight, cut her hair short, and she now dressed in clothes she wouldn't have once worn to do the housework in. She held the dog under her arm. It still squirmed and snarled at him, but at least if she held the little bastard, it couldn't do him any damage.

"You!" she said contemptuously, what little colour she possessed draining from her face.

"Lauren," he said, turning on the smile that always worked with women—especially her. "I've been going out of my mind waiting to hear from you."

"How did you find me?"

"It wasn't easy, but when I didn't hear from you, I got worried and tracked you down." He smiled for a second time and reached out a tentative hand. She backed away as though he was offering her poison. "Why didn't you get in touch?"

She curled her upper lip disdainfully and didn't answer the question. "What do you want?" she asked instead.

"Can I come in?"

"No!" She made to close the door. "Just leave me alone."

"No can do, darling. We need to talk." He pushed hard against the door, sending her staggering backward into a miniscule front room. "Look, I can see that you're still angry but—"

"Angry?" She made a scoffing sound that was most un-Lauren-like. "You have no idea!"

He wanted to touch her, but she still held the dog, and he didn't trust the horrible mutt not to take a lump out of his arm.

"Can't you put the dog somewhere else whilst we talk?"

"Why would I want to talk to you?" she asked, appearing to regain a modicum of composure and going on the offensive.

“Darling, I know you feel let down, but really, there was no point in—”

“Let down.” She waved the hand that wasn’t holding the dog. “Don’t give it another thought.” She abruptly changed tack. “Just get out. I have nothing to say to you.”

“But there’s so much that we need to discuss.”

“Which would explain why you didn’t come near me for the three years that I was inside.” She glared at him. “Not so much as a letter or even a message through a third party.”

Jeff suppressed a smile. He’d always been able to read her so easily. Her feelings toward him hadn’t changed. She was just upset by his silence, but he’d soon sort that.

“I couldn’t risk it. What was the point in us both going down?” He smiled again, his jaw aching from the effort. “God, but I missed you so much.” He reached out a hand and touched her face. She slapped it away. “Don’t be like that, Lauren. You know there’s never been anyone for me but you. Nothing’s changed in that respect. I’ve been going out of my mind, waiting to see you again.”

“Get out!” She threw an empty mug at him. Her aim was spot on, and he only just ducked before it hit him. “Get out and leave me alone.”

“You don’t mean that.” He spread his hands. “Lauren, think about all we once were to each other.”

“I’m doing my best to forget.”

“Come on,” he said, reaching forward with both hands this time. “You know I couldn’t come near you. It would have been the end of all our plans, but that doesn’t mean that I stopped thinking about you for one second.”

Her eyes sparkled with such bitter hatred that Jeff realized he’d grossly underestimated the extent of her disillusionment. She wasn’t the same trusting little accomplice who’d hung on his every word, and he’d have his work cut out to talk her round. It would next to impossible unless she put the mutt down. It kept up its rumbling growls, its teeth snapping toward his hand when he reached for Lauren, preventing him from drawing her against him.

"Oh, excuse me," she said sarcastically. "I hadn't realized that you'd kept all the money safe so we could sail off into the sunset as planned. Just give me a moment, and I'll pack my bags."

"Me? The money?" He stared at her. "What do you mean?"

"You might have forgotten about all that money I diverted on your instructions, but I certainly haven't. That's obviously why you're here. You feel an overwhelming desire to make it up to me by taking me away from these salubrious surroundings."

Jeff scratched his head, his mind going into overdrive. What the hell game did she think she was playing now?

"I don't know what you mean, darling," he said, suppressing his irritation with difficulty. "I don't have the money. I assumed you moved it before the police closed in, which I thought showed considerable resourcefulness."

"Me!" She looked as astounded as he felt. "How could I possibly have it?"

Jeff dropped into the nearest chair. It had wonky springs that attacked his backside, but he was so stunned that he barely noticed.

"You must have."

"You're the second person to accuse me of having it. The first was recently murdered, in case you're wondering, but don't worry, I'm sure the same fate won't befall you."

"Lauren, get rid of that bloody mutt," he said, no longer able to control his temper when he reached for her, and Kermit bit the back of his hand. He rummaged in his pocket until he found a handkerchief and tied it round the wound, not even feeling it. "We can't talk like this."

"There's nothing to talk about." She shrugged, still clinging to her ratty dog. "Do you really think I'd be living here if I had three million quid tucked away?"

"Well, you'd be silly not to. The police are still looking for the money, and they think you have it." He paused, fixing her with a gimlet gaze. "They *think*, but I *know.* You see, I don't have it, so you're the only other person who possibly could."

She looked straight at him and blinked several times. "But I don't understand…I was so sure."

"Lauren, darling, please." He stood again and paced the small room. "You've had you bit of fun. Now can we please kiss and make up, and I'll show you just how sorry I am for what happened to you."

"I haven't got the money," she said, shaking her head, ignoring his olive branch. "You swear that you haven't, and I believe you, Why else would you be here?"

"Well, because of you and me—"

"Don't treat me like an idiot," she said venomously. "I know you only used me. If you had the money, I'd never have seen you again."

"Lauren, that's just not true."

"I assume you didn't confide in anyone else."

He shot her a look. "Of course not."

"Nor did I. Which means…hum, I wonder."

"You wonder what, darling?"

"Well, that morning, before the police came to accuse me of murder, I'd just accessed the account when Sandra came in."

"Sandra?" He tried to sound casual, as though he didn't have a clue who she was talking about. She couldn't possibly know that he'd been screwing her for a good six weeks before Lauren's world collapsed.

"Yes, I'm sure you remember her," Lauren responded, her eyes levelled squarely on his face. "She's the attractive woman from accounting that you'd had a lot of meetings with. Well, I assume that's what you were having because she seemed to find reasons to call round every other day when previously we'd not seen anyone from that department."

"But she wouldn't have had access to the account," Jeff said, almost to himself.

"Well, that's the thing. The police came whilst she was there, and I was so shocked that I don't remember actually logging out of it."

"Oh, Christ!" Jeff ran his wounded hand through his hair, leaving a trail of blood down the side of his face without knowing it. "Do you really think—"

"Well," she said, shrugging. "I don't have the money, you say you don't, and I can't think of anyone else that would even know about it."

"Even if Sandra saw the details on your screen, she wouldn't have known what they were."

Jeff's words were designed to convince himself as much as her. He tried to remember what promises he'd made Sandra to get her to drop her knickers. She'd always been jealous of Lauren and had taken every opportunity to belittle her. Jeff enjoyed having two women vying for his attention, but still, he really didn't think Sandra would have…but would she? Jeff felt physically sick, convinced that Lauren couldn't possibly have got it right. Almost sure that she had. Sandra showed no signs of having come into a fortune, but then she'd be stupid to do anything to draw attention to herself.

"It was bedlam when the police came," Lauren said in a distant voice. "I hadn't thought about it before because I was convinced you'd cleared the account, but now you've got me wondering."

"I need to talk to her," Jeff said, getting up and almost running to the door.

"Oh," Lauren said behind him. "I thought you wanted to get reacquainted."

Jeff didn't even bother to say good-bye.

"Don't forget to get a tetanus jab," she called after him. "Kermit hasn't had his shots."

Chapter Twelve

As soon as Lauren heard his car drive away, reaction set in. She fell onto the settee, clutching her face in her hands, tears streaming down her face. God, but she hated him! How could she have fallen for his slick line and reptilian charm? She cursed her stupidity for latching on to a substitute father figure—one whom, unlike her actual parent, she stood some chance of impressing. In retrospect she suspected that he'd picked up on her need to be noticed, and exploited her vulnerability for his own purposes. Understanding that didn't make it any easier to cope with the consequences.

She could still smell his aftershave and threw open the window in a desperate attempt to rid the shack of all trace of his presence, wishing now that she'd let Kermit go. He would have bitten his calves just as severely as he'd done with Fowler. Never mind, he'd still taken a chunk out of his hand. Quite a big chuck if the flow of blood was any indicator. Hopefully it would need a stitch or two and permanently disfigure his hands. Jeff had smooth hands that he took a pride in. Laruen felt a twisted sort of satisfaction from knowing Kermit had marred their symmetric lines. Absently she stroked his wiry head, glad he'd been there to defend her. Williams would have grabbed her otherwise, and the thought of him touching her ever again—a thought that had once reduced to her to a quivering mass of desire—now made her skin crawl.

She didn't know how long she sat there, lost in her own version of hell. Darkness fell, and the only illumination in the room came from the dwindling fire. The wind rattled against the open window, sending a chill breeze through the room, but still she didn't move.

Footsteps outside made her start violently. Jeff must have returned. Her heart hammered against her ribcage, and her breath came in short, painful gasps as she looked frantically for a weapon, grabbing the poker and getting ready to crack it across his skull. He obviously hadn't believed what she'd told him and was going to do something horrible to her under the cover of darkness to make her talk. She'd made it easy for him by leaving the windows flung wide. Oh God, where could she hide? Would this torment never end?

Only when the door opened and Kermit went crazy with delight did she remember that Nate had said he'd come back.

"Hey," he said frowning. "What are you doing sitting here in the dark?"

"I was sleeping."

"With the windows wide open? It's freezing in here." He closed the window, sat beside her, and took her hand. "What's really wrong?"

"I…I had a visitor." She gulped back her anguish. "Williams came to see me."

To her horror, she burst into tears. Nate held her, stroking her back, soothing her until the worst of the flood abated.

"Did he hurt you?" he asked, his tone glacial.

She blew her nose on the handkerchief he handed to her. "No, not physically, but it was a shock to see him here. I wasn't prepared to face him and didn't know what to say."

Nate scowled so ferociously that the vertical lines above his nose almost met. "But he didn't touch you, did he?"

"He tried to, but Kermit bit his hand."

"Good!" He got up and banked up the fire. In his usual efficient manner, he soon had flames leaping up the chimney. "I hope the bastard gets rabies."

"We couldn't get that lucky."

Nate cupped her chin and smiled at her. "What did he want?"

"Well, that's the funny thing. He seems to think that I've got the money and wanted to know where it is."

Nate's eyebrows shot skyward. "Why would he think that?"

She shook her head. "I just don't know."

"Did anyone else have access to the account?"

"Only if they knew the passwords."

Nate stood up, rubbing his chin, clearly deep in thought. "He knew it would be a risk coming to see you," he said slowly. "Why would he do it, unless he really doesn't have the money?"

"Well, it was cleared out on the day the police came to question me, so I could have done it." She frowned at him. "But why would I have, unless I killed Drake and was expecting a visit?"

"And I know you didn't kill him."

"Thanks, but you're in the minority."

He smiled at her in such an intimate manner that it sent her mind on a sensual detour, reminding her of their activities the night before. She wondered how that was possible, given the seriousness of her situation, but Nate Black just had that effect on her. Jeff Williams once did, too. God forbid that she'd fallen for another no-good scumbag. One glance at Nate and she knew that wasn't true. There was an innate sense of integrity about him that somehow reassured. In spite of his tawdry profession, this guy had standards, and she was lucky to have him in her corner.

Hold that thought, Lauren. You're strong, you've spent three years plotting your revenge. You'll achieve it, too, even if you don't have the front-row seat you were hoping for. Stop being so feeble and get a grip.

"If it's any consolation," Nate said, "Peter Reed doesn't think you killed anyone either. If he did, then he'd be moving heaven and earth to prove it, and I happen to know he's not doing that."

"So that begs the question, why would I have moved the money when I knew nothing about the murder and had no reason to be worried about it?"

"You wouldn't have. Someone else obviously did, if Williams really doesn't have it." His gaze locked on her face. "Any ideas?"

"No," she said, looking away first. "But if he doesn't have the money, will our scam still work?"

"Oh yes. He'll 'borrow' company funds."

She shook her head. "I wish I shared your belief."

"Trust me, I'll have him salivating, unable to resist a no-lose situation, just you wait and see."

"Well, if that happens, then revenge will be sweet indeed. Instead of just blowing his own ill-gotten gains, he'll put the company in debt, get booted out, and lose everything that matters to him."

"Which is precisely our intention." He flashed that damned smile again. "Come on, Lauren, we can do this."

"How did he find me?" she asked.

"Same way I did, I would imagine. He probably had someone looking for you the moment he knew you were out. Were you followed when you left prison?"

Lauren shrugged. "I don't think so. I wasn't paying much attention at first, other than hoping that no reporters were about. But if anyone had trailed us into this part of the forest, they would have stood out and I'd have noticed."

"Well, they wouldn't need to know precisely where you were. As long as they knew you'd settled in this area, they'd know which probation office you'd attend, and then it would just be a waiting game."

Lauren bit her lip. "Surprised someone didn't sell tickets," she said sarcastically.

"Well, I reckon that's how Fowler found you, for what it's worth. Williams's guy told him where you were, and he told Fowler."

"Which gets us precisely nowhere because we can't prove it."

"We don't need to. We have other plans, remember."

"Yes." She stared at her hands, folded in her lap. "I remember."

"What's wrong?" he asked, crouching beside her. "Having a change of heart?"

"Yes…no—oh, I don't know." She stood, too, and tried to pace, but there wasn't room for them both to move about the miniscule room. "I just wish I could be involved, that's all."

"You are."

"No I'm not. I'm stuck in that bloody café six days a week whilst you and Sophie have all the fun."

"She needs to do this," he said quietly. "You saved her sister, and she feels she owes you."

Lauren flapped her hands. "I know that. I'm just a bit shaken up after Williams's visit."

"Have you eaten anything today?"

Lauren couldn't remember and didn't much care. "Why are you always trying to feed me?"

"Perhaps because you need looking after." He took her jacket from the peg on the back of the door. "Come on, we'll walk into the village and get something to eat in the pub."

Nate whistled to Kermit, who wagged enthusiastically, and Lauren didn't have the strength to argue.

"Okay," she said. "But I can't be late. I have to work tomorrow. No Sundays off for me."

"Me, too," he said. "I'm spending the day working with Melanie on Brad Frobisher's online presence."

"How far have you got?" she asked as they trudged along the lane.

"Well, I've drafted a couple of newspaper reports that Mel will put up. There's also a believable family background thingy on yours truly. I'm a recluse who doesn't court publicity," he said, grinning.

Lauren burst out laughing. "Hope you're a good actor because a less likely recluse I've yet to find."

"You have a lovely laugh," he said softly. "You ought to use it more often."

"You've said that before, and I've told you that I haven't had much reason to over the past few years."

"Well, I aim to do something about that." He tightened his hold on her hand. "You can count on it."

"What else have you done?" she asked, uncomfortable by the sincerity in his tone, unsure what precisely he wanted from her when this was all over.

"I've contacted a…well, a contact back home who's helping me to fake some impressive-looking geological surveys."

She furled her brow. "How do you know what's needed?"

"Easy, I looked it up online, which is precisely what Williams will do."

"But if you want him to invest so much, won't he require independent confirmation of your reports? He isn't as daft as you seem to think. He's bound to want his own expert to do something."

"You worry too much. The reports are drawn up by someone who really does work in the profession."

"What does he owe you that's makes him willing to commit fraud?"

Nate chuckled. "Trust me, honey, you don't wanna know."

"No, you're probably right about that."

When they reached the pub—not The King's Arms of course—Nate forced a large vodka and tonic on her.

"Cheers!" He touched his beer bottle to her glass. "Now what do you want to eat?"

She didn't really want anything but ordered a salad anyway and pushed it round the plate when it arrived.

"Talk to me, Lauren," Nate said at one point. "You're worrying me. What's wrong, honey?"

"I guess I'm still unsettled by Williams's visit."

"Want me to stay with you tonight?"

"No, he won't come back."

"Well, if he does—" Nate delved into his pocket and produced a mobile phone. "I meant to give you this earlier. I've programmed in my number and Melanie's and Sophie's. It's fully charged. The charger's in my car, and I'll let you have it when we get back."

"Thanks." She put it in her pocket, already feeling more confident now that she had a means of communication. "Not sure if I'll get a signal at the shack though."

"You will. I checked."

"That's good."

"If you take it to work, make sure no one sees it."

She lifted one brow. "Why?"

"Just in case someone's watching you."

"No one in the café takes a blind bit of notice of me." She paused. "Except you."

He chuckled. "If they're good, then you won't know they're there."

"Well, even if I am being watched, why should it matter that I have a phone?"

"Because it's a change in your routine, and we're trying to make them believe that you're not up to anything."

"Hum, I think you're being over cautious, but I take the point."

"If Williams comes anywhere near you again, dial 999. If nothing else, it'll show Peter and his colleagues that he does have more than a professional interest in you."

"No, he'd pass it off as avuncular interest," said Lauren with a cynical little laugh.

"He might well try."

"Wish I'd thought to record his visit today." She shrugged. "Not that I had anything to record it on, but it would have proved his culpability and your elaborate scheme wouldn't be necessary."

"Hey, are you out to spoil my fun?"

"I knew it! You're enjoying this."

"If you're suggesting that I look forward to bringing that smarmy bastard down several pegs, then you're spot on."

"Yes, but I still don't understand why you feel the need." She pushed her plate away and spun a spare drip mat round in circles. "It's not your fight."

"Well, it looks as though it is now." He leaned back in his chair, the expression in his eyes soft and compelling. "Tuesday your day off?"

"Yes."

"Well, I reckon a trip to Southampton would be in order to see what progress we've made."

The prospect cheered her. "Okay, but I'd better take the bus. If I am being watched, then your hanging about might set alarm bells ringing."

"Good point. Come on," he said, standing up. "You obviously don't want to eat, and like you said, you have to be up early."

They strolled back through the forest hand in hand. The earlier breeze had settled down and barely rustled the leaves on the trees. A full moon lit their path, and they took their time making their way back to the shack, as though neither of them wanted the evening to end. Lauren couldn't have said what she wanted. She needed to be alone, to think and to plan, but the notion of Nate leaving her to her own devices filled her with loneliness. Since meeting him, she—one of the most decisive people she knew—had become a morass of uncertainty. As though reading her thoughts, he suddenly stopped, pulled her into his arms, and kissed her with a passion that stole what little breath remained in her lungs clean away.

"Are you sure I can't keep you company?" he asked, breathing hard.

"I'm not sure about anything anymore, Nate," she said, pulling out of his arms. "But I have got to stop relying on you so heavily."

"You don't hear me complaining."

She sighed. "I don't know what you want from me, but I'm not in a position to offer anything right now, don't you see that?"

"You're not as strong as you think you are."

"Which shows how little you know me. I survived three years in the tough regime of a women's prison, so I think I can take care of myself."

"Let me in, Lauren," he said passionately, grasping her forearms. "Not all men are out to hurt you."

"Aren't they?"

"This one sure ain't."

She wrenched her arms out of his grasp, pacing in some agitation. "I've lost the ability to trust," she said softly.

"That's understandable, and it's one of the reasons why I worry about you."

"Well, don't. I'm fine on my own. If you want to help me, then get together with Mel and get this scheme of yours off the ground. Something tells me that I haven't got long before the plod pay me another visit."

* * * *

Jeff drove home, cussing and swearing fit to bust a gut. His hand hurt like hell, and he'd have to get it sorted before he went home or Gloria would ask awkward questions he could do without. They both knew he wasn't the devoted, monogamous husband he made himself out to be. The arrangement suited them both, just so long as he was discreet and did nothing to affect their social standing. The one golden rule she rigidly policed was that he didn't get tangled up with any of the women from work. She had never quite believed that he wasn't involved with Lauren and had been on his case ever since.

He stopped at a row of shops in Wimbledon High Street to buy Band-Aids and antiseptic cream. Then he visited the gents in a nearby pub, unwound the blood-soaked handkerchief, and winced. The cut still oozed blood and hurt like hell. He should probably go to the hospital and get a tetanus shot but couldn't be arsed. He smeared cream clumsily on the cut, blotted it with toilet paper and stuck a couple of Band-Aids over it, hoping they were tight enough to seal the wound. That bastard little rat of a dog had one hell of a bite, sinking his teeth in and refusing to let go. If Jeff ever saw it again, it would be dead meat.

He walked into the bar and ordered a large whisky that he needed badly. Taking it to a quiet corner table, he thought about all Lauren had implied. It was hard to concentrate because his hand throbbed so much that it was giving him a headache. He would have laid out good money on…well, on her having the money, but she'd just put severe doubts in his mind. She wasn't stupid and had had plenty of time to lay her plans. In prison she could have forged contacts who'd supply her with false travel documents—at a price—and she would have been long gone. If she really had the dosh, she wouldn't have hung around this long after her release unless she still wanted to share it with him. That was the only conclusion he'd been able to come up with when she didn't flee. Funny, but even after everything she'd endured, he'd been confident of her devotion and hadn't seriously believed that she'd renege on their deal.

It had been a hell of a shock to discover the money gone on the day following the murder. At the time he'd simply assumed that Lauren had panicked when she saw the police stomping in her direction. She must have thought they knew about the stolen money and had the foresight to shift it before they got to her. After all, it only took the flick of a couple of buttons. Lauren had no reason to move it before that because she actually knew nothing about the murder. He swore aloud, drawing curious glances from nearby drinkers. Could Sandra really be the one who was responsible?

Jeff ordered a second drink and retreated to his table again, worrying away at the problem. She had often hinted that she knew Jeff was up to something underhand. She worked in accounts, knew her way round computers, knew where to look, and knew how to read a spread sheet. Even so, to have found out about the account and just happened to be in his outer office when Lauren was arrested—could it really have happened that way? He racked his brains, thinking back to that fateful day when he thought everything was going to plan, trying to remember if Sandra *had* been there.

He had a horrible feeling that she had.

If she had the money, she was biding her time, maintaining the relationship with him and waiting for him to ask her about it. He was willing to bet that she'd share it with him in a flash.

At a price.

One that he wasn't willing to pay.

Jeff sighed, drained his glass, and left the pub. Blood seeped from beneath the plasters on his hand, but he barely noticed. Instead, he wrestled with the problem of Sandra and what he would have to do to get his hands on *his* money.

Chapter Thirteen

Nate waited outside the shack long after the light in Lauren's bedroom went out, fretting about her. He didn't know why he felt the need. Like she'd so robustly pointed out, she was more than capable of taking care of herself. Or so she thought. But Nate had seen how badly shaken she'd been by Williams's visit. Even so, she was just a broad. A means through which to get a good story and right a few wrongs, like Sir-bloody-Galahad. He rolled his eyes, accepting that she'd well and truly got under his skin. Her vulnerability, the downturn in her situation—even if it was partly of her own making—and the total lack of parental concern would have tempted him to champion her cause even without the prospect of a story. Well, that and the fact that he enjoyed taking her to bed.

He wandered toward his car, frowning as he dwelt upon her restraint between the sheets. She couldn't completely disguise her enjoyment but was totally passive, afraid of emotional commitment. She wasn't levelling with him about Williams, either. His journalistic sixth-sense told him there was more and she didn't trust him enough to come clean.

He drove to his hotel, resisting the urge to ring her on her new phone and wish her good night. She had to be up early and wouldn't welcome the intrusion. Nate sighed with a combination of frustration and…well, frustration.

"A cold shower for you, sunny Jim," he told himself, heading in that direction.

Nate rose early and arrived at Melanie's as soon as he decently could. They made a good team, each an expert in their particular field, and by midafternoon they had a good base from which to launch their scam.

"Do you think we're doing the right thing?" he asked her during a coffee break.

She looked at him with surprise. "Of course! Don't you?"

"Yes, but Lauren seems to have doubts."

"She has trust issues," Melanie said, echoing his thoughts of the previous day. "Hardly surprising really. But don't let that deter you. Your idea for getting back at Williams is far better than anything we'd been able to come up with."

"What was Lauren like before she went inside?" Nate asked, helping himself to a biscuit.

"I didn't know her that well. She joined Whytelake's after me, and we didn't work in the same area. We were both high-flyers, dashing round in business suits with phones glued to our ears, ready to change the world." Melanie's chuckle was devoid of all humour. "We were also rivals for Williams's affections, of course, which hardly made us bosom buddies."

Nate elevated a brow. "She knew that?"

"No," Melanie said, grimacing. "But I did. I sensed I was losing him because I wouldn't be his patsy. I also knew he'd move on to his next victim. I watched him, and it didn't take me long to figure out who it would be."

"But you didn't warn her?"

She shrugged. "Right then I was in full corporate mode, out for number one. Then I got pushed out the side door and…well, you know the rest."

"Has Lauren changed much since she went inside?"

"What do you think?" Melanie's expression was reflective. "It would be enough to change anyone. I can't begin to imagine what it must have been like for her. But she survived, and that's the main thing. I'd only seen her once since she got out, before we all met here the other day that is. We had coffee together in Southampton after she'd seen her Probation Officer. I didn't recognize her at first when she walked into that café." She dropped one shoulder, almost like an inverted shrug. "Oh, I'm not just referring to the physical differences. It was more like she was dead inside, as though someone had turned out a light and drained her of all vitality. I was horrified, to tell the truth."

"But she was as keen as ever for revenge on Williams."

"Emphatically so. She said the thought of bringing him down was the only thing that had kept her going but that we needed to bide our time. She thought people would be watching her, to see if she had the missing millions, and that things needed to settle down before we made our move."

"Well, she's right about that, which is why she can't play an active role." Nate sighed. "It would help if she could, and then perhaps she'd trust me."

"You're a newspaper man," Melanie reminded him. "Not a profession known for its ethical approach, and one that hasn't done her any favours recently."

Nate grinned. "Yeah, you're right, I guess." He glanced at his watch. "Lauren will be home after her shift at the café. I'll give her a call and update her on our progress."

"Good idea."

Monday slipped by in a similar fashion, and Tuesday afternoon saw the arrival of a whey-faced Lauren. Sophie was there, too, and Melanie and Nate between them briefed the other two on their progress.

"Come and see all the stuff we've put up on the web," Melanie said, taking Lauren's hand. "This is Nate's, I mean Brad Frobisher's website showing his Colorado property and its history of silver mining."

Lauren examined it closely, clearly impressed. "How did you get all that together so quickly?" she asked.

Nate winked at her. "Where there's a will," he said.

"Well, I know it's fake, and yet I'm almost convinced."

"That's the idea."

"There's no mention of recent silver finds," she said, frowning.

"Of course not. It's hardly the sort of thing that would be advertised."

"I suppose not."

"We have other, more subtle things in place to drop hints about that," Sophie said. "A few archived press articles speculating about the possibility and stuff like that. If it's too obvious, he'll smell a rat."

"The best news is that we know Williams still uses that bistro pub at lunchtimes," Melanie said gleefully. "My contact at Whytelake's has confirmed it."

"He always was a creature of habit," Lauren said bitterly.

"And so, ladies…" Nate imitated a drum roll on the surface of the desk. "If it's okay with you, Sophie, we reckon we'll be good to go this Thursday."

"That soon?" Lauren asked.

"Sure, why not?"

"I'm game," Sophie said, giving Lauren a quick hug. "Do you want to see what I'm going to wear to nail the bastard?"

"I guess I do."

Sophie disappeared into Melanie's bedroom and emerged a short time later wearing a clinging business suit in sapphire blue. The skirt finished just above her knee, and the jacket was sculpted to her body, highlighting every valley and curve. The camisole beneath it just covered her cleavage, until she leaned forward, giggling as Nate struggled to hide his reaction. Her legs were encased in fine, almost-black stocking, and four-inch heels set off those endless legs to perfection. The outfit managed to look entirely respectable and yet totally sexy. Nate let out a low whistle.

"Wow!" he said. "That oughta do it."

"He won't stand a chance," Melanie said.

"He won't know what's hit him," Lauren agreed. "Sophie," she added, frowning, "are you absolutely, completely sure about this?"

"Stop worrying," Sophie said, kissing the top of Lauren's head. "Nate will be there to look out for me."

"That's what I'm worried about," Lauren responded, making them all laugh.

"Anyway, if it all goes pear-shaped, I'll simply bail. There's no danger."

"It seems too easy," Lauren said, biting her lower lip in a manner that made Nate want to sweep her into his arms and make that worried expression disappear.

"The best plans usually are."

"How do we know he'll actually be there on Thursday?" Sophie asked. "I'd hate to waste this lovely suit if he's not."

"Well," Melanie said, looking up from her computer screen, "my informant tells me that he has no lunch plans for that day, so it's a fair bet. We just have to take the chance. If I ask any more questions, she'll get suspicious."

"Game on!" said Lauren almost to herself.

* * * *

Four days on and Sandra hadn't responded to Jeff's phone calls or e-mails. What the hell did she think she was playing at? Now that he was finally giving her some attention, she'd blown *him* off, just like that ungrateful tart Lauren had done. His concentration was shot to pieces, not helped by that bloody dog bite. Gloria had asked him all sorts of questions about the injury, but he refused to be drawn, making out that he'd cut his hand on a piece of broken glass in the golf club bar. He knew she didn't believe him but wouldn't let her take a look. She'd know at once that it was a bite of some kind, and that would only lead to more intrusive questions. Fortunately she wasn't the caring type and lost interest when a programme she wanted to watch came on the telly.

His hand throbbed all night, preventing him from sleeping. He finished up at his private doctor in Harley Street on Monday morning. No hanging about in the local emergency room for him. His quack gave him a tetanus shot, put a few stitches in the cut, and bandaged it properly. The painkillers he prescribed were worse than useless, and he'd stopped taking them anyway because they didn't mix with alcohol. The only really painful aspect of the whole fiasco—apart from Lauren's scathing contempt—was the charlatan's bill. Jeff couldn't put it through his insurance. Questions would be asked that he didn't care to answer, so he footed it himself with bad grace. Right now his life was going to hell in a handcart, but he wasn't one to sit passively by and wait for matters to right themselves. He worried away at every little detail because he hated being out of control, wondering whether to launch a charm offensive with Sandra or pay Lauren another visit.

He was no nearer deciding when he went to lunch at the bistro pub on Thursday. Even though he didn't fancy socialising and wasn't hungry, it was important to keep up appearances and stay in the loop. More deals were struck and useful tips dropped casually over lunch than in any business setting. That's how the system worked, and Jeff was still a player to be reckoned with. He joined another couple of financial gurus, Mike and Alan, at their usual table and flirted with the pretty waitress who came to take their order, even though his heart wasn't in it.

"Did you see that Marshall's stock dropped four points?" grumbled Mike. "I had them set to go up."

"Bad luck," Jeff said insincerely.

"You made a killing on that print company last week," Alan reminded Mike. "Rough with the smooth and all that."

"Talking of smooth," said Mike. "What do we make of that?"

Three heads turned to watch a statuesque woman with pale coffee-coloured skin traverse the crowded bar as though she owned it. She walked with swaying hips and all the confidence of a model at the height of her career, looking to neither left nor right, even though she must have been aware that conversations had stalled and every male head in the place had turned to stare. She settled herself at the table next to Jeff's, completely ignoring their gawping faces. When the waitress approached her, she ordered a mineral water but declined a menu.

"I'm waiting for someone," she said. "We'll order when he arrives."

"Damn!" muttered Alan, turning his attention to the food that had just been placed in front of him.

Jeff toyed with his club sandwich and watched the woman out of the corner of his eye. For the first time since Lauren's release, his mind was taken up with something other than her and the missing millions. This was a truly beautiful woman—all the more so because she wasn't trying to make an impression. Her confidence disarmed him, and just for a moment he forgot that this was a game, most of the rules of which he'd invented himself. This woman couldn't possibly be immune to the stir she'd caused, and Jeff, just for the hell of it, decided he'd linger and give her a crack once his companions went back to work.

The woman rummaged in her bag and produced a ringing phone. She turned her back to Jeff's table and answered it curtly.

"I'm glad that at least you have the balls to answer my calls," she said, sounding furious.

"What name did she give?" asked Mike.

"Didn't hear," Jeff said, not taking his eyes off her.

They fell quiet again, all blatantly attempting to eavesdrop. It became unnecessary when the woman's voice rose. She turned to stare straight ahead and berated the unfortunate person on the other end of the phone.

"You journalists are all bloody vultures," she said savagely, thumping a newspaper Jeff only just noticed, opened to the business pages, on the table in front of her. He thought it was that rag, the *Inquirer*. He wouldn't admit to reading it himself, but like just about everyone else, he did. Surprisingly for such a low-end paper, its business reporters were usually ahead of the game and right on the money. The person on the other end of the phone must have said something to try and placate the woman, but it didn't work.

"You promised me that Mr. Frobisher's find wouldn't be disclosed until I gave you the word."

Jeff and his mates exchanged an intrigued glance.

"Of course it counts if it's in the financial pages. What the hell do you think this is all about?" She listened some more. "I don't care! You promised me! Mr. Frobisher is American, and he'll sue you to hell and back if you screw this up from him."

The profanity, slipping from such beautifully sculpted lips, turned Jeff on. She'd dropped her voice a little, and he leaned slightly toward her, anxious not to miss a word.

"To say nothing of what he'll do to me," she added. "I guarantee my clients confidentiality and have built my career on discretion."

Ah, so she was a publicist, or fixer of some sort. Jeff struggled to think if he'd come across her before. Somehow he doubted it. She wasn't the sort of woman he'd be likely to forget.

"No," she said. "Don't print a retraction, just let the story die. You'll be hearing from me."

She snapped her phone shut, mumbled something incomprehensible, and left it on the table in front of her.

"Well," said Alan, raising a brow, "entertaining as this is, I'm afraid I have to leave. I have a one-thirty meeting."

"Yes, me, too," said Mike. He cast a quick glance at the adjoining table. "Pity that."

"I'm waiting for Ed to join me," Jeff lied.

The other two left without questioning Jeff's non-existent appointment. They all eyed up women given half a chance, but neither of the departing executives played away from home, nor did they suspect Jeff of doing so. They all had too much to lose both personally and professionally if they got caught. As soon as they were out of the door, Jeff turned toward the woman.

"Having a bad day?" he asked.

She glanced at him and frowned. "Do I know you?"

"Not yet," he responded, flashing his sexiest smile.

She half turned away, ignoring him. The paper was still in front of her, and Jeff could see now that it was definitely the *Inquirer*. He made a mental note to check out what article had got her so steamed up.

"I couldn't help overhearing you say that you're a publicist," he said, undeterred by her cold shoulder.

She arched a brow. "Did I say that?"

"My name is Jeff Williams." He offered her hand, and she briefly made contact with his fingers but didn't tell him her own name. "Perhaps I could put some work your way."

"I'm not taking on any more clients right now."

She bent to take something from her bag, and her top fell forward, giving Jeff a front-row view of her full breasts, encased in a pretty lace bra. His prick sprang to attention, making him more determined than ever to find out who she was. This woman was classy, but even if that hadn't been the case, something told him this chance meeting could turn out to be mutually beneficial. His instincts were seldom wrong, and he learned a long time ago to go with them. If he charmed her into submission, she'd certainly be able to handle his personal frustration, but his business antennae were on full alert. If something in the financial pages had got her so steamed up—something that had leaked too early—there could well be profit in it for him.

Before he could open his mouth again, her phone chirped.

"Stella Grant," she said abruptly into it.

Great, so now Jeff knew her name.

"Oh, Mr. Frobisher." Her entire attitude thawed. "You're running late. That's perfectly all right. I'll wait. We need to talk." She paused to listen. "Yes, I've seen it. It's regrettable, but I'm sure we'll be able to contain it."

* * * *

Nate closed his phone. Sophie had used the code words, *we need to talk*, the pre-arranged signal that Williams was there and had taken the bait. He entered the pub ten minutes later, dressed in jeans with a white dress shirt open at the neck and the sleeves rolled back. He had his hair gelled back to make it look darker, and he wore horn-rimmed glasses with clear lenses, plus coloured contact lenses that itched like hell, just in case anyone was in the pub who might recognize him from the *Inquirer.*

He approached Sophie's table, noticing Williams almost salivating as he tried to engage her in conversation. She was doing a brilliant job of blanking him, but then a woman who looked like Sophie must have had plenty of experience in fending off unwanted attention. She saw Nate approaching and stood up.

"Mr. Frobisher," she said, smiling. "You're here."

"What the hell is this all about?" He slapped his own copy of the *Inquirer* in front of her, his raised voice drawing the attention of other patrons. "You guaranteed me complete anonymity, and yet my business is plastered all over this bloody rag." Nate made a mental note to thank his mate of the paper for planting the snippet. He owed him one.

"Please sit down, Mr. Frobisher," she said, looking suitably contrite.

"The hell I will!"

"People are listening. Best not to make matters worse."

"Difficult to see how they could be any worse," he said, making a big thing of showing his reluctance before sitting. "Explain," he said succinctly. "Beer," he added to the waitress hovering above him. "I don't give a damn what kind. Whatever you got." He waved the menu she was brandishing away. "Now talk," he said to Sophie when the waitress scurried off.

"That reporter on the *Inquirer* saw us together at Jenson's reception the other night," she said apologetically, her voice only just loud enough to carry to Williams's table. "He figured out who you were, must have done his own research, picked up on the rumours in The States, and printed that piece."

"I told you I don't like having my name in the papers."

"I'm sorry. He didn't call me for a comment or tell me he was going to print it. I only saw it when you did."

"What I don't understand," Nate said, letting out a long breath and pretending to calm down, "is how he could think I'm looking for an investor."

"Because Jenson is known as an entrepreneur, I guess," Sophie said, sipping at her water. "That reporter was hanging about outside like the lowlife he is, trying to get a heads-up on who was there." She spread her hands. "I'm sorry, I should have anticipated that."

"Not your fault, I suppose," Nate said ungraciously. "I got a call from Jenson this morning. He saw the paper and won't be investing. Says he doesn't like the tabloids calling the shots."

"Damn, I'm sorry."

"I should have stayed at home and looked for funding," he muttered. "I knew this was a mistake."

"Not necessarily. I'm sure I can find other people who might want to get involved."

"I'm particular who I do business with."

"I know that, Mr. Frobisher, but—"

"This is a bloody disaster," Nate said, about to run a hand through his hair but remembering about the gel at the last minute and making do with stroking his face.

"Perhaps the banks would consider—"

"I've already told you, I want to get out from under their grasping clutches."

"But you only need a two day extension," Sophie said, frowning. "I don't understand their attitude."

"Join the club. Come on." Nate drained his beer, threw enough cash on the table to cover their drinks, and stood up, reckoning that they'd done enough to pique Williams's curiosity. Anything more would be overkill. "This isn't the place to talk about this. We'll go back to yours and brainstorm."

They swept from the pub without a second glance at Williams. As soon as they were a safe distance away, Nate pulled out his phone and called Lauren. She answered on the first ring.

"How did it go?" she asked anxiously.

"Great, he's hooked."

"Thank goodness!" Nate smiled at the relief in her voice. "How did Sophie do?"

"She was great, just great! She missed her vocation."

"So what happens now?"

"Now," he said, sighing, "we wait. The next move has to come from him."

Chapter Fourteen

As soon as Frobisher and his lovely companion left the pub, Jeff settled his own bill and followed them out the door. He watched the American hail a cab, his mobile phone jammed against his ear. The cab stalled in traffic right next to him, but he strode away and gave no indication that he'd seen them inside it.

Back at the office he grabbed a copy of the *Inquirer* from reception and shut himself in his office with it. It took him a while to find the piece that had so upset Frobisher. It was just a couple of paragraphs stuck at the bottom of the page, speculating about the reasons for a recluse like Frobisher attending Jenson's reception, hinting about his requirement for an investor and referring to rumours about a the discovery of a new vein of silver in his family's worked-out mine. Jeff sat back, pondering what he'd read. He wouldn't have seen it, much less given it any credence, had it not been for that chance encounter in the pub.

Jeff put Frobisher's name into his search engine and was surprised by the amount of stuff that came up. From an old Colorado family, he was now the sole owner of a huge spread where he lived alone, not encouraging friendship. The silver mine that had founded the family's fortune was long since played out and was now a tourist attraction. He jumped from one hit to another, not learning much more about the family, or about Frobisher himself. There were a few old articles from American papers, speculating about alternative uses for worked-out mines that might boost the local economy but no mention about a new discovery of silver at Frobisher's place. Jeff wondered why the English journalist hadn't contacted his American counterparts to check out his theory. Laziness, he supposed. The *Inquirer* didn't employ the brightest sparks in the industry, and if they did, they soon moved on to better things.

Having learned all the web could tell him about Frobisher, Jeff put in Stella's name. He had that tingling feeling like he used to get when he fed Lauren information that paid off, and somehow *knew* he was on to something. There was much less to learn about Stella, but Jeff wasn't discouraged. The people with most to offer seldom shouted about it. She obviously didn't court clients because she had no website. Her name came up on a few professional sites, but there were no contact details. Immediately Jeff wanted to know more. He called his investigator, gave him Stella's name, and told him he wanted an address or phone number as soon as.

He sat back, still wondering what he'd stumbled upon, when his internal phone rang.

"Williams."

"You left a message," Sandra's cool voice responded.

"I left several," he said, forcing a conciliatory note into his tone.

"What can I do for you?" she asked stiffly.

This wasn't good. First Lauren shutting him out and now this slut. "Are you free for a drink this evening?" he asked, turning on the charm even though it almost choked him.

"Why?"

"Why? Well, we haven't seen each other for a while, and I thought—"

"You weren't exactly the life and soul the last time we got together."

"Sandra, look, I'm sorry, but I'm under a lot of pressure at the moment. You understand, I'm sure."

"Oh, I understand all right." Sensing that she was weakening, Jeff said nothing, waiting for her to fill the silence. "All right," she said, sighing. "When and where?"

They made the appropriate arrangements, and Jeff hung up, feeling mildly euphoric. She had the money, he just knew it, and somehow he'd persuade her to tell him where it was. And then, just possibly, he'd hit on a brilliant scheme to increase it.

* * * *

Lauren wiped her brow and then cleared the mess from the table in front of her. With the exception of Tuesday, when she'd gone to Southampton, she'd been working double shifts for almost a week, covering for Cindy's holiday. That way she could take several days off without it seeming peculiar. She knew it was madness, but she absolutely *had* to be there when Williams sniffed round Sophie and Nate. She hadn't told Nate because he would attempt to talk her out of it, and he'd probably be right to do so. It would be stupid for her to chance being seen, but she wouldn't let that stand in her way. She'd risk going back to jail before she gave up on her ultimate moment of revenge.

It was gone six in the evening when she got back to the shack. She wasn't altogether surprised to find Nate waiting on the doorstep. Her heart gave a little skip that she tried to ignore. Kermit was less circumspect and went delirious at the sight of him.

"Hi," he said when Kermit finally stopped jumping all over him. "Where have you been? I've been waiting awhile."

"Shouldn't you be in Southampton?" she asked, ignoring his question. "In case anything breaks."

"It won't. Williams will do his homework first and needs to find out where Sophie lives."

"You've left her alone?" She scowled at him. "Is that safe?"

"You worry too much. Have you never heard of telephones?"

Lauren stepped round him and opened the door to the shack.

"I suppose you want to come in."

"Hey," he said, stepping up behind her and making it feel as though her tiny front room had shrunk. "What's with all the animosity? I thought we were friends."

"I'm tired. I just did a double shift." He didn't need to know that it wasn't the first time.

"Well then, let your Uncle Nate make you a drink and rustle up some supper for us both." He grinned at her, and her heart did another wobble. She absolutely *did not* want to be attracted to him but couldn't seem to help it, especially when he looked at her like that. "Tell you what, why not have a nice long soak in the bath and get rid of the day. By the time you get out, I'll have the fire going and supper ready."

"You'd make someone a lovely wife," she said, too tired to argue with him.

He rolled his eyes. "Wouldn't I just."

It was almost an hour before she could pull herself out of the wonderfully hot water and push her limbs into clean clothes. True to his word, there was a roaring fire sending flames leaping up the chimney, and an appetising smell emanated from the kitchen. There was even a bottle of red wine on the table, open and breathing. She didn't bother to ask where the food and drink had come from, used by now to his habit of bringing stuff with him. He poured her a glass of wine.

"Sit!" he ordered, as though she were Kermit.

Smiling in spite of herself, she fell into one of the old wooden chairs at the kitchen table and watched him work. She liked watching him. There wasn't much about him that she didn't like, and that bothered her. Men weren't to be trusted. That was especially true when they looked like they'd stepped off the pages of a gent's magazine *and* worked for the tabloid press.

After they'd eaten and cleared away, they sat opposite one another in front of the fire, and he told her more details of the confrontation with Williams in the pub.

"And you really think he'll bite?" Lauren asked for the third time, still full of doubt.

"I really think he'll bite." He stretched his arms above his head and grinned. "Have a little faith, woman! The guy's a greedy bastard, we already know that, and we've presented him with an opportunity he won't be able to resist."

"Yes, he's greedy, but he's wily, too." She shook her head. "I just can't believe he'll fall for it. It seems so obvious."

"My guess is that he'll make contact with Sophie, if only to try and chat her up."

Lauren screwed up her face. "That I can believe."

"Once he's in Sophie's lair, it's up to her and me. We'll soon know. Something tells me if this is going to go down, it'll happen soon."

"Let's hope so. My nerves can't take much more of this."

They held one another's gaze for a protracted moment, and Lauren knew her words didn't just apply to Williams. The atmosphere crackled with sexual tension as she fought her increasing attraction toward this annoyingly proficient man who appeared determined to involve himself in her affairs. She enjoyed sex but hadn't missed it whilst she'd been inside. A lot of women indulged in single sex relationships whilst banged up, claiming it took the edge off and helped them to forget the horrors of incarceration. Lauren understood that but had never been tempted herself. Physical intimacy promoted an exchange of confidences, and Lauren wasn't ready to share her thoughts and aspirations with another woman. It would be akin to relinquishing control.

Common sense, her closest ally, deserted her as she regarded the handsome planes of Nate's face, cast into shadow by the flickering flames of the fire. Unbelievably she was on the verge of actually trusting him simply because she wanted him—needed him—so desperately. Desire flared like a physical ache. Temptation had never seemed more compelling as she slowly drowned in the depth of grey eyes that reflected her own feelings. The overwhelming need pooling in the pit of her stomach deprived her of the ability to think straight. His eyes remained focused on her face, and she didn't have the strength to look away. Would it really be such a bad thing to let him stay the night again, even if she had vowed it wouldn't happen? He'd done so much for her and asked for nothing in return. It wouldn't mean she'd placed her complete trust in him. Not really. People had flings all the time. She'd just got out of practise, that's all.

"Stop analysing everything to death, Lauren," she silently berated herself. "You need to get laid. Why make everything so complicated? Just go with your instincts and get it out of your system."

As though hearing her unspoken thoughts, he stood up and held out a hand, saying nothing because the situation required no words. She hesitated but then stood as well and took his fingers in hers. He lifted their joined hands to his lips and kissed the back of hers, his tongue lingering as it drew swirling patterns across the inside of her wrist. She gasped as fire lanced through her, swamping her reason. He pulled her toward him with one strong arm, the fingers of his other hand still entwined with hers.

"You're killing me," he whispered into the top of her head. "You know that, don't you?"

Any response was quite beyond Lauren, but then the situation didn't need words any more than she needed his reassurances. Something that felt so right couldn't possibly be wrong. The inexorable, pulsating desire she'd hadn't thought to feel for a man ever again was building inside her at a quite-alarming rate, and there was absolutely nothing she could do, short of ordering him from the shack immediately, to suppress it.

He would go if she asked him to, but Lauren didn't seriously consider sending him away. She buried her face in his shoulder so that he wouldn't see the conflicting emotions playing across her features and guess the nature of her thoughts. Reaching a decision, she tilted her chin until her lips were within range of his and covered them in a bold invitation that drew a strangled oath from Nate. Without missing a beat, he took control, crushing her mouth possessively as he deepened the kiss. There was a raw carnality in his actions as his mouth, warm, mobile, and demanding, played against hers. Lauren, her awareness of him raised to the point of insanity, fully participated in that searing kiss, feeling alive in ways she'd forgotten were possible. His tongue plundered her mouth, and she parted her lips to allow him full access to it, capitulating with a soft sigh.

He broke the kiss and smiled down at her, his eyes darkened by swirling passion as the full and impressive extent of his erection pressed against her thigh.

"Shall we take this upstairs?" he asked, watching her closely.

She merely nodded, still incapable of speech, and led the way. He followed her up the stairs, appearing to understand her disinclination to talk. Had it been otherwise, she might well have lost her nerve, but he seemed to understand that, too. This guy got what made her tick in a disconcertingly reassuring way. They reached her bedroom, which was in darkness. Somehow it was better that way, and she knew he wouldn't reach for the light switch. Instead, he reached for her, and she was more than ready to fall into his arms.

They tumbled in a clumsy embrace onto the bed and kissed again. A deep, incendiary kiss that sent a fine tremor through her body and overstimulated her senses. She emptied her mind of everything except the determined progress of his lips. They had left hers and were now paying attention to the erogenous zone beneath her left ear. The tremor became a shiver as her turbulent emotions struggled to keep pace with his actions. Her hands reached for the buttons to his shirt but were clumsy, and it was sometime before she managed to unfasten them and push the shirt from his shoulders. All the while his lips continued to work their magic. They were on her breasts now, sucking and nipping at her nipples through the fabric of her bra. She was mildly surprised to discover that her top had disappeared. She had no recollection of his removing it. Her hands explored the broad planes of his chest, her fingers tangling with the wiry hairs adorning it and tugging gently. He groaned when one finger gently circled his nipple.

"Lauren, baby, I—"

"Shush." She placed a finger against his lips. "No words. Just deeds."

She sensed his smile in the darkened room. "Yes, ma'am!"

His fingers reached for the waistband of her jeans and unfastened the snap. The zip sounded unnaturally loud as he jerked it downward. She lifted her hips so he could pull the denim down and apply those magical lips of his to her abdomen, nipping and lapping his way toward her panties in a manner that made her squirm restlessly against his tongue.

"Patience!" he said, his tone full of molten tenderness as he raised his head and dropped a light kiss on her lips. "I'm in charge here."

Lauren obediently stilled. Let him think he had the upper hand. He didn't, of course. He might temporarily be master of her body, but he couldn't see inside her head. No man would ever share her thoughts ever again. Dreamily she relaxed, her head thrashing from side to the side on the pillows as pleasure spangled, tumbling through her limbs in response to his gossamer-light touch. His mouth was again on her navel, moving slowly—far too slowly—toward her clitoris. She clawed at his back, both comforted and tormented by his vital strength, readiness coursing through her entire body as it quivered and shook in anticipation.

"Nate, I need this," she said breathlessly." I need you to make me feel whole again."

He dropped a kiss on the outside of her panties. "Just trust me."

"You wouldn't be here if I didn't."

"I know that, too."

He stood up so abruptly that, just for a wild moment, she thought he'd had a change of heart. Then she understood he'd only got up so he could rid himself of the rest of his clothes. She heard them hitting the floor. Then the mattress sagged as he rejoined her, his erection so solid that it was almost painful as it pressed against her stomach. She reached a hand between them and touched it. It jumped violently, and so did he.

"Hey, this is for you, baby." He spoke through gritted teeth. "Best not do that, or it'll all be over in a flash."

She wrapped her arms round his neck and lifted her hips toward his penis, rubbing her clit against it. It was enough to stimulate that rushing, soaring feeling that heralded the onset of a climax. Her breath hitched as she swung her hips from side to side, letting the feeling consume her. She sensed Nate watching her as the sensation in her midsection intensified. His teeth flashed in the darkness, and he thrust himself toward her. She cried out as her world exploded, and the tremors hit like a mini-tornado.

"I guess you did need it pretty bad," he said, kissing the end of her nose, his erection still pushing against her.

"I guess I did."

"Glad you didn't get involved with the lesbians inside," he murmured, as though sensing her earlier thoughts.

"No, I didn't do that. I wasn't even tempted."

"Wanna do it properly now?"

"And if I said no?" she asked flirtatiously.

"Then I might just have to kill you." He laughed and groaned simultaneously, reaching behind her to remove her bra.

Her breasts fell into his hands, and he bent his head to pay his respects, subliminal sexuality in his movements as his tongue expertly carved intimate pathways across her sensitised skin, making her shiver. First one hardened nipple and then the other fell victim to a tongue that rasped, licked, tantalised, and promised so much. It wasn't long before Lauren was again aroused to the point where she thought she'd go out of her mind. He appeared to know it and turned his attention to her panties, now soaked through with her own juices. She lifted her hips, and he removed them, throwing them carelessly on the floor. He used his fingers to separate her soft folds and delved inside. Lauren groaned. It felt sublime, but it wasn't enough. It wasn't what she truly wanted. She needed every inch of his penis buried deep inside her, exorcising the ghosts of her past, making her feel desirable and complete.

"You," she said breathlessly. "I need you."

"I know you do."

He leaned over, delved into the pocket of his discarded jeans, and produced a condom. He opened the packet with his teeth, rolled it down his length, and then rolled onto her.

"Just so you know," he said in a deep, gravelly voice, "I'm not usually a missionary position sort of guy, but seeing as how this is so urgent—"

"Is it urgent?" she asked innocently. "Personally speaking, I could last all night."

"Liar!"

He nudged his prick into her vagina and then immediately withdrew again.

"Hey!"

"I thought you could last all night," he said, a smile in his voice.

"Sure, but I didn't mean all night, only once."

She regretted the words as soon as they left her lips. He'd got her all steamed up and confused. It sounded as though she was asking for a repeat performance—or as many performances as he could manage, and she wondered what she could say to explain herself. Then the feel of his penis entering her again made her forget all about it. She lifted her hips and wrapped her legs round his waist.

"That's it, baby," he said, his voice husky. "Take it all."

He thrust hard into her, driving himself all the way home. Lauren helped by lifting her lower body still higher, glorying in the tight, snug feel as he pulsated inside her. How could the woman in prison ever have thought that what they did to each other came anywhere close to this?

"Are you all right?" He paused, and she could sense the concern in his voice.

"More than all right," she gasped. "Just don't stop."

He chuckled. "It's a bit late for that."

He picked up the pace again, and she moved with him, selfish longing flooding her mind as he brought her to a pinnacle of need that left her breathless, close to sensual meltdown. Sensations of dizzying shock ricocheted through her body as wave after wave of the most cataclysmic pleasure threatened. She was conscious of her fingers clawing at his back, of the ache inside her thighs as they clung to him in this unaccustomed position, of the explosive amalgamation that built as they moved in perfect harmony. Prurient noises slipped past her lips as the wild sensations ebbed and peaked, leading them to a precipice that they would negotiate together.

Lauren bit hard at her lower lip, drawing blood.

"Nate, I can't…I don't think I can—"

"Me neither."

With a final thrust and deep guttural moan, they came together. Nate's penis throbbed deep inside her for what felt like an eternity. A wave of pleasure hit Lauren broadside. She thought she'd been ready for it but knew now that she'd never experienced anything like it before. She screamed his name, begging him to plunge deeper. She wanted—absolutely had to have—every last inch of him sheathed tightly inside her. She'd settle for nothing less.

Lauren rolled on her back afterward, sweating, out of breath, already wondering if she should have lost control quite so comprehensively. In her own defence, she simply hadn't been able to help herself. She thought she was a girl of the world and understood sex in all its guises. Now she knew that wasn't true. She glanced at Nate, also flat out on his back, his half-erect penis still covered by the condom. He turned toward her, and even in the dim light of the room she could see lines of deep emotion etched on his face.

It had been special for him, too.

Chapter Fifteen

"I thought I made it plain the last time we met that if you're going to hit me, I don't want to know you anymore." Sandra's voice was shrill. "I'm not into that sort of thing."

Jeff attempted to look contrite, offended by the sharpness to her features that he'd always found unattractive. He could imagine her in later years wearing one of those expressions hinting at permanent disapproval. He suppressed a sigh. What was it with her? He'd only given her a gentle tap for saying it didn't matter when he couldn't perform. What the hell else did she expect when she called his manhood into question? And how come she'd suddenly adopted this "hard to get" act? They both knew she was devoted to him and would never let him out of her clutches. No, her fit of pique had nothing to do with that little slap. She was more upset because he'd called out Lauren's name instead of hers when he did finally climax.

"Sorry about that," he said in the low, persuasive drawl that always worked with the women. "I was going through a tough time."

"That's no reason to take it out on me."

"Sorry." He covered her hand with one of his own. It wasn't something he'd ever risk doing in public as a rule, but she didn't seem to appreciate the magnitude of the gesture. "I'll make it up to you, I promise."

She regarded him with suspicion but a little less aggression. The sanctimonious little madam was obviously going to make him grovel. Jeff quietly seethed. He hated women who thought they could manipulate him. They never could—especially not this one. Then his thoughts veered toward all that money *she'd* stolen from *him*, the lack of which had severely curtailed his plans, and knew he'd do whatever it took to get it back.

"Sandra, you're obviously upset, and I—"

"Huh, don't kid yourself." She flashed a spiteful half smile. "Perhaps it's time to call it a day."

"What!" She couldn't be serious. Panic flared. "You're hurt because you think I've treated you badly." He spread his hands, skewering her pinched features with an intense gaze. "That was never my intention. It was just that I was going through a bad patch. It won't happen again. Just give me another chance."

She appeared mollified. "Yes, well, you were unkind to me and that hurt more than anything. I thought we had something special going."

Jeff valiantly refrained from rolling his eyes. "We most definitely do. How can I make it up to you?" he asked seductively.

"I expect I'll think of a way," she said, finally smiling at him.

An hour later they were back at her flat, and Jeff forced himself to perform. She wasn't a bad screw as it happened. As soon as it was over, she headed for the shower. Jeff sprang from the bed when he heard the water running, went back to the lounge, and examined the locks on the front door. A bog standard Yale and a Mortis that wouldn't present any problems for his guy.

He didn't intend to ask her about the money. She'd been clever and bided her time, carrying on with her usual routine as though nothing had changed. She thought she was safe because no one suspected her, and that's the way he wanted it to remain, but there had to be some clues as to its whereabouts in this flat somewhere. There was one other bedroom that she used as a study. He prowled round it, taking a close interest in everything. A laptop sat in the centre of a neat desk. That was bound to lend some clues. He tried the drawers. The usual crap in the top two—nothing to interest him. The bottom one looked as though it held files but was locked. That's where his man would need to concentrate his efforts.

He got out of there as soon as he reasonably could, feeling fractionally better about life. A safe distance away, when he was sure she wouldn't be able to see him if she was watching from the window, he pulled out his phone and rang his investigator.

"I need you to get into this place on Monday morning," he said, giving him the address. "There's a Mortis and Yale but no alarm."

"Fair enough. I take it you don't want the owner to know I've been there."

"Correct."

"What am I looking for?"

"I need you to copy the hard drive on the laptop and examine the bottom desk drawer. Photograph anything to do with the woman's financial affairs but make sure you put everything back the way you found it."

"You've got it."

"Let me hear from you Monday night."

Jeff cut the connection, finally feeling in control again. Now all he had to do was work on the Frobisher guy. If that was kosher—and Jeff had that tingling feeling that told him he'd stumbled upon the opportunity of a lifetime—he'd be able to recover all his losses without the help of any conniving females. And if things really went his way, he'd be able to use the money Sandra stole from him to do it.

* * * *

Nate felt euphoric. Not just because the sex had been phenomenal but because Lauren had finally opened up to him. For the duration of their tryst she had been completely and absolutely his. She held nothing back, and he'd bet his bank balance that she enjoyed it every bit as much as he did. But his victory was short-lived. As soon as she regained her breath, she left the bed without a word and disappeared into the bathroom for a long time. When he tried to follow her in there, he found the door locked. Frowning, he returned to bed and waited. She'd have to come back eventually, and then they'd talk.

After what seemed like forever, she did return but wouldn't look at him and didn't say a word. With her back toward him, she curled up so close to the edge of the bed that she was in danger of falling out of it. He tried to pull her into his arms. He *so* wanted to hold her and watch her as she fell asleep, but she shrugged off his hand and buried her head beneath a pillow. Nate let out an elongated sigh, wondering what it would take to break through her defences. Wondering what it was that she was afraid to tell him.

Nate slept badly and was awake well before the alarm went off. Lauren hadn't moved a muscle all night, but he'd been able to tell from her shallow breathing that she'd not really slept either. When they got out of bed, they tiptoed round one another, each politely offering first use of the bathroom to the other. She was speaking to him, being icily polite, but wouldn't meet his eye. She asked if he'd like breakfast, which he declined. They were like strangers rather than two people who'd just shared mind-blowing sex.

Nate conceded that he was firmly back to square one with her.

It would be useless trying to get her to talk about it. She needed space and time to get her head together. Perhaps when this thing with Williams was over she'd be able to think more rationally. One could but hope. Nate dropped her at work and asked when she'd been around again.

"I'm still working double shifts," she said. "Thanks for the lift."

She got out of his car and headed toward the café without a word of good-bye. She didn't look back or watch him drive away.

Sighing, Nate put the car in gear and headed toward London. He'd given up his room in the local hotel now that he and Lauren were friends. Perhaps that had been a mistake. No, he thought, angry now at receiving the cold shoulder. She was acting as though he'd somehow forced her into having sex, and they both knew that wasn't true. Okay, so perhaps she regretted it, but that was hardly his fault.

He hammered the steering wheel with the heel of his hand and veered dangerously into the adjoining lane. A loud blast on a horn alerted him to his inattention, and he waved an apology to his aggrieved fellow road user. His only reason for being in the New Forest was to get close to Lauren and see if there was a story there. Perhaps he'd got closer than was wise. Whatever, they had the sting operation in place to catch Williams, and Lauren had made it crystal clear that was all she was interested in.

I get the message, lady. You ain't that special.

Nate returned to his flat in Battersea, had another shower and changed from the clothes that he'd been wearing for over a day. Then he wondered what to do with the rest of the weekend. There really wasn't any more help he could give Melanie. She was every bit as proficient when it came to computers as Lauren had implied. All the other pieces were in place, and Williams, if he planned to get in touch at all, wouldn't do so until Monday at the earliest. At a loose end, Nate immersed himself in catching up with a few leads he'd been chasing for his book on miscarriages of justice. He'd neglected it recently whilst pitching for Lauren.

He didn't call her over the weekend, reminding himself of her bizarre reaction to their lovemaking whenever he felt tempted. She had a phone now, and his number was programmed into it. It might be juvenile, but as far as he was concerned the next move was hers.

His phone rang at midday on Monday. Not Lauren but a breathless Sophie saying she'd just taken a call from Williams.

"Did he call on the landline number we set up for you?"

"Yes, but the divert to my mobile worked."

"What did he say?"

"He said we'd met in that pub, but I pretended not to remember for awhile."

"Good girl. Then what?"

"He said he wondered if we could meet. He had something he wanted to discuss with me. I was short with him, told him I couldn't talk because I was expecting someone, and that anyway, I wasn't looking for more clients."

"Carrot and stick," Nate said, nodding his approval.

"Yes, it seemed to work because he said it was more a case of what he could do for one of my clients. He wouldn't say more over the phone, so I told him I worked out of my apartment at Canary Wharf and he could call at three this afternoon."

"Okay then. I'll ring about ten past and say I need to see you unexpectedly, then I'll arrive whilst Williams is still making his pitch."

"That should work."

"Sophie, are you still okay with this? It's not too late to call it off if you have any doubts at all."

"Are you kidding me? I'm having the time of my life."

"Okay then." Nate chuckled. "I'll see you later."

Nate hung up, not even asking if Sophie had told Lauren and resisting the urge to do so himself.

* * * *

Lauren treated herself to a lay in on Monday morning, still tormented over her lapse with Nate. It shouldn't have happened, but she wouldn't weaken again. There would be no repeat performance. She felt bad about the way she'd used him and then ignored him afterward, but her feelings were complicated, impossible to articulate, and giving him the silent treatment seemed like the easiest way to deal with the aftermath. It had obviously worked because he hadn't tried to contact her since, which showed just how much the interlude had actually meant to him. Perversely, the deafening silence from his end disappointed her. Why that should be when all she wanted was for him to leave her alone, she couldn't have said.

Cindy was back on duty, and unbeknown to the rest of her friends, Lauren had the next few days off to compensate for all the extra hours she'd put in. Her boss was too much of a tight wad to pay her extra, but this arrangement suited her just fine. Nate could put up all the objections in the world, but there was not a hope in hell of her staying quietly in the country whilst they took all the risks. Despite what Nate seemed to think, Williams was anything but stupid, and she was still far from convinced that this whole silver-mine scam would work. How hard would it be for him to find out if the mine actually existed and who owned it? Those were the sorts of checks any rational person would make before doing anything.

What worried Lauren the most, the problem that niggled away and was turning her into a Grade-A grouch bag, was that if her mates got caught, then they'd finish up in prison. She'd tried to point that out to them, but they weren't deterred. She ought to have told them a few home truths about life on the inside. A few of the things she'd seen and heard that still kept her awake at night. Perhaps then they'd have had second thoughts. Prison life was a damned sight tougher than the media made it out to be.

Damn it, why had she let Nate take over? Their original plan might not have been rocket science, but it would have worked. Williams would have pursued Sophie simply because he was a hound and couldn't help himself. They would have got proof of it, and that would have been enough to satisfy Lauren.

She arrived at Melanie's without having told her friend to expect her. Sophie was there, too, and they both seemed delighted to see her.

"You should have said you were coming," Sophie said. "Does Nate know?"

Lauren quirked a brow. "Any reason why he should?"

"I don't know, you tell us." Melanie sat down, rested her chin in her cupped hand, and grinned at Lauren. "You two seem pretty tight, you lucky devil. He asked me a ton of questions about you when we were working on the web, and I got the impression that—"

"That he wants a good story."

Sophie and Melanie exchanged a loaded glance.

"If you say so, dear."

"What worries me is this damned silver mine," Lauren said. "How do we know if it even exists?"

"Oh, it does," Melanie said confidently. "Nate told me it belongs to friends of his and that they won't mind what we're doing. He's told them about it, and if anyone calls asking questions, they know what to say."

"Blimey," Sophie said, clearly impressed. "He's obviously got clout."

Lauren snorted, refusing to be impressed. Melanie made coffee, and the girls settled down to have a good natter whilst they waited for Williams's call.

"I must be losing my touch," Sophie said, glancing at her watch.

"He'll be in a partners' meeting until eleven, unless they've changed their routine," Lauren told her. "Relax, whatever else might go wrong, he'll definitely call you."

Not long after that, he did.

"I'd better let Nate know," Sophie said.

Lauren's pulse quickened. "Don't tell him I'm here."

"Okay, if you'd rather I didn't."

As soon as Sophie hung up and repeated the conversation, Lauren spoke up.

"I'm coming to London with you," she said determinedly.

"Don't be stupid!" Melanie and Sophie said together.

"It's not up for negotiation. Oh, I know I can't be seen, but I can hide in the bedroom and listen."

"You could, I suppose," Sophie said. "But why take the risk?"

"Because I've waited three years for that right."

"True, but if he catches on that you're there, you could blow the whole thing."

"Well then, I'll have to make sure that I don't give myself away. Can I leave Kermit with you, Mel?"

"Yes, of course."

"Come on then, Sophie," she said, bustling her friend out the door before she thought to ring Nate and tell him she was tagging along, "the train won't wait for us."

* * * *

Jeff wasn't best pleased. Sandra was home all day with a stomach bug, and his man couldn't get into her apartment. He needed to know that she definitely had the money. Once he did he'd find a way to get it back. He wanted to use it if he got involved with this Frobisher thing. Still, provided Sandra was back at work tomorrow, it wouldn't be too late. Frobisher couldn't be in that much of a hurry.

Jeff had spent a considerable amount of time over the weekend checking out the Frobisher angle. He'd phoned the sheriff's office in the local town, making out that he was a tourist, asking after the mine. He was told that it was a local landmark, open to the public six days a week during summer months. It was owned by the Frobisher family, but when the mine stopped producing enough silver to make it viable, it was turned into a tourist resort.

"For a modest entrance fee, you get to mine your own silver," some Yank told him proudly. "You ought to stop by."

"Perhaps I'll just do that," Jeff said, smiling to himself as he hung up. He was definitely onto something here.

He was inexplicably nervous as he rang the bell to Stella Grant's apartment in Canary Wharf. Her voice echoed through the entry phone.

"It's Jeff Williams," he said.

"Third floor."

The door buzzed open, and he made his way across a polished entrance hall to the elevators, pressing the button for three. A door opened as he stepped out of it, and there she was, dressed in an expensive-looking dress that fit in all the right places. She was even more glamorous than he remembered. That made him nervous, which annoyed him. He liked to be in control. He *was* the one in control, he reminded himself. These people had a problem, and he could sort it for them. They needed him—not the other way round.

He squared his shoulders and extended his hand to Ms. Grant.

"Mr. Williams," she said, ushering him into a minimalistic yet expensively furnished lounge.

"Ms. Grant." He took her outstretched hand and held on to it for a little too long. "Thanks for seeing me. This is a nice flat," he said, giving it a cursory once-over.

"It's a short-term rental," she said dismissively, "and serves its purpose. I dislike hotels."

"I can certainly relate to that."

"Now, what can I do for you? It will have to be quick, so you'll excuse me if I don't offer you any refreshment," she said, taking a seat on one of the two leather settees and motioning him toward the other.

"I didn't come here for coffee."

"Then, excuse the bluntness," she said, glancing at her watch and tapping her fingers against its face, "but what is it that you do want?"

"You represent Brad Frobisher."

She raised one superbly shaped eyebrow. "Is that a question or a statement of fact?"

"You said it yourself," Jeff responded suavely. "You're busy, so I won't waste your time dancing round the issue. You represent Frobisher, he needs funds, and I might be able to help you there."

"What makes you suppose that he's looking for backers?" she asked warily.

Jeff started to relax. He had her now and could play this game of cat and mouse a hell of a lot better than her. Hell, he invented most of the rules himself.

"Because you're an exceedingly expensive, very exclusive facilitator."

That eyebrow elevation again. "Am I now?"

"You don't advertise your services, avoid publicity, but are known to work across Europe, representing only the wealthiest clients when they're in need of discreet, temporary funding." He flashed a smile. "You have contacts in the highest places and have in the past introduced clients to Giles Jenson, a reclusive multi-millionaire who, like you, shuns publicity."

"I might dislike publicity, but I'm no multi-millionaire."

"No, but you're acquainted with a number of people who are and only work for one client at a time. I saw you with Frobisher the other day and so…" His modest smile transcended the need for words.

"You've done your homework," she said reluctantly.

"Frobisher is the owner of a silver mine in Colorado."

"A worked-out silver mine," she said, checking her watch again.

"A mine in which the local bank holds a majority share because they bailed out Frobisher's family when it was on the verge of bankruptcy."

Stella shrugged. "That's a matter of public record."

"The bank insisted, against the family's wishes, to convert it into a tourist attraction, and it's now turning a profit."

Stella inclined her head. "Go on," she said cautiously.

"Everything's going along nicely, but all of a sudden Frobisher turns up in England, in the company of an exclusive facilitator, and goes berserk when some third-rate hack publishes unsubstantiated comments about his mine. What am I supposed to make of that?"

"You've added two and two and come up with seventeen," Stella said, looking bored. "My client enjoys his privacy and doesn't like seeing his name in the tabloids, that's all."

Jeff merely smiled. "Credit me with a little intelligence."

"All right," she said impatiently. "What is it that you think you know?"

"I think this business of producing silver for the tourists has accidently hit upon an unmined vein." Jeff shifted his position and shot her a challenging smile. "Since the downturn in the economy, the price of silver has skyrocketed, so this find couldn't have come at a more opportune time for your client. He can close his doors to Joe public and have the family land all to himself again." Jeff paused, his gaze fastened on her face. "But only if he can raise enough money to repay the bank and get them out of his affairs."

"Really." Stella stretched remarkably long, slender legs in front of her, causing Jeff to temporarily lose his thread. He moistened his lips and pursued his original train of thought.

"If the bank stays involved, then they'll take a hefty portion of the profits, and any self-respecting businessman would resent that, especially since their irresponsibility caused the economic implosion in the first place. If I'm right, then Frobisher must be desperate because the silver discovery can't possibly remain secret for long. If the bank finds out about it, they probably have a clause in their agreement that allows them to remain involved, even if the debt's repaid."

"What makes you say that?"

He shrugged. "Banks always write agreements in their favour. So Frobisher needs short-term loans to pay off the bank and is willing to pay whopping interest rates for the privilege of getting rid of their involvement before the news of the find breaks."

"And even supposing this little hypothesis of yours is right, and I'm not saying for a moment that it is, what interest would it be to you?"

"Well, perhaps if Jenson isn't willing to bridge the gap, then I might step in."

Stella's phone rang.

"Excuse me," she said, checking the display. "I have to take this."

Jeff waved a hand, thoroughly pleased with himself. "Please, take all the time you need."

She moved away from him and had a short conversation in hushed tones. Jeff couldn't hear what was said, but she appeared to be trying to convince someone about something. She closed her phone and returned to her seat.

“Well,” she said, “that was Mr. Frobisher. I briefly told him about you. He’s on his way here now, and you can talk to him for yourself.”

Chapter Sixteen

Lauren had promised to stay in the bedroom and not make a sound. Easier said than done, she now realized, since apart from their low voices next door, the place was deathly quiet. No noise from adjoining apartments—presumably because the occupants were out at work—and Sophie could hardly put the TV or radio on in the middle of a business meeting.

Lauren crouched behind the bedroom door, ear pressed against it. She could hear Williams's voice, smug and full of self-confidence. It made her skin crawl. Sophie's tone was pitched low, and it was hard to make out what she said. Never mind, it seemed to be going exactly to plan. Nate was on his way, and her heart did a peculiar little skip at the thought of seeing him again. He'd be angry with her for turning up, but she didn't give a damn about that. All that mattered was that he pulled this thing off.

The doorbell rang. He was here already. Lauren's heart rate accelerated, and perspiration trickled between her breasts when she considered the risks he and Sophie were taking. Williams was a powerful man and, she had good reason to know, dangerous when crossed. He had almost certainly arranged the murders of two men to protect his own skin. There was no saying how he would react if he discovered they were trying to play him. This was lunacy, a huge error of judgement, and she had to stop them before it was too late!

She heard the sound of Sophie's heels on the wooden floor as she crossed it to open the door. She wanted to reveal herself and tell Williams to clear off. Better that than have him wreak revenge on her friends when this stupid scam failed. She tried to stand up, but her limbs refused to move, rendered immobile by fear and indecision. Her warning cry remained mute in her throat, and by the time she recovered from her panic attack, it was too late to act because Nate's voice reached her, loud and aggressive.

"What's all this bull about someone trying to muscle in?" he demanded.

"Look, Mr. Frobisher," Sophie said in a placating tone, "I know it's unusual, but I think you should hear him out."

"I don't like surprises. They make me nervous."

Sophie said something she couldn't quite hear.

"Who is the guy, anyway?" Nate asked.

"His name's Williams, and he works for a firm of stockbrokers. Come and meet him."

"Oh, what the hell! Come on then, but I'm highly suspicious of him."

"Of course. So am I."

Lauren heard more footfalls and then Jeff's oily voice.

"Mr. Frobisher," he said. "Thanks for seeing me."

There was a slight pause during which Lauren assumed the men were shaking hands and sizing one another up. She thought she'd be content just to be here and eavesdrop, but that was no longer enough. She'd give anything now to be able to open the door a crack and actually see them.

"I'm not sure why I am." Nate sounded irascible. "What do you want?"

"To help you out."

Jeff repeated his theory about Frobisher's silver mine.

"I told you that bloody hack would queer our pitch!" Nate yelled. "Now we've got every two-bit hustler in London on our backs."

Lauren covered her mouth with her hand to stifle a giggle. She'd love to see Jeff's reaction to being called a two-bit hustler, especially since he was the one being hustled.

"I'm a senior partner at Whytelake's, a respected firm of city stockbrokers," Jeff said with commendable calmness. "I have considerable resources at my disposal for the right investment and no one to answer to for my decisions."

"I doubt you're even in my league," Nate said disparagingly.

"On the contrary, Mr. Frobisher, I rather think it's the other way round."

"Oh right, got a spare five million bucks doing nothing for the next few days, have you?" Nate either laughed or sneered, Lauren wasn't sure which. "Thought not."

"I could raise that amount if I was convinced it would be worth my while."

"Yeah well, that ain't gonna happen. I need it by tomorrow if—"

"Tomorrow?"

"Yeah, tomorrow. You seem to know a lot about my damned business, but what you probably don't know is that the next quarter's interest is due on Wednesday. If I don't clear the whole loan by then, the bank gets to stay involved for another three months, even if I pay it off the day after it's due. That's the tight-ass agreement the bloodsuckers insisted upon. There ain't no way this silver business can stay secret for another three months," he added moodily.

"Are you absolutely sure this find is genuine?"

Nate glared at him. "You think I'd be flitting round the world like a blue-arsed fly if it wasn't?" He sighed. "Sorry, what do you know about silver?"

"Not a lot."

"Well, let me educate you. Hell, Colorado ain't known as the silver state for nothing. There's been silver ore in the Aspen mountains since the mid 1800s. It's mined underground just like coal and found in veins of rock with hot water flowing through and round them."

"Go on," Williams said.

"Well, we take the punters to a section of the mine where we know there are still a few weak veins. We get them to chip off a bean-sized sample of rock, and once we're above ground we use chlorine-free water in a test tube, mix it with nitric acid and the specimen of silver ore, and boil until the silver dissolves. After that we add a few drops of hydrochloric acid, and if it turns milky, it means there's silver present." Nate chuckled. "Gives the paying customers a hell of a kick when that happens."

"So what happened this time that was so different?"

"I should have made myself clearer. When the solution turns milky, it means there's low quality silver present, just like we could have told them in the first place. But," added Nate, pausing for emphasis, "if it turns into a thick, curdy mass—"

"The silver is high grade," Williams finished for him, sounding a little breathless.

"Exactly, and that's what happened a week or two ago. We've closed off that area of the mine, but it's only a matter of time before—"

"Presumably Jenson was satisfied that the find's genuine."

"We never got that far."

"What, you didn't supply him with proof, and he still would have invested had it not been for that leak of his name in the papers?" Williams sounded flabbergasted.

"Oh, sure I brought proof. Notarised proof of finds, geological surveys, stuff like that, but also rock samples, sealed by independent witnesses—"

"And where's that ore sample now?"

"Jenson sent the one I gave him to an expert geologist."

"Who?"

Nate came up with a name without missing a beat, and Lauren had to assume he was genuine. Hell, listening to him, she believed Nate's every word, and she was in on the scam. How the hell had he found a respected geologist prepared to go along with him? It wasn't an aspect of the plan he'd bothered to tell her about, or one that she'd even considered.

"And so," Jeff said, "if Jenson wouldn't mind asking his geologist to talk to me about it, if he confirms it's genuine, I might be able to find the funds. I'd want independent collaboration, obviously."

"Obviously."

Lauren heard a rustle of papers. "I brought several notarised copies of the survey and more rock samples."

"Hum, looks just like a lump of rock," Jeff said. "Mind if I keep it."

"Be my guest. You can keep a copy of all the documents if you like. I have more."

"I dare say you do." Jeff paused, obviously reading the papers Nate had given him. Lauren's respect for the American increased by the second. How had he managed all this so fast? He appeared to have all the angles—things that wouldn't even have occurred to Lauren—covered. "What rate of interest are you offering?"

"For a three-day loan, five percent."

"Ten."

"Seven and a half," Nate said.

"You're really not in a position to negotiate, Mr. Frobisher," Jeff said smugly. "I'm your last hope. Ten percent or nothing."

"This guy is bad news," Nate said with a heavy sigh. "Forget it. I'll go home on the next flight and somehow find a way to hush this up." She heard him pacing the room. "My mine manager's been with the family since before I was born. We can count on him keeping quiet."

"Mr. Frobisher," Sophie said. "I really think you ought to consider Mr. Williams's proposition. You said yourself that news this momentous won't remain a secret for long."

"I'll find a way," he said. "This guy is as bad as the frigging banks."

"I'll take that as a compliment," Jeff said, a smile in his voice.

"It wasn't intended as one."

Jeff sighed. "All right, Mr. Frobisher, you drive a hard bargain. Seven and a half percent for a three-day loan of five million dollars, and we have a deal."

There was a long pause and more pacing on Nate's part. "Yeah, okay, I guess I don't have much choice."

"But," added Jeff, "I shall need to make a few enquires of my own before we seal the deal."

"You'd be a fool if you didn't."

"And, obviously, I shall want something in writing."

Lauren gasped. She hadn't thought of that, but Nate obviously had because he didn't miss a beat.

"Sure. We can meet with your lawyers first thing in the morning if you like."

"Lawyers?" Sophie said. "I thought secrecy was vital, Mr. Frobisher."

"It is, but as we're moving so quickly, I guess we can rely on the legal profession to keep it under its hat for a day or two. That's all we need. Besides, I can't imagine Mr. Williams would want to part with that sort of money without a binding agreement."

"You're right about that but no lawyers," Jeff said. "We'll keep this between ourselves."

"It's your call." Lauren could hear the surprise in Nate's voice. "What do you need from me?"

"Well, obviously, I shall need collateral. We sign an agreement that allows me to take over the bank's position on the property if you renege."

Jesus!

"Not a problem," Nate said smoothly. "Wanna take a look at the current agreement I have with the bank?"

"Naturally."

More rustling of paper, but Lauren barely heard it. Her head was still reeling.

"I think this calls for champagne," Sophie said.

"Make that call to the geologist first," Nate reminded her.

Lauren held her breath, convinced that this was where it would all go disastrously wrong. To her astonishment, Sophie dialled a number and handed the phone to Jeff. He had a short conversation, hung up the phone, and then spoke to Nate.

"I think we do potentially have a deal," he said. "This guy confirmed what you told me, but I'll get someone else to run the tests for my own peace of mind. If he agrees, then we're on."

Just like that? Lauren fell onto the bed, unable to believe it could possibly be that simple, still wondering where the catch was.

"Well, that's great, and I'm sorry if I came off a bit strong at the start," Nate said. "If you don't mind my saying so, I thought you were trying to scam me."

Oh, Nate don't be such idiot! You're pushing your luck.

"How soon do you need the money?"

"By close of business tomorrow."

"Shouldn't be a problem, but I need to make some calls to set the ball rolling," Jeff said. "Can I use your phone?"

"Sure," Sophie said.

"I'll take a bathroom break." Nate opened the door to the bedroom with such force that he almost caused Lauren, who was once again crouching behind it, to topple over.

"Ouch!" She covered her mouth to smother the sound.

"What the hell?" Nate closed the door behind him. "What are you doing here?" he whispered, picking her up.

Her arm burned where he grabbed it but not because he'd hurt her. "Listening," she said scathingly. "What does it look like?"

"Well, I get that, but you really shouldn't—"

"Later, he's off the phone and chatting Sophie up," Lauren said, pressing her ear to the door.

Nate used the toilet. On his way out again he threw a scowl Lauren's way that told her she'd have some explaining to do when Williams left.

"Shouldn't be a problem," Jeff said. "I have to go to a reception at the Dorchester tonight, but it'll be over by nine. Can you meet me in the bar afterward, and I'll give you a definite answer. I'd prefer not to communicate by phone on such a sensitive issue."

"Yeah, I guess we can do that," Nate said.

Lauren heard Sophie taking Jeff to the front door. As soon as it closed, she braced herself for the onslaught and didn't have long to wait. The door to the bedroom flew open again, and Nate's formidable body filled the aperture. His expression of blistering rage shook her. She'd expected him to be annoyed, but this was extreme. Way beyond any mood she'd seen him in before. He was like a stranger suddenly, and she was a bit frightened of him. Lauren swallowed back the lump in her throat, threw her shoulders back, and faced him, damned if she'd back down beneath the force of his irate glower.

"What do you think you're doing here?" he demanded.

"Shush!" Sophie said, coming up behind him. "Give Williams a chance to get clear. If he's waiting for the lift, he'll hear you."

Nate paced the distance between the bedroom and lounge for what seemed like an eternity, muttering and cursing, fit to bust a gut. Apart from his rumbling monologue, it was deathly quiet in the apartment, Sophie instinctively taking up a position beside Lauren as the girls waited to see what he'd do next. They glanced at one another, both uneasy, as he walked toward the window and glanced out. Apparently satisfied that Williams was clear of the building, he swivelled on his heel and pointed a finger at Lauren.

"Of all the harebrained, ridiculous stunts to pull." He lifted a hand to his hair, appeared to remember the gel at the last minute, and dropped his arm against his side with a loud thwack. "You could have ruined everything."

"But I didn't," Lauren said in a commendably even voice, "so I don't understand what you're getting so steamed up about."

"If he'd needed to use the bathroom, he'd have had to come in her and—"

"And I would have heard him ask and hidden in the closet," she snapped back at him.

"Why did you let her come, Sophie?" he asked, only moderating his tone a fraction.

"It's nothing to do with Sophie. I'm a big girl and make my own decisions."

They stood on opposite sides of the bed, glaring at one another like prize gladiators, both furious, neither prepared to back down.

"Look," Sophie said, pushing her hands toward them palms out. "You two need to sort this out. I'm going back to my place to sort out something to wear to the Dorchester and catch up with a few things. Shall I see you there, Nate?"

"Yeah sure," he said, sighing and calming down a little. He walked up to Sophie and placed a hand in the small of her back. "Thanks, you did great with Williams. Played it exactly right."

"I think we've got him hooked," she said.

"Let's hope so." Lauren watched as he kissed her on both cheeks, annoyed at the spurt of jealousy she felt. "I'll see you in the bar at the Dorchester at nine. We'll get there before his reception finishes and establish ourselves."

"Good thinking." Sophie turned back toward Lauren. "Bye, sweetie. Will you be all right?"

"I'll be fine."

"You can stay here tonight if you like."

Lauren hadn't given any thought to her sleeping arrangements and didn't fancy catching a train back this late in the afternoon. Besides, she wanted to be in on the spot at crunch time, which would be over the next day or so, if at all.

"Thanks," she said, "I'll do that."

The girls hugged. Nate walked Sophie to the door and closed it behind her. He took his sweet time turning to face Lauren, frazzling her nerves by deliberately making her wait, or so it seemed. She hadn't moved from her place in the bedroom, partly because she wasn't too sure that her limbs *could* move right now. She was frozen with indecision, unsure how to deal with Nate in such an uncompromising mood. One thing she did know was that his anger was about a lot more than her appearing here without telling him. She took a deep breath and forced herself to walk toward the lounge. He blocked her path at the doorway.

"Excuse me," she said, as though addressing a stranger.

"That's asking a lot."

"Nate, stop acting like a Victorian father protecting his child."

"Then stop behaving like a child."

She whirled away from him, unsettled by the subdued menace in his stance. The atmosphere seemed to vibrate with his displeasure, and she withdrew mentally to a place where it couldn't reach her—a habit she'd picked up in times of despair whilst in prison.

"I wouldn't be reduced to underhand tactics if you told me what was going on."

"What do you mean?" He regarded her with an icy expression. "I told you everything."

"No you didn't. I knew nothing about the finite details. I kept trying to make suggestions when we were at Mel's, and you wouldn't listen because you thought you knew better." She glowered at him. "Did it occur to you that I might be worried about you and Sophie putting yourselves in the firing line?"

He made a scoffing sound. "We weren't in danger."

"Nate, the man has sanctioned two murders that we know of. His pride is the size of Wembley stadium. If he even suspected that you were trying to get one over on him, then he would retaliate without a second thought."

"He didn't suspect."

"No!" She shouted the word in her anxiety to make him understand her concerns. "Because you'd taken care of all the details, but I didn't know that. It would have saved me a lot of heartache if you'd let me in on the act."

"Perhaps so," he said, his tone changing from glacial to a quiet, scornful indifference that she found infinitely more hurtful. "I intended to tell you everything when we last met. We got distracted, if you recall, and afterward you wouldn't even look at me, much less talk to me." He shrugged. "What was I supposed to do? Send you a memo?"

Colour flooded her face. There was absolutely nothing she could say without making the situation ten times worse—unless she was willing to open up to him and explain things that she barely understood herself—and so she remained silent. But it seemed that Nate wasn't willing to accept silence. He moved round the bed, caught her by the shoulders, and drilled her with a look so full of smouldering anger that she barely contained a startled gasp.

"What is it, Lauren? Why won't you let me in?" When she didn't, couldn't respond, he shook her gently. "Talk to me, damn it!"

"Nate, you don't understand. It's hard for me to—"

"Sure I understand. That bastard really hurt you. You wouldn't be human if you weren't now slow to trust men, but you know me well enough to realize I'm not like him. I'm trying to help you, for God's sake!"

"I know you are." Lauren dropped her head, resisting the urge to rest it on his broad shoulder. A nerve twitched in his forehead, probably caused by her intransigence. "It's just that I'm…I'm scared."

"Goddamit!"

He pulled her into his arms so fast that her body collided against his with a hard thump.

"I am so angry with you that I'm spitting nails, you realize that, don't you?"

Without giving her time to respond, his lips covered hers, and she inhaled sharply, stealing his breath and taking it deep into her lungs because her own supply appeared to have run out.

"What do you wanna know about the plan?" he asked, breathing heavily as he broke the kiss.

"Well, Giles Jenson for a start. How does he fit in?"

She felt the shirt being pulled from the waistband of her jeans. "I helped him once a few years back when a reporter on the *Inquirer* was set to print a load of personal stuff about his daughter." The buttons on her shirt fell open. "I got it pulled, and he reckons he owes me."

"So you asked for his cooperation?" She returned the favour and pulled his shirt free, running her hands across his ripped abdomen. "Before you had that piece placed in the *Inquirer* about you and Sophie leaving his party?"

"Of course. I wouldn't have embarrassed him by having it printed without his knowledge." Her shirt hit the floor.

"What if Williams tries to call him?"

"I'm counting on him doing that. I certainly would in his position. Jenson will play along."

"How did you get the owners of that silver mine to cooperate?" His shirt went the same way of hers.

"They're friends of mine." Her jeans fell round her hips.

"They must be good friends." Her voice sounded unsteady as she reached for his zipper.

"They are."

"And those rock samples and all the paperwork?" She reached inside his jeans and cupped his prick. He exclaimed sharply but then closed his own hand over hers, showing her what he wanted.

"Couriered over from America." His hands claimed her naked breasts. What the hell had happened to her bra? She neither knew nor particularly cared.

"How did you manage that?"

There was a definite quaver in her voice as desire overcame common sense. She so didn't want this to happen again. It complicated everything. She was also quaking with desire and couldn't have stopped if her life depended upon it.

"God, I love your tits," he said, bending his head and suckling.

"They're too small."

"I like them small and pert, and you have fabulous nipples."

He sucked one into his mouth and gently bit it. Lauren dissolved as liquid heat flooded her body, quelling any lingering doubts about the wisdom of her actions. Nate sank onto the side of the bed, taking her with him. One moment she was sitting on his bare thighs, the next she was across them, looking down at the floor.

"What the—"

As quick as a flash, he pulled down her panties and slapped the palm of his hand across her bare buttocks.

"What was that for?" she demanded, desire evaporating as a stinging pain gripped her.

"For disobeying me." *Thwack.* "I told you to stay in the forest." *Thwack.* "Not only did you not do that, but you also compromised our plan by coming here." *Thwack.*

"How dare you…ahh!"

This time, instead of spanking her, two fingers made their way inside her vagina. "Yes," he said, his breath peppering her ear as he bent close. "Pleasure and pain, such a thin dividing line."

"I didn't…wasn't aware."

"Do you think you deserve the pleasure?" he asked, adding a third finger and rubbing his thumb against her clitoris.

"I'm sorry, Nate."

She felt tears dripping from the corners of her eyes. Immediately her world righted itself as Nate upended her again and cradled her against his chest.

"I'm sorry, too," he said. "I didn't mean to make you cry. I thought you might like it, is all."

"I did, but I…"

Appalled, she didn't seem able to stop the flood of tears. Nate soothed her, whispering that everything would be all right. But it wouldn't be, unless he could undo the past, and not even he could work that sort of magic.

When the tears finally stopped, Nate pulled her into strong arms corded with muscles, lay down with her, and simply held her. They were both naked, and he was exceedingly aroused, but he didn't make a move on her. Instead, he seemed mortified to have made her cry. She reached up and touched his face.

"I'm better now," she said softly.

"Hey, welcome back. Sorry if I got carried away." He grinned. "I've wanted to do that to you since the first time I saw you in the forest and your reaction to me was so prickly."

"Actually," she said, leaning up on one elbow. "It *was* rather stimulating."

He chuckled, icy fury giving way to soft admiration. "That was the idea."

"I thought you were angry."

"I wasn't angry. I was furious because you shut me out after—"

"After we made love last time." She shook her head against his chest. "I'm sorry. It wasn't anything you did."

"Glad to hear it."

"It was more a case of giving up control. I've had to look out for myself for the past three years, and I've learned not to place my trust in anyone." She blinked back fresh tears. "But letting you get so close, that's what it felt like I was doing, and it scared me."

"Yeah, I get that, but I also know for a fact that we ain't gonna use this," he said, brushing a hand across his erection, "if you'll live to regret it and go all silent on me again."

She sucked her lower lip between her teeth, trying to quell a smile that managed to escape anyway. "It would be a shame to waste it, don't you think?"

His grin was broad and infectious. “Honey, you really don’t wanna know what I’m thinking right now.”

“Actually, I can read your mind like a best seller.” She flicked a finger across his prick. “The clues are rather obvious.”

Nate cursed, rolled on top of her, and slid straight into her. His cool attitude had obviously been just that, and he was on the brink of losing control. He wasn’t wearing a condom, she realized as his penis filled her so gloriously and completely, and they began to move in unison. She was too far gone to care.

“Lauren,” he said urgently, “I don’t think I can—”

The desperation in his voice was infectious and brought her to an immediate, cataclysmic climax. Her nerve ends still tingled as he withdrew, cried out her name as though he was physically in pain, and shot his load all over her breasts.

Chapter Seventeen

Nate lay flat on his back beside her, regaining his breath. This time he was determined that she wouldn't shut him out. He pulled her toward him, mindless of his sperm still drying on her body.

"If that's what happens when we argue," he said, kissing the top of her head, "then I guess we should fight more often."

To his relief, she responded immediately. "It was pretty special, I'll give you that," she said, punching him lightly in the ribs. "I guess you Yanks really do rule some areas of the world."

"Happy to give satisfaction, ma'am." He stroked the curve of her face, drinking in her flushed features, thinking that she'd never looked more beautiful. Melanie, and especially Sophie, were tons better looking than her, but for Nate there was something about Lauren's attitude of self-containment that vied with her vulnerability, setting her apart. If he had to choose between the three women, it would be no contest, and Lauren would win hands-down every time. "Talking of which, how did you cope in prison?"

"I abstained," she said.

"Not through lack of offers, I'm sure."

"I don't go for other women."

"Shame," he said, chuckling, "I wouldn't mind watching you and—"

She slapped his chest. "What is it about two women together that so gets to men?"

His chuckle turned into a full throaty laugh. "I'll tell you one day."

"There was a lot of it going on, and I could understand why. It was a way to forget for a short time, that's what some of the girls told me anyway, but it wasn't for me."

They lapsed into momentary silence, but Nate was pretty sure she hadn't withdrawn from him.

"Are you ready to move the money the moment Williams parts with it?" he asked her, reminding her of her vital role in the operation.

"Yes, I've got several accounts opened in places where they don't ask too many questions."

"Or pay much attention to banking rules, I trust."

"Of course!"

He ran a finger across one of her breasts. "Just checking."

"How about the account he's paying the money into?" she asked.

"It's kosher."

"I'm not even going to ask you how you managed that."

"Contacts, baby, contacts." He grinned and tapped the side of his nose. "Networking is what it's all about nowadays. Anyway, presumably he'll use that three million he stole, and you'll get your money back."

"Perhaps," she said. "Unless he thinks a figure that large would alert the fraud people in America."

"If he uses that stolen dosh and sends it all in one hit, it will, so he probably won't be that stupid. That's why I shall suggest that he splits the transfer into six."

"You have six accounts ready to take it?" She sat up and stared at him. "How did you manage that? No, no, don't tell me…connections." They both laughed. "I hate to say this, Mr. Black, but you do seem to have thought of everything."

"Yeah well, either way, six accounts are necessary. To cover the stolen cash or, if he takes it from Whytelake's, he'll have to take it from different accounts. I recall you saying that anything over a million would raise a red flag."

"Yes, it used to, and I'm betting security's even tighter since I left."

"Well, I'm hoping he does use the firm's money, and then he'll be comprehensively finished when the fraud comes to light. If he uses his own funds, all he'll be is broke."

"Yes," said Lauren, turning away from him. "I expect he'll borrow from the firm, just like always."

He was losing her again. She was still sensitive about any references to the stolen millions, and he guessed he could understand that.

"How did you get that geologist to confirm your findings when Jeff rang him?" she asked.

"Well, actually Jeff didn't ring him. Oh, Sophie rang the number, but someone at the paper diverted the call to a reporter who took it for me."

"Ah, so all this phone tapping stuff the press *doesn't* do—"

"Hey, I called in a lot of favours to get the guy's cooperation."

"What did you have to do in return?"

"The paper's been after me for a while to do an exposé on an illegal puppy farm in Essex. Not my sort of bag, but for your cause," he said, dropping a kiss on her left nipple, "I took it on. Have to go back out there in a couple of days and finish it off."

"Thanks," she said quietly. "That can't be a pleasant assignment."

"It's not, and I really didn't want to work for the *Inquirer* again, but it'll be worth it to put those money-grabbing bastards down in Essex out of business."

"What if Jeff calls that geologist again?" Lauren asked.

Nate elevated a brow. "If he does, we're screwed."

"Then let's hope he doesn't."

"It's unlikely, given that he's going to get independent tests done." He patted her rear. "Right, come on, let's get in that shower, and then you're coming back to my place in Battersea. That way, I'll know where you are, and when I get back from the Dorchester, I can give you a firsthand account."

Nate didn't know what to make of things as they caught the tube across town. She'd not turned away from him this time, but she hadn't completely opened up to him either. She was still hiding something, and the hell if he knew what it was.

They reached Battersea, and Nate opened the door to his converted loft.

"Be it ever so humble, it's home," he said, ushering her in before him and watching her look round with interest.

His London pad was a large L-shaped room, with a kitchenette off to one side and a separate shower room. The living section was arranged round a log-burning stove and large flat-screen TV. Next to that, an alcove housed his desk and bookshelves, the walls covered with framed copies of some of his finer front-page exposés. One side of the L was completely taken up with his bed and closets. The view over the old Battersea power station was front row.

"It's very homely," she said, nodding her approval.

"I've kept it on even though I don't work on the *Inquirer* anymore," he said. "The rent's not too bad, and I still spend a lot of time in England, so it makes sense. Make yourself at home," he added. "What can I get you?"

"Just coffee, please," she said, sitting in the corner of an overstuffed couch and tucking her feet up beneath her. "Hum, I could get used to this. Television, what a treat!"

"Don't get too excited. It's usually a load of crap."

"Even so." She picked up the remote and channel surfed. "Hum, I see what you mean."

She turned the set off again and fell asleep before the kettle even boiled. She was still zonked out when it was time for him to leave for the Dorchester.

"Probably better that way," he mumbled to himself, leaving her a note telling her where to find everything. It felt good knowing she was there and would be waiting for him when he got back. He paused before leaving, standing in the open doorway to watch her sleep. His heart lurched as the truth dawned. It explained so much about his volatile feelings toward her. How she could rouse him to passion and anger simultaneously, like no other woman had ever managed. How he didn't want to cross the line with her but couldn't keep his hands off her. She belonged here.

She belonged to him whether she knew it or not.

Nate and Sophie arrived at the hotel at almost the same time. As always, Sophie looked the part in a pale-green cocktail dress that caused even staid old men to stop and stare. Nate guided her into the bar, where they took a quiet corner table. A waiter took their order, and only when their drinks had been delivered did they talk.

"How's Lauren?" Sophie asked.

"Better now. I took her back to my place so I can keep an eye on her."

Sophie chuckled. "Is that what they call it nowadays?"

"I don't trust her to behave herself, left to her own devices. Hell, I wouldn't put it past her to turn up here if she was still at Canary Wharf. This way I know where she is."

She appeared amused. "You don't have to justify yourself to me, Nate. If anyone's overdue a little fun, it's Lauren."

"Try telling her that." Nate sighed. "She's freaked out on guilt and remorse, and I have a hard job getting through to her."

"Give her time. She's been through a lot and doesn't find it easy to trust."

Nate rolled his eyes. "Tell me something I don't know."

There was a commotion at the entrance to the bar as an influx of monkey-suited men made a beeline for it.

"Showtime," Nate said, raising a hand as he saw Williams hovering in the doorway.

Williams was distracted by someone speaking to him, and it was his wife Gloria, deadly in a tight-fitting beige creation. Her gaze lingered upon Nate as though she knew him from somewhere.

"Damn it!" he muttered.

* * * *

Jeff wasn't best pleased. His investigator had got into Sandra's flat that afternoon when she went out shopping, and by the time he got back from his meeting with Frobisher, there was a fat envelope sitting on his desk with all the information he'd asked for. Much good it was proving to be. There was absolutely nothing out of the ordinary about her bank accounts—one checking and two savings with modest credit balances—just as he'd expect from someone on her pay grade. Anything to do with the stolen funds must be kept on her computer records, but thus far he hadn't been able to break her password and get in. He thumped his desk in frustration. Time was getting on, and he was due at the Dorchester. It was a company beano for valued clients, and he couldn't afford to miss it or be late. He'd just have to spend more money and get someone to break the code for him. He picked up his phone, arranged it, and left the disc at reception to be collected.

Then he changed into evening clothes and headed downtown to meet Gloria. She excelled at these events, and tonight he'd be grateful for her presence. The last thing he felt like doing was chatting up stuffy investors when his own ambitions were finally on the brink of being realized.

"Where are these people you want to meet?" she asked him when the idiot who'd detained Jeff with banal conversation finally drifted away.

Jeff scanned the bar with his eyes. "Over there," he said, leading her toward Frobisher and the delectable Stella.

Frobisher stood as they approached. Jeff made the introduction, and Frobisher shook Gloria's hand.

"Please to meet you, ma'am."

His accent sounded more pronounced than Jeff remembered it and slightly more southern, too.

He was too preoccupied to pay much attention to it and quickly turned the conversation to business—business that he had no intention of discussing in front of his wife.

"If you ladies will excuse us for a moment," he said. "Mr. Frobisher and I have a few things to discuss."

"Don't be long, darling."

Gloria spoke testily. She hadn't been happy about this delay and wouldn't appreciate being left with Stella. She wasn't too keen on other women at the best of times, and one that outshone her in every department wouldn't do much for her mood. She'd wanted to go on to a nightspot somewhere, and Jeff had said that they might. Not that he had any intention of doing so, but she didn't need to know that yet. He and Frobisher stepped into the foyer and found a quiet spot. Jeff wasted no time in getting down to business.

"I've made a few more calls this afternoon, got your rock sample independently tested—"

"You work fast."

Jeff cracked a smile. "Time is of the essence, is it not?"

"True. Anyway, I guess everything panned out, pun intended," he said, "or we wouldn't be having this conversation."

"Absolutely right. I also had a brief chat with Mr. Jenson, and he reassured me."

Frobisher raised a brow. "Surprised he took your call. He doesn't usually speak to strangers."

"I keep telling you," Jeff said, an edge to his voice. "I do have some influence in this town."

"Right, okay, where does that leave us?"

"Well, provided you don't need the money for more than three days, then I can help you out."

"Gee, that's great, thanks."

"Ten percent, right?"

"Here, I thought we agreed seven and a half."

"You're not in a position to negotiate."

The American scowled at him. "Yeah, okay, I suppose. Geez, half a million bucks for three days. Nice work if you can get it."

"You'll make a great deal more than that from your silver mine."

"Yeah, that's true. So, what do you need from me?"

"Your passport, please."

Frobisher produced it from an inside pocket. Jeff flipped through it, appeared satisfied, and motioned to the concierge, who joined them immediately.

"Photocopy this for me if you wouldn't mind, Jason."

"At once, Mr. Williams."

Williams pulled a thin sheaf of papers from his inside jacket pocket and handed them to Frobisher. He read the papers quickly and scrawled his name in the appropriate place.

"Here you go."

Jeff signed as well, suppressing a smirk. This guy really was a hick. He ought to have this document checked out by a lawyer. If he bothered to do so, he'd see that Jeff had slipped in a clause that gave him a little more than ten percent. Not that lawyers were an option. If he *had* insisted upon involving them, Jeff would have run a mile.

"We'd best get Ms. Grant to witness our signatures," Jeff said.

"Just a minute. Don't you want the account details?"

"Oh, of course."

It was Frobisher's turn to produce a sheet of paper. "You can pay it all at once if you like to the first account number, but I figured it would fly under the radar if you split it into smaller payments." He shrugged. "Your choice."

Jeff quirked a brow. Perhaps this guy wasn't quite as daft as he looked because he'd just solved a problem that had been bothering Jeff.

"Smaller payments would probably be better. We don't want everyone knowing our business, do we?"

They returned to the bar and found the two women struggling to make conversation. Predictably, Gloria perked up when the Yank returned and tried to engage him in conversation.

"Do I know you from somewhere?" she asked, squinting in the dim light to get a better look at him.

"I don't think so, ma'am. I'd sure remember if I'd met a beautiful woman like you."

She shook her head. "I never forget a face."

Jeff tuned out, concentrating on getting Stella Grant to witness their signatures and then handing Frobisher one copy of the agreement.

"Well, I guess that's that then," he said, holding out his hand to seal the deal. "You'll have the necessary by midday tomorrow."

"Thanks, I appreciate it."

"The pleasure's all mine, but now, if you'll excuse us."

"Do we have to go so soon?" Gloria asked petulantly. "We were just getting to know these people."

"I'm afraid I have a lot of things to catch up on," he said, taking Gloria forcefully by the elbow. "I'm sure you understand."

"Oh yeah, sure." Frobisher stood and took Gloria's outstretched hand. "It's been a pleasure, ma'am. Let's do it again some time."

"Oh you Americans with your *ma'am this and ma'am that.*" She did that false tarty giggle thing that made Jeff want to throttle her. "It makes me feel ancient."

"Well, you sure don't look it."

Frobisher produced the compliment she'd shamelessly fished for, and Jeff finally got her away, his mind on that computer disc. It would be waiting for him at his London flat, and he'd know where the funds were before morning.

"I wanted to stay," Gloria protested as they left the hotel.

"Sorry, business comes first."

"Business always comes first with you."

"It's what keeps you in diamonds, darling."

"No, *darling*," she said spitefully. "That would be Daddy's money."

Jeff ground his teeth. Was it any wonder that he wanted out? Every time they had the slightest disagreement, she raised the matter of her father's money, rubbing salt into an open wound by implying he couldn't keep her in style.

"Hey, where are we going?" she asked when he gave the taxi driver the address of his flat. "I thought we were going on somewhere."

"Be my guest," he said, hoping she'd take the bait. "I've got stuff to do."

She slid into the corner of her seat, clearly a little tipsy, and sulked.

"That American," she said after awhile. "I'm sure I know him from somewhere."

"I doubt it. He's only been in the country for a few days."

"No, I'm sure we've met before."

Jeff wasn't listening. His mind had drifted back to the question of the money. He'd spent a lot of the afternoon deciding which accounts he'd borrow it from if it came to that, pretty sure he could put it back again before it was missed. But it would be so much safer if he could use the money Sandra had taken from him.

"Jeff, are you listening to me?"

"Sorry dear, did you say something?"

"About the American, I—"

"Oh, do give it a rest," Jeff said, losing patience, still smarting from the crack about her father's money. "I know you fancied him.

You made that patently obvious and made a bit of a fool of yourself into the bargain."

She shot him an evil smile. "Have it your own way," she said as the cab drew up outside his flat. "I won't bother to tell you who I think he is."

As Jeff got out, she was telling the cabbie to take her on somewhere else.

* * * *

When Nate got back to his loft, Lauren, curled up in the same corner of the settee, was now awake and had the television on with the sound low.

"Hi," he said. "Sleep well?"

She smiled at him. "Sorry, the least I could have done was stay awake until you left."

"No problem." He sat next to her. "What are you watching?"

"Some corny old black-and-white film." She switched it off. "How did it go?"

"He bit."

She looked dazed. "Is he really going to do it then?"

"Looks like it."

"I can't quite believe that you pulled it off."

"Thanks very much," he said, feigning hurt.

"I didn't mean it like that. It's just that there were so many things that could go wrong."

"Well, he had the rock sample tested, rang Jenson, and thinks he's screwed me by adding a clause in the agreement that ups the interest payable."

"He hasn't changed then."

Nate stretched his arms above his head. "Don't look like it."

"What else did he ask you for?"

"Oh, just a copy of my passport."

"Nate!" She sat bolt upright and gaped at him, her eyes round with fear. "How did you…you couldn't possibly have—"

"Relax, baby. I had a passport in Frobisher's name, all worn and full of visas, including one letting me into Britain a few days ago. He flipped through it, and he didn't suspect a thing."

She relaxed. "How on earth did you manage that? How come you even thought of it?"

"With any international transaction, a passport is always the first thing that's asked for."

"And you just happened to know someone who could knock you up a fake in record time."

"Hey, I'm an investigative journalist. I wouldn't be much good at my job if I didn't have those sorts of resources."

"And people who can divert phone calls, friends in high places who owe you favours, and by the sound of it, half a town in Colorado prepared to perjure itself on your behalf." She sighed. "Does the president call you when he needs a hand sorting world peace?"

"We did what we set out to do," he said, the adrenaline rush that had kept him focused giving way to a deep weariness. "That's what counts."

"Yes, we did, thanks to you." She leaned across the space that divided them and smiled. "Thanks, Nate."

"Don't thank me yet. We still have to wait for that money to come through."

"Well, he'll move the funds by lunchtime tomorrow, unless he loses his nerve. That way they'll go with all the other transactions and won't stand out."

"You think he'll use company funds?"

She nodded. "Yes, that's what I think he'll do."

The silence between them lengthened. It was almost companionable, but there was tension there, too. Nate didn't want to make it worse, but she needed to know about Gloria.

"Williams's wife was there."

"Oh hell! You should have said. Did she recognize you?"

"I think so."

"Damn! She could ruin everything."

"Nah, I think she *did* know we'd met before but couldn't remember where. I don't look quite the same, remember."

Lauren blew air through her lips. "Designer stubble, glasses, and slicked-back hair. It doesn't change the basic you."

"People see what they expect to see. You'd be surprised what a difference little changes can make."

"Let's hope you're right."

"Well, if it does come back to her, she'll only remember me as the guy she flirted with at her gym, and she's hardly likely to tell hubby that."

"I suppose not, but still, it worries me."

"Don't let it. We only have to get through until lunchtime tomorrow. If she tells him after that, it'll be too late."

"So, what do we do now?"

"We get a good night's sleep, and then tomorrow morning we pick Sophie up and get out of Dodge."

"We go back to Southampton?"

"Yep. We wait with Melanie for the funds to come through. Or not. If they do, then you're on. You move them pronto. If they don't and Williams comes looking for us, there'll be nothing for him to find."

Lauren sighed. "You make it all sound so simple."

"It is." He smiled at her, stood up, and reached out a hand. "Come on, your look beat."

"Not that beat," she said, returning his smile in a way that made his forget all about his own tiredness.

By ten the next morning they were back in Southampton. Nate and Lauren received a rapturous welcome from Kermit, who ran round their legs in tight circles, scrabbling at them until Lauren picked him up and gave him a cuddle. Melanie had been kept up to speed on developments by the others. She produced breakfast for them all, even though Lauren protested that she was too wired to eat.

"Gotta keep your strength up," Nate told her, forcing bacon and scrambled eggs onto her plate and winking in an intimate way that brought their activities of the previous night graphically to mind. She blushed, eating her breakfast because she knew Nate would keep on her case until she did. It was a way to keep her head down and avoid the curious glances the others were shooting her way.

Lauren helped Melanie clear up after breakfast and then walked Kermit several times round the block, too anxious to keep still.

"Now we wait," she said to the others with a heavy sigh when she returned to the house.

At eleven Melanie took up a position in front of her main computer, eyes glued for any signs of wire transfers. They all tried to keep busy, but there really was nothing to do but wait. It got to them all, and their desultory attempts at conversation faded into a brittle silence. Sophie flipped through the pages of a magazine without reading it, Lauren checked for the hundredth time that there was nothing wrong with the accounts she'd set up to receive the money, Nate checked his e-mail and made some calls.

The first transfer came in just before midday for just under a million dollars.

"Game on!" Melanie cried.

The transfers came thick and fast after that. Lauren's fingers flew over the keys as she moved each one on—and then moved it again. With her brain in top gear, in some ways it was like she'd never left the business she'd once loved but never wanted to be involved with again.

"What now?" asked Sophie when Lauren moved the last of it to an account in Venezuela.

"First of all, we remove all the stuff we planted on the web," Nate said.

"Already on it," Melanie said, working on half a dozen screens simultaneously.

"After that," Nate added, looking over Melanie's shoulder in case she forgot anything, "we wait to see what happens to Williams."

"How will we know?" Sophie asked.

"Oh, we'll know. Melanie will pick up any office gossip from her friend at Whytelake's, and I'll get the lowdown from my police connections on any criminal charges."

"I doubt if Whytelake's will prosecute him for stealing," Lauren said. "They'll cover the losses and keep quiet because they won't want to rock the boat and worry their clients. They'll just kick him out and pretend nothing's happened."

"Which is what we want, right?" Nate smiled at her. "Don't sound so defeated. He won't be able to claw his way out of this one."

"I suppose not."

"In the meantime we all go back to our normal lives," Nate said. "It's important, especially for you, Lauren, just in case Williams starts throwing wild accusations about. When do you have to be back at the café?"

She screwed up her nose. "Tomorrow morning."

"Then you'd best go back to the shack tonight," he said.

"I shall be here as always," Melanie said.

"And I'll go back to London," Sophie chimed in.

"I'll drive you," Nate said. "I have a story I have to follow up on."

"Essex?" asked Lauren.

"Yeah, one of those calls I just took was to say I have to be out there when it gets dark to catch the bastards moving the puppies," he said, his expression grim.

"We'll keep in touch and get together again for a proper celebration when we know Williams is finally out of the picture."

"You're on!" said Sophie, sharing a high-five with them all.

Lauren didn't envy Nate his night's activities and figured that perhaps going back to work at the café wasn't so bad by comparison.

She insisted on catching the bus so that Nate could get back to town with Sophie, wondering why she didn't feel more satisfaction at having achieved the objective that had kept her going throughout her three-year ordeal.

* * * *

Jeff pressed the button to transmit the last of the money, lent back in his chair, and smiled with satisfaction. He'd had a good gut feeling about this one all along, and nothing had happened to change his mind. It wasn't the first time that he'd picked up a useful lead in a lunchtime crowd, but it was certainly the most lucrative bit of eavesdropping he'd ever indulged in. People were so careless about what they said in public locations that really they deserved to be fleeced. He'd checked it every which way he could think of, and there didn't seem to be a downside. He'd have the money safely back in Whytelake's coffers within three days, with appropriate interest rates according to the futures trades he'd supposedly made on each deal. If by any miracle the discrepancies were found at a later date, he'd be long gone by then.

This opportunity couldn't have come at a better time. He'd never intended to abscond with the money he persuaded Lauren to appropriate, not until some years later when the dust had settled and there was no longer the slightest possibility of him being implicated. Well, that time had come. He'd get the money back from Sandra, take a healthy profit from that hick Frobisher, and disappear into the sunset, leaving Gloria to enjoy her father's money alone. It was all coming together beautifully.

Except for one thing. His computer expert hadn't been available to pick up the disc yesterday. Apparently he was away for a few days, working on another job, and Jeff didn't trust anyone else with something so sensitive. It was annoying but not the end of the world and could wait another day or two. He had his back covered.

He was about to leave for a well-earned lunch when his private line rang. He noticed his home number flash up and smiled. Gloria hadn't come back to the flat in town last night and was now calling him from Wimbledon. As always, after one of her nights out, she'd be contrite, thinking she'd pushed him too far. She still didn't get it. He didn't care what she did because he'd long since stopped giving a toss.

"Good morning, Gloria," he said into the receiver. "Good night out?"

"Lovely, thank you, darling. Did you complete your business deal?"

"Oh yes. That's all tied up now."

"Good. Well, I thought you should know that Daddy's invited us for the weekend. He has some people staying that he thinks we might like to meet. I said we'd go."

Jeff gritted his teeth. As usual, she'd made the arrangements before consulting him. "Of course," he said urbanely. "Tell him I look forward to it."

"I already did." She paused. "Oh, by the way, I think I remember where I've seen that American before."

"Really." Jeff glanced at his watch, only half listening.

"Yes, I've seen his picture lots of times. You wouldn't have done, of course, because you don't read the *Inquirer* but—"

"The *Inquirer*?" That was the paper that leaked the rumour about Frobisher's silver find. She had his full attention now. "What do you mean?"

"That American. Do pay attention, darling. I tried to tell you last night, but you were too preoccupied to listen. His name's Nate Black, and he's an investigative journalist for the *Inquirer.*"

"No, he's not." Jeff laughed, still not unduly worried. "His name's Brad Frobisher, and he's from Colorado."

"Oh well, I'm sure you know who you're dealing with. I must have got it wrong."

A nasty feeling wormed its way into Jeff's stomach. Wasn't the Yank who'd been hanging round Lauren called Nate? As soon as Gloria got off the phone, he did an Internet search on Nate Black.

And found himself staring at Brad Frobisher's face.

Chapter Eighteen

"Jesus, no!"

Jeff tore at his hair, refusing at first to believe it. This had to be some sort of eerie coincidence. The man on his screen looked like Frobisher, but there were differences, too. He didn't want to accept that the differences were easy to fake. His hair, the designer stubble, the glasses—all bog standard disguise material. He grabbed his phone and rang the numbers he had for Stella Grant and Frobisher. Both were unobtainable, which was when he accepted that he'd well and truly blown it.

Jeff phoned Jenson again, but he wasn't available, adding to his feeling of impending doom. Were they all in this together? Inspiration struck, and he phoned the geologist whom he'd spoken to from Stella's apartment. He got put through to a university somewhere, which he didn't remember happening yesterday, but Stella had placed that call, hadn't she, and handed him the receiver when she got through? In his agitated state, Jeff couldn't be sure. He got the geologist's department but was told the person he required was on leave for the entire month.

"But he can't be. I spoke to him just yesterday."

"Not on this number you didn't."

"Is he available on a cell phone?" Jeff asked, clutching at straws.

"No, he's on a dig in an area outside of mobile-phone reception."

Jeff replaced the receiver and dropped his head in his hands. He'd been well and truly taken. They'd been so bloody good that he hadn't suspected, not even for a moment. Jeff forced himself to calm down, intent upon damage limitation. He was five million dollars out and wouldn't see it again. He had those documents Frobisher or Black or whoever the hell he was had signed, but they weren't worth the paper they were written on. He could go to the police, claiming fraud, but he'd committed fraud, too, by using company funds for his personal use. That's where they'd been so smart, trapping him in a web of his own greed.

There was only one thing for it. He'd have to get Sandra to give up the money she'd stolen from him. He didn't have time to wait for his computer guy to find where she'd hidden it. He'd go round there, tell her he knew what she'd done and get her to give it back. And she *would* give it back. Jeff ground his teeth as he thought of the methods he'd employ to persuade her. He'd put up with her whining and nagging for quite long enough, and she would finally get what she deserved.

Somehow he managed to function for the rest of the day, giving up all thoughts of going to the pub for lunch. Food would have choked him right then, and he was beyond making small talk with his fellow brokers. He called Sandra on her internal phone, told her to leave early and that he'd see her at her place. She agreed without question.

She had a bottle of wine open and breathing when he arrived.

"Darling," she said, "what a lovely surprise."

He gave her a brief kiss and accepted the glass of rich red that she offered him.

"You look exhausted," she said. "Bad day?"

She had no idea. He couldn't think how best to get her to surrender the funds voluntarily and didn't have time to muck about. He pulled her by the hand until she was sitting beside him on the couch.

"I've finally had it with Gloria," he said, knowing it was what she wanted to hear.

Her face lit up like a Christmas tree. "What do you need from me to make leaving her easier?"

"I have to do this carefully," he said, feigning regret. "Her father has so much influence that he could crush me if I don't cover my tracks." He paused. "And he will, if he thinks I've upset his darling daughter."

"Then what?" She frowned. "We've been through this before, and you always said you couldn't leave because of her father's tentacles. What's changed?"

"How do you fancy leaving England and setting up together somewhere where it's harder for him to get at us?"

Her illuminated expression told him all he needed to know. "Where?" she asked breathlessly.

"As far away from here as we can get. Somewhere warm."

"I'll start packing."

"I need the money, though."

"The money?" she quirked a brow. "What money are you talking about? I have a little bit saved, and you're welcome to that but—"

"The money you stole just before Lauren was arrested."

She furled her brow. "I didn't steal anything. How could I? I was—"

He hit her face so hard that her head snapped back. She must have bitten her tongue, and blood poured from her mouth, dripping over his white shirt. "I know you have it, so don't play games. I need it, and I don't have time to ask nicely."

"Jeff, please, you're frightening me. I honestly don't know what you're talking about."

He put her through it, enjoying himself in spite of his plight, doing all the things that she'd previously drawn the line at. She screamed, she pleaded, she begged, but it merely drove him on. He didn't doubt for a moment that she knew where the money was. It was her way of keeping him with her. Well, he'd had enough of manipulating females. He'd been chained to one in marriage, held hostage by another even when she was in jail, and now this one thought she could hold out on him. It was too much, and his temper snapped.

"Jeff," she pleaded, tears coursing down her face. "Has it occurred to you that whatever's happened to put these weird ideas into your head, it's only occurred since Lauren got out of prison?"

Jeff had his hands round her throat but stopped squeezing when the truth behind her words struck home. Why the hell hadn't he realized it for himself? Lauren and the Yank were in this together.

Sandra spluttered, coughing as she drew deep breaths and reinflated her lungs. She looked petrified, as well she ought. Perhaps she didn't have the money after all and Lauren had put the idea into his head to save her own skin. She'd picked up on his interest in Sandra somehow and used it to her advantage.

Sandra quivered, naked and covered in her own blood where she'd bitten her tongue so badly. She couldn't live, of course. She would never keep quiet about what he'd done to her. Besides, his days at Whytelake's were over, so she'd outlived her usefulness.

In a psychotic rage, his eyes veiled by a dark mist of anger at the unfairness of his life, he replaced his hands on her neck and squeezed, getting a buzz from the fear in her eyes as she realized she was about to die. She made a choking, gurgling sound at the back of her throat, her eyes rolled back in her head, and her entire body went limp.

So that was how it felt to actually kill someone, he thought dispassionately as he calmly wiped all the surfaces he'd touched, took anything that referred to him from the flat, and left, clicking the door softly shut behind him.

His next stop would be the New Forest.

* * * *

Lauren told herself she'd be glad of the solitude at the shack, but once she got there she couldn't settle to anything. The events of the past few days whirled inside her head like a disjointed kaleidoscope. Restlessly, she traipsed through the forest with Kermit, even though it was almost dark. The territory was so familiar to her that she barely needed a flash light.

Why the hell couldn't she feel triumphant? They'd done it! They'd beaten the master manipulator at his own game. But it all seemed too easy, and she had a bad feeling about it. Nate was resourceful and clever, but Williams was no slouch, and she was still astounded that he'd fallen for the sting, even one as meticulously planned. Nate had said his greed would be his downfall, but Lauren had still had her doubts. And those doubts were stronger now than they had been before this thing got under way. They'd missed something. Something obvious that ought to have occurred to her long before now.

When a fact eluded her, she'd discovered that the best way to bring it back was to think about something else. Lauren threw a stick for Kermit and switched her mind to Nate Black instead. Conflicting emotions assailed her from all angles. The man was quite disgustingly self-confident, turned heads wherever he went, *and* possessed an unsettling intellect—a heady combination that would once have turned her on.

Oh hell, admit it, Miller, it still did.

She had no idea why he was so determined to fight her corner. Until recently she had supposed he just wanted a scoop. The reasons behind her crime was a subject that had once been speculated upon at length in the press, and he wanted the inside story. She was no longer quite so sure it was that simple because Nate was a complex man. The extent of his anger when he found her at Canary Wharf with Sophie was way too extreme. Just as perplexing, there was something in the depths of his eyes whenever he looked at her that melted her resistance and, despite everything, made her feel inclined to trust him.

Lauren didn't want to trust any man ever again, and yet she'd not only fallen for Nate's charm but let him take over the sting to snare Williams, too.

"You're totally pathetic," she said aloud.

She hadn't treated him particularly well, enjoying mind-blowing sex with him at the shack and then shutting him out. He'd been furious, and she didn't blame him. Her behaviour was enough to confuse anyone. How long before he sent for the little men in white coats and had her taken away?

Without realising it, she'd done a complete circuit of her corner of the forest and was now back at the shack. It was full dark, but fortunately she'd left the outside light on and a lamp in the sitting room. She didn't recall doing so.

"Come on then," she said to Kermit. "Supper time for you."

Kermit growled, but before Lauren had a chance to figure out what had bothered him, a shadow emerged from the treeline, aimed a savage kick at Kermit that elicited a howl from him and sent him spiralling through the air. He landed with a thud, moaning but still bravely attempting to growl. He didn't seem able to stand. Lauren gasped, horrified, but before she could get to him, a strong pair of arms grabbed her from behind and propelled her toward the door to the shack.

"What kept you?" asked Williams in a voice that made her skin crawl.

* * * *

Nate felt completely drained, sickened by what he'd just been forced to see. They'd caught the men behind the foul puppy farm business, and they were being handcuffed by the police and taken away. The animal welfare people were there, too, gently removing the pathetic pups and their exhausted mothers. Nate had got his exclusive for the *Inquirer*, but it had left a bad taste in his mouth. Animal cruelty of any sort really got to him.

"That's it then," he said to his photographer, having taped an interview with the guy who'd tipped them off about the operation. "I'll file the copy in time for the Sunday edition."

"Right you are then."

Nate's mobile rang, and he excused himself to answer it.

"Nate, it's Peter Read."

"Hello, Peter, what can I do for you?"

"I thought you'd like to know that we just got a 999 call from a woman who'd almost been strangled."

"Anyone I know?"

"Nope, but you know the man who tried to kill her." Peter paused. "His name's Jeff Williams, and apparently he's now on his way to the New Forest."

* * * *

Jeff was on a roll. He'd got rid of Sandra and would soon be leaving Gloria in the lurch to face the ignominy of his fall from grace alone. That would be a greater punishment for her than divorce or anything else he could have inflicted on her. He ought to have thought of it before. And now, the *coup de grace.* He had the meddlesome Lauren at his mercy. He'd get that money out of her, shag her every which way to Christmas, and then kill her, too. These women all thought they could get the better of him. He took a deep breath, feeling invisible, and pushed his struggling captive toward the front room, kicking the door closed behind him just in case that horrible mutt wasn't badly injured enough to stay down. Lauren clearly knew what was in store for her and fought him every inch of the way.

"Stop fighting, damn it!"

He took one hand from her arm and gave her a belt across the face. It must have hurt, but instead of subduing her, she stopped walking altogether, their bodies collided, and she kicked backward, catching him squarely in the nuts. He yelled. She was only wearing sneakers, but her aim was spot on, and it hurt like hell. He pushed her into a chair. She fell heavily and didn't move.

"Right," he said harshly. "Where is it?"

"Like I'd tell you even if I knew," she said, not pretending she didn't know what he meant.

"Oh, you'll tell me," he said, enjoying himself now in spite of the dull throb in his scrotum.

She leaned one hand down the side of the chair as though reaching for something. Jeff grabbed the poker before her fingers could make contact with it and threw it across the room, shattering an awful picture on the opposite wall.

"Nice try," he snarled.

"Why are you doing this?" she asked him. "Why did you set me up to take a fall? If you're going to kill me, at least tell me that."

"Because you were available," he said, smirking. "Because you were naïve, trusting, and would do absolutely anything I asked you to."

"So it was all a lie. You didn't love me and didn't want to spend the rest of your life with me."

"If I had, we wouldn't be having this conversation." He strode about the small room, confident that she couldn't move, or do anything to defend herself, without him having the last word. "You were getting too clingy, asking too many intrusive questions. You didn't do that to start with and were grateful for whatever time I spared you, but it got to the stage where you became a liability."

"Let's see if I've got this straight," she said. "I'd outlived my usefulness, but you couldn't just end the affair because I knew all about the stolen money. Hell, I stole it on your orders, and you couldn't risk me making accusations about that. The tip from the electrical company would give you enough money to do…" She glanced up at him, frowning. "What did you want to do?"

"To get shot of the whole darned life," he said savagely. "You'd go down for Drake's murder—"

"A murder that you organized."

"Absolutely." He was proud of that, his only regret being that he'd never had anyone to boast to about his achievements before now.

Well, it didn't matter if Lauren knew all the details because she sure as hell wouldn't live to tell anyone. "You'd be accused of that, and of stealing the money, which would have disappeared."

"Well, obviously it did, because you took it."

"Don't be stupid. If I had it, do you think I'd still be here?"

"How the hell would I know what goes on in the mind of a megalomaniac?"

Jeff frowned. This wasn't going according to plan. She was supposed to be quaking with fear, begging for her life like Sandra had. Instead, she looked at him with derision in her expression, and it infuriated him. He swung back his arm and hit her so hard across the side of her face that this time she did scream.

"Now," he said, "the fun's over. Tell me where the hell it is."

* * * *

Nate ran toward his car, phone still glued to his ear. He was an idiot to have left Lauren alone. He ought to have anticipated something like this.

"Did the woman say anything?" he asked Peter.

"Not much. Her trachea is badly bruised, and she can barely speak. We're guessing here, but it looks as though he thought he strangled her and left her for dead. We gather from the books we found in her place that she's heavily into yoga."

"So knows how to control her breathing. To make it shallow."

"Right. That's probably what saved her. As soon as Williams left, she dragged herself to the phone and hit the three nines."

"Who is she?" Nate put his car into reverse, spinning the wheels as he steered it back onto the blacktop.

"She worked for the accounts division of Whytelake's."

"Ah, I see. His latest floozy, presumably."

"That's what we're thinking."

"How do we know Williams is going to the forest?" Nate asked, hitting the main road and flooring the accelerator.

"She wrote one word."

"Lauren," Nate finished for him.

"Right."

"I'm on my way, but I'm a couple of hours away. If he was in London, he'll have a head start. How soon can you get there, Peter?"

"Don't panic. Williams didn't have a car in London, so he'll have to go back to Wimbledon, get his car, and get down there."

"We should be close behind him then, but can't you get the local boys to intervene?"

"I thought you might prefer to keep them out of it."

Darn it! How much did Peter know about their little scam? Obviously quite a lot.

"Yes, so long as you're sure he hasn't got too much of a head start. It doesn't matter about anything else, Peter," Nate said, a catch in his voice. "Just make sure she's safe."

"I'll see you there," he said, breaking the connection.

Nate drove without thought for anything or anyone except Lauren, cursing his stupidity at leaving her alone when he knew she was in danger. And she was in danger because she knew where the stolen money was. That's what it had always been about for Williams. It was so obvious, he berated himself some more, this time for not realising that she must still have it. Had it been otherwise, Williams would either have been long gone by now or he would have used the funds to finance the silver-mine scam.

He left the motorway and overtook a slow-moving car on a dangerous bend, pulling back into his lane before a collision with a car coming the opposite way became inevitable. Its driver laid on the horn and waved a fist at him. Nate barely noticed. Why the hell hadn't she told him the truth? If she still didn't trust him after all they'd been through, then what hope was there for them? His thoughts brought him up short. How long had he been considering a future with Lauren in it?

"Since that first day when you saw her in the forest, you crazy, love-sick fool," he muttered, willing himself to get to the shack in time to deal with Williams personally.

* * * *

Lauren was running out of ideas. The prospect of help arriving was nonexistent. Nate was the only visitor she ever had, and he was in Essex. Her phone was in her pocket, but even if she could somehow divert him for long enough to call for help, it would never get here in time. She was most definitely on her own. Her only hope was to keep him talking. Let him boast about his crimes, even if no one else but her would ever hear him admit to them. She could see that he was enjoying showing off, and perhaps that would make his a little less vigilant. For the first time she wished the room was larger. That way she'd have more of an opportunity to take him by surprise. As it was, he was never more than two strides away from her. It looked hopeless, and she ought to be petrified. Instead, she felt a strange sort of enveloping calm—a steely determination to learn all the facts, if only for her own satisfaction.

"Drake wasn't the man who'd leaked the information though, was he," she said, wiping the blood from the side of her face with the back of her hand.

"No, Fowler was too cautious to deliver the message himself. I hadn't counted on that."

"So you had an innocent man killed."

He made a scoffing sound. "Hardly innocent. He was a petty crook willing to do anything for a few bob, no questions asked."

"So when I got out, you found me and put Fowler on to me so you could get rid of him and pin that on me, too."

"You seem to have figured it all out," he said, smirking.

She had, that was the problem. She was running out of stalling tactics.

"It's a shame it has to end this way, Lauren," he said, offering her a significant glance. "If it's any consolation, you were the best I've ever had."

"Not much, no."

"Now then, my dear. For the last time, where's the money?"

She looked him straight in the eye. "It seems to me that right now that money's the only thing keeping me alive, so even if I know where it is, I'd hardly tell you and sign my own death warrant."

"Ah, but there are so many different ways to die. Personally, I hate pain," he said, picking up the bottle of Jack Daniel's Nate had left behind and taking swig, "but the choice is yours. It doesn't matter much to me either way."

"Jeff, the more you threaten me, the less likely I am to be intimidated," she lied. "If nothing else, three years in prison taught me how to stand up to bullies."

Her calmness, the fact that she could look him straight in the eye without displaying any fear, appeared to anger him. He was a control freak and needed to know that he was calling the shots.

"Then you've only got yourself to blame." He put the bottle down and approached her, hands moving toward her neck. "Where is it?" he said, his fingers closing round her throat.

* * * *

Nate and Peter arrived at the lane to the shack almost at the same time. DS Taylor, the woman detective who'd interviewed Lauren was already there, along with several uniformed officers. There was a Jaguar parked crookedly across the path.

"It's registered to Williams," Taylor told them.

"Let's hope we're not too late," Nate said, moving forward.

DS Taylor frowned. "Are you allowing a civilian in on this, sir?" she asked.

"Mr. Black knows the layout better than any of us," Peter said. "Is there a back door?"

"No, but there's a bathroom window."

Peter, moving stealthily, deployed the uniforms round the shack. It was obvious that DS Taylor wasn't going anywhere except in the front door with them. This was her patch, and although Peter outranked her, she was determined to be in on the kill.

The three of them approached the front door when a soft whine caused them to pause. It was Kermit, lying on his side, panting hard. He didn't seem to be able to move. Nate ran a hand softly along his side. The dog winced when he touched his ribcage but didn't show any other signs of distress.

"Looks like the bastard kicked him," Nate said through gritted teeth. "I've had just about a gut full of animal cruelty today."

"Doesn't look as though anything's broken, or he wouldn't let you touch him," Peter said.

"Stay here, boy, and we'll sort you in a minute," Nate murmured.

As though understanding him, Kermit lay back and closed his eyes.

They crouched below the front window and listened. They could hear loud demands from Williams, muted responses from Lauren.

"At least she's still alive," Nate whispered, as much to himself as to the others. He cautiously lifted his head above the sill and peered in. "She's in a chair, not tied up as far as I can see." Nate watched for a second and then sprang to his feet. "He's trying to throttle her. I'm going in!"

Before either officer could prevent him, Nate put his shoulder to the front door and burst in. The commotion caused Williams to release Lauren's neck and look at him with a combination of surprise and consternation.

"What the—"

Nate didn't stop to listen. Instead, he strode across to Williams, ready to deck the bastard and put all his pent-up frustration into the blow. Before he got close enough, Lauren picked up a bottle of Jack Daniels and brought it down across the back of Williams's skull.

The she turned toward Nate, smiled, and fell to the floor in a dead faint.

Chapter Nineteen

"Hey," he said. "Welcome back. You okay?"

Lauren came to, disorientated, and cautiously lifted her head. Someone must have laid her on the lumpy sofa because a spring was aggressively attacking her butt. Nate balanced precariously on the arm of the settee, holding a cold compress to her forehead. There were people everywhere, but the sound of Williams's voice rose about the hubbub.

"It's those two you ought to be talking to!" he screamed manically, pointing a finger at Nate and Lauren whilst holding a cloth to his bleeding head with the other hand. "They tried to defraud my company of five million dollars. I was attempting to stop them like any responsible director would."

"Of course you were." Lauren shot him a disarming smile, finally enjoying her moment of revenge to the full.

"I can prove it," Williams shouted hysterically. "I have a contract signed by him. It's in a false name, but the picture on the passport is his."

Lauren and Nate shared a glance. That could prove to be a sticking point.

"And you felt the need to strangle the young lady, just to get her to admit it," Peter said calmly.

"I wouldn't have killed her."

"It's still assault, isn't it, Inspector?" Lauren said, sitting up. "I learned a lot about the law these past three years," she added helpfully. "Not much else to do where I was living."

"You enjoy assaulting women, don't you, Mr. Williams?" the inspector asked.

"I don't know what you're talking about. I was just trying to save my company an embarrassing loss."

"Tell that to Sandra Dawson."

"Sandra?" Jeff blinked at the inspector. "Sandra's dead?"

"Not to my knowledge, sir," he said offhandedly, "unless you know something that I don't."

"No, no, I saw her earlier, and she was fine then. It's just that you made it sound like—"

"Oh, we know all about your meeting with Ms. Dawson. She's in intensive care, telling us as much as she can, given the delicate state of her throat."

What little colour that remained there drained from Williams's face.

"The paramedics are here, sir." Peter indicated the latest posse traipsing into Lauren's tiny front room. Some of the policemen had to go into the kitchen to make enough space for them. "They'll deal with your injury, make sure you're fit and well, and then you'll be charged with all sorts of crimes." Peter smiled at DS Taylor. "He's all yours, sergeant. Perhaps you'd care to read him his rights?"

She looked surprised by Peter's generosity. He'd just handed her a career-making collar. "With pleasure," she said.

"What about you, Ms. Miller?" Peter asked. "Do you need medical attention?"

"No, I'm fine. I'm more worried about my dog. Williams kicked him."

Nate disappeared and came back with Kermit cradled carefully in his arms. "No permanent damage," he said, placing the dog on Lauren's lap. He was a little subdued, but she made a huge fuss of him and received a few tentative wags for her trouble.

"Do you think we need to call a vet?" she asked anxiously.

"No, I don't think so," Nate said, running his hands down his body again. "He'll be sore for a day or two, but that's all."

"Well," said Peter, rising to leave. "We shall have to take statements from you both, but that can wait until tomorrow."

"Inspector," Lauren said. "This might help you."

She got up, crossed to the chair that she'd sat in for the duration of her ordeal, reached to the side of it, and extracted a digital recording pen.

"Is that what I think it is?" he asked, quirking a brow.

"Son of a bitch!" said Nate at the same time. "You were fighting for your life but had the presence of mind to remember that?"

"Yes," she said, answering Peter's question. "Nate gave it to me. Williams paid me one previous visit, you see, and Nate said if he came back I was to switch this on and let him incriminate himself. I made an obvious move for the poker, and whilst he was taking it away, I grabbed the pen from that shelf by the chair, switched it on, and hoped for the best. Providing it worked, it's all on there. How he masterminded the crimes I committed, how he arranged two murders, the whole thing."

Peter switched the device on and heard Williams's voice, a little muffled but clearly him, boasting about his achievements.

"Thank you," Peter said. "If it's any consolation, I never believed that you acted alone."

"I took responsibility for my stupidity, Inspector. All I ever wanted was for the world to believe that I didn't act alone."

"Leave it to me," he said. "The truth will come out before very much longer."

It was very quiet in the shack once Peter left, taking his troops with him. Nate and Lauren looked at one another. The atmosphere seemed to vibrate with emotion—a combination of unanswered questions and unfulfilled promises. Lauren knew she had some explaining to do. The time had finally come to be completely honest, but she had a more immediate concern.

"Is Sandra really going to be all right?" she asked.

"Yes, apparently her yoga breathing exercises saved her. She realized Williams was going to kill her, and so she played dead, hoping to fool him." He paused. "It obviously worked."

"Thank goodness!"

Nate drilled her with a gaze. "Why didn't you tell me that you had the money all the time?"

She sighed, not entirely surprised that he'd guessed. "That would have required a degree of trust I just didn't have in me." She stood up, leaning one arm against the mantelpiece. "Oh, I almost told you several times but couldn't be absolutely sure whose side you were on." He made to protest, but she silenced him with a wave. "Look at it from my perspective, Nate. You're an investigative journalist, and my story's a major scoop. Everyone still wants to know what happened to the money, and I know what stratagems journalists will stoop to." She shuddered and wrapped her arms round her torso. "I had plenty of experience of their underhand tactics after I was charged. Anyway, I was through trusting any man."

"Which is why you kept withdrawing from me?"

She nodded. "I couldn't take the chance."

"What made you take the money? I mean, you moved it before you knew Drake was dead and that you were a suspect."

"It was Jeff," she said. "At first I was besotted with him and believed every word he said to me, idiot that I was. I so needed his approval, and I just didn't care about anything else. But then, as time went on, I couldn't help noticing little things. Like how he'd never be seen in public with me unless it was for a legitimate reason. Oh, I knew he was married…but still. And then his psychotic personality occasionally showed. He was careful in front of me, but we worked in close proximity, and I often saw him lose it with others. He'd go totally berserk for no real reason, and it scared me. I hated stealing, but he kept telling me this would be the last time and then we'd have enough to get away together."

"But you started not to believe him."

"Yes. I hadn't wanted to believe Melanie when she warned me about him, but I was never able to get her words completely out of my head. I convinced myself that she was jealous because my star was in the ascendency and Jeff was my mentor. Whytelake's working conditions are highly competitive, and I'd upstaged Mel."

"But you started to wonder if perhaps you were going to be replaced?"

She quirked a brow. "I can see why you're so good at what you do." She sat down again and stroked a still-subdued Kermit. "I noticed Sandra hanging round a lot. She was the accountant responsible for Jeff's area of operation and liaised with the auditors, so I guess he had to keep her sweet, but still, she didn't need to see him as often as she did. I wondered about that. When I asked him about her, he said we needed her on our side so she didn't look too closely at the accounts we were manipulating. That made sense in a way, but her attitude didn't. She didn't hesitate to take swipes at me, both professionally and personally, and as far as I knew I'd done nothing to deserve them. Then one night I was working late in another office, came back to my desk to get my bag, and saw them in his office."

"Getting it on?"

She sighed. "Yes. And yet he was obsessively careful about that sort of thing with me. That's when the blinkers came off, and I accepted that I'd been a prize idiot to fall for the oldest line in the book."

"And so you moved the money to bring him to his senses."

"Yes, I'd finally had enough of being used." She stared at the unlit fire, lost in her own version of hell. "To my detriment, if he'd really wanted to go away with me, I'd have probably still gone. I was that smitten, God help me. Either way, it was time for him to decide."

"But before you could have it out with him, Drake was murdered."

"Yes, that was the day when my life as I knew it fell apart."

"You so didn't deserve all that crap."

"I stole the money, Nate," she said starkly. "No one held a gun to my head. I deserved everything that came my way, *and* I know I still got away lightly. Whether I'll ever be able to reconcile what I did with my conscience is another matter."

"It's only money."

She shuddered. "Easy for you to say."

Nate perched on the arm of the chair and gently massaged the back of her neck. She rotated her shoulders, and his fingers dug deeper, flattening out the kinks in her rigid posture.

"Hum, that feels good," she said with an elongated sigh.

"When Williams came to see you here, you told him that Sandra had the money, right?"

She looked at him sharply. "How did you know that?"

"Hers was the first name to pass your lips once Peter left." He lifted his shoulders. "Your conscience obviously bothered you."

"Yes," she said on a long breath. "I knew he didn't have the money, obviously, and that he'd come looking for me. I decided that if he found me before I was ready to try and catch him in a lie, then I'd cook up a story to convince him that Sandra had it. If nothing else, it would buy me some time, and she'd been so horrible to me that I didn't feel bad about it. Until…until I—"

"Until you thought she might have been killed because of you."

"Yes. If that had happened, I'd never have forgiven myself."

"You weren't to know that he'd resort to murder."

"I didn't know for sure but should have guessed. I've had enough time to think about it, and I knew that for him money transcended everything." She paused. "He really does hate women, you know. You were right about that."

"Yeah, his wife used her money to control him, so I guess his resentment stemmed from that." He took her hand and pulled her back to the sofa. "You still should have told me."

"Well, you held out on me."

He blinked. "What do you mean?"

"The Colorado silver mine." She fixed him with a gaze. "It's yours, isn't it?"

He quirked a brow. "How did you figure that one?"

"I'm not stupid, Nate. You couldn't possibly have pulled a scam that complicated together without an inside line. It's either yours or belongs to someone very close to you." She flashed a brief smile. "Besides, I remember you telling me you were just a Colorado country boy at heart. I had images of you in a cosy log cabin, though. Obviously I wasn't thinking grand enough."

"Yeah," he said. "It's mine, and it is called the Frobisher place. The geological reports were knocked up for me by a local outfit that owes me a favour. The rock samples came from one of the few remaining rich veins. A decent geologist would know the origin of the rocks, so it had to be genuine." He spread his hands like it was no big deal. "The rest is true. We do open it to the public in the summer."

"Why Frobisher?"

"It belonged to my maternal great-grandfather. He had no sons, so his daughter inherited. She married and produced my mom, who married Mr. Black."

"Do you still live on the property?"

"When I'm in the States and don't have to be in New York. It really is pretty much worked out and relies on the tourism in the summer to keep it solvent. There is no bank loan, but if I didn't write books and do groundbreaking investigative journalism, there might have to be."

"Thank you," she said quietly.

"For what?" he asked.

"Oh, nothing much." She leaned her head against his shoulder. "For believing me when no one else did. For pulling off the scam. For not asking all the questions that had to be plaguing you." She ran a hand down his thigh. "Oh, and for saving my life just now."

"You're more than welcome," he said, dropping his head and covering her lips with his own.

"What are we going to do with the money?" she asked when he broke the kiss.

"The money we extorted from Williams we'll return anonymously to Whytelake's, once we're sure that he's been charged and fully disgraced, of course."

"Good, I never want to steal anything ever again. But what about the money I have?"

"I don't know. What had you intended to do with it?"

"I was willing to die in this room today rather than tell Williams where it was." She glanced up at him. "You know that, I suppose."

"Yes, it occurred to me when I was dashing to your rescue. I figured that as long as you didn't tell him where it was, it would keep you alive."

"It would have been my ultimate revenge, dying and not telling him, I mean."

"But you must have had plans for it when you moved it out of Williams's grasp."

"Well, as I say, I intended to force him into a decision, but I can see now that by taking control of it, I would have turned myself into another Gloria. Anyway, I figured that if I couldn't get him to commit to me, then I'd find a way to put the money back where it belonged."

"Well, it's too late for that now."

"Yes, but keeping it doesn't seem right."

"No, it doesn't, but deciding who its rightful owners are is next to impossible." He paused, still massaging her neck. "We could share it round a few good causes."

"Melanie's business and Sophie's drop-in centre," Lauren said without hesitation. "They deserve something."

"Absolutely, and I'm sure we can think of other deserving cases but—"

"But what, Nate? You suddenly look all pensive." She was worried by the abrupt change in his attitude. "What else is wrong now?"

"Nothing's wrong, but my concentration's shot to hell."

She frowned. "Why?"

"Because right now all I can think about is kissing you again."

He did precisely that, until a knock at the door had them springing apart like guilty lovers.

"Now what?"

Nate strode across the room and pulled open the door. Peter Read stood there.

"Oh, Nate," he said, "sorry to interrupt, but I forgot earlier, what with all the excitement. My men searched Williams's London apartment and found this in a locked drawer. It seems to have lost its way *en route* to the evidence locker," he said, smirking. "No idea what it is, of course, but I'm sure it's nothing important." He looked round Nate's shoulder and winked at Lauren. "We're even now," he said to Nate and disappeared into the night.

"I'll be damned!" Nate said, grinning.

"What is it?"

Nate chuckled. "The agreement I signed with Williams."

"Yes, I was wondering about that."

"It would have cast uncertainties on Williams's total guilt, and Peter knows it. There's no saying what a clever brief would have done with it. He'd certainly dig up the connection with me, pillory the methods of the tabloid press and put doubt in a jury's minds."

She fixed him with a level gaze. "You knew that, but you took the risk anyway."

He sat down and pulled her into his arms. "I did it for you, sweetheart, and would do it again without a second thought."

She looked at him through eyes misted with emotion. "But why?"

"I think you know the answer to that one."

"I'm still traumatised," she said, unable to prevent a tiny smile tugging at the corners of her mouth. "I need to hear you say it."

"Okay, I'm not sure this is the right time, but here we go." He cleared his throat, suddenly looking nervous and unsure of himself, which was a first in Lauren's experience. "Lauren Miller, I love you to distraction. You're beautiful, clever, resourceful, principled—"

"Nate, I appreciate the compliment, but I'm actually a convicted felon."

He grinned. "We all make mistakes."

"True, but this one—"

"Will you stop interrupting me when I'm pouring my heart out?"

"Sorry," she said sweetly. "Carry on. I'm listening."

"Oh, the hell with it." He ran a hand through his hair, his smile so predatory, his eyes so full of unguarded passion that her entire body trembled with desire. "Will you spend the rest of your life with me?"

"Yes."

"Yes, just like that?" He regarded her with tender amusement in his expression. "Aren't you supposed to ask for time to think about it?"

She shrugged. "I've no idea. I've never been proposed to before, so I don't know the drill, but it doesn't seem like a good idea to muck you about and risk having you slip out of my clutches."

"Sounds good to me," he said, pulling her into his arms.

"After all, another good story might come along and you'll be off chasing it, and I won't know what to—"

"Will you please stop talking when I'm trying to kiss you, woman."

Her smile lit up the entire room. "Gladly," she said.

THE END

HTTP://WWW.WENDYSOLIMAN.COM

ABOUT THE AUTHOR

Wendy Soliman was brought up on the Isle of Wight in Southern England but now divides her time between Andorra and west Florida. She lives with her husband Andre and a rescued dog of indeterminate pedigree named Jake Bentley. When not writing she enjoys reading other people's books, walking miles with her dog whilst plotting her next scene, dining out and generally making the most out of life.

Also by Wendy Soliman

BookStrand Mainstream: *A Class Apart*
BookStrand Mainstream: *Shalimar*

Available at
BOOKSTRAND.COM

CPSIA information can be obtained at www.ICGtesting.com
Printed in the USA
BVOW021152180312

285455BV00003B/16/P

9 781619 266452